Brendel

Richard R Hall

Shadow Angels Trilogy
Book Three

Brendel
By
Richard R Hall

True Look Publications

658 Central Ave.
Albany, NY
12206

ISBN-13: 978-0998780023
ISBN-10: 0998780022

For Christopher and Jennifer, wherever you are.

Books by Richard Hall

Shadow Angels Trilogy:
Shadow Angels
Rise of the Queens
Brendel

Chapter One

T he Demon Slayer stood back from a busy street on a terrace of a sky tower, watching humanity hurry past. He lived in the shadows for over a millennium and had become skilled at hiding himself from the mortals. He stayed in the darkness of the night, or a thought placed in their heads to trick their minds and eyes into not seeing his strangeness, to make him appear like any one of the multitudes of other humans passing by.

This was a time when flying cars filled the sky, and the streets were used for walking. The city was York, and it was the year of our lord 3148 AD. His blond hair cut short, and his new age clothes worn smartly, Shawn Bryce was his name. The flash of his eyes, the power in and around him for the few who could truly see, told he was not of the human world but a vampire of the Archangels Michael's making. The lesser god Eos, also known in this world as The Mother, had given this man high power, and he was both vampire and warlock and now known in heaven as a guardian.

An ordinary looking woman stood on the far side of the street, and Shawn hid from her. Shawn used the crowds to hide from this woman and a powerful spell to cloak himself. A spell that came from Eos filled with energies of heaven, so this evil witch did not know he was near.

He slowly stepped forward, looking down the walkway at another witch wearing the same shroud of secrecy. She was his changeling, a mother's witch turned vampire – unlike him, a vampire turned witch – and she too was a Guardian. Gwyn had been with him for more than a hundred years now. This woman had saved him, and he loved her dearly. Giving him a nod of agreement, she too turned her powerful senses on the woman. They had finally found Samil—meaning Brendel must be near.

The night was cool, and a gentle breeze blew against his face, bringing a multitude of odors. He easily could turn his powerful sense on the mortals, smell their blood and emotions, hear the onslaught of their whispers and their thoughts floating in their minds. Few creatures of this world were as powerful as he was. York, a city located in the District of Penn, was known for its nightlife, and tonight the streets were crowded. He heard the noise of the city and the hum of the aircars overhead. Holograms of advertisements, giant faces of attractive women, hovered over the street, hawking their wares, trying to draw the crowd to another level of the sky tower. Shawn smiled at the bustle of the humans as they passed, with speech and symbols filling the brisk air around their faces.

Then a smile came to his face as the scent of cooking food floated in the air. He only drank blood, but still, after a hundred years, he could remember what food tasted like. Before Malin took him captive and turned him human, he had lived a thousand years as a vampire and forgot what food tasted like. Victoria, his love of a thousand years, turned him back to a vampire, and now she was his maker and queen.

The demon Brendel was only a hundred years old and already had brought war back to this world. Istanbul was in flames and had been burning for a week. The territories of Jerusalem and Istanbul had started hostilities over long ago forgotten differences between them. A young man – a Westerner – started a cult in Istanbul and stirred old religious sentiments. This is what demons do, and this had been the clue that Queen Victoria and Shawn were waiting for. Brendel was a master at using old religious hatreds to turn humans against each other and finally had raised his head. Suspicious, the queen sent Shawn and Gwyn to York to find the demon.

The woman continued to walk, and Shawn slowly crossed the street and followed. Stealth was of great importance, for this woman was Samil, a powerful and evil witch of Lucifer's, sent to guard the demon, Brendel. Soon Gwyn joined him, and they kept their distances from Samil in hopes she would lead them to Brendel.

"This woman doesn't look like Samil," Gwyn whispered.

"I know, but she is," Shawn replied. "The witch has shapeshifted and uses this form to hide."

They followed the evil witch for blocks, avoiding the glances over her shoulder, blending into the crowd, whispering a spell to make their shroud stronger.

"Do you think she knows we're here?" Gwyn questioned.

"I don't think so!" Shawn quickly whispered as he used all his stealth to probe at the witch.

They continued to follow Samil. Finally, she turned and entered a theater. A hologram of a marquee formed over the street with the name of the play and many different flashing colored lights, the letters grew big, bounced and exploded, shooting light trails into the night, then the process repeated. It was a small theater for this age.

As Shawn came close, he stopped and looked at Gwyn. "Can you feel the dark energy, Gwyn? Hear the grind of evil? It is Brendel," Shawn whispered, hardly believing what he spoke.

"We finally have found the demon," Gwyn agreed. "I wonder if he wants this?"

"This time, it did seem easy!"

The demon Brendel was a direct spawn of Lucifer's, not brought from some other world, and wielded tremendous power. He was of the flesh, but nothing could penetrate the dark energy that surrounded him. Queen Katherine discovered Brendel a hundred years before, born of a mortal woman, and the very act of his birth tore the woman apart. Lucifer was his father, and within Brendel was unspeakable evil and dark energy.

They stood at the entrance to the theater and spoke low to one another.

"Brendel and Samil are in this building," Gwyn said. "We have your slayer."

"We do!" Shawn replied as he reached back and felt the blade under his coat. "I hope The Mother gives us her power."

"She will! I wish you had your staff!"

"Then we won't need the staff."

"Do you still want to enter?" Gwyn questioned.

"We have to see what Brendel looks like! We will go in cloaked. I know this is dangerous, Gwyn, but it has taken a long time to find Brendel. Once we get near, we will know him, and he will be much easier for us to find again. Then we will leave!" Shawn glanced toward Gwyn, looking for her reassuring look, her resolve that always steadied him, but he saw none. "Follow me!" he sighed.

They paid their admission, entered the theater, and found themselves in a small lobby. Shawn turned to Gwyn and whispered, "The demon is on the other side of the door."

Going to the door, he placed his hand on it and felt the overwhelming evil on the other side. He cracked the door slightly, looked through, and saw a large crowd sitting in plush, theater chairs watching the actors strut and give their lines on the stage. In disbelief, he saw an actor, dressed in clothes of a time long gone, acting out lines of the play, and it was Brendel. The demon appeared as a handsome young man with long dark hair slicked back and a perfectly chiseled face.

Gwyn looked in and then back at him and said, "His face changed for a second to look like you!"

"It did—That's not good!" Shawn glanced around and did not see Samil. "Let's go take a seat. Be ready!"

Shawn and Gwyn made their way to two empty seats in the back. Shawn prayed their supernatural defenses were enough to hide them from the demon. Brendel did not notice them taking their seats as he was absorbed in his performance. They watched the show unfold, and as it was ending, Shawn looked and now saw Samil. The plain woman was standing against the sidewall of the theater staring at them. With a pang of fear, Shawn realized that Samil knew who they were.

The play ended, the lights rose, and Brendel walked to the center front of the stage, glaring out at them. His face shapeshifted to look the same as Shawn's and then back to a grotesque demon face. The demon knew they were there. Brendel shouted to the people, "It seems, ladies and gentlemen, we have some supernatural creatures in our audience. I'm sure you all heard of Guardians or vampires."

Brendel pointed the finger at them with an evil grin on his face, and Shawn saw that Samil now looked like herself, the bald witch, and she too had a wicked smile on her face. This was a trap; the audience was becoming uneasy, as their senses wavered when the stench of evil and death filled the theater.

"Right there, ladies and gents are two vampires sent by pathetic angels. How are you, Shawn and Gwyn Bryce? You dare stalk me. You thought you could get this close to me, and I would not know. I am Brendel, and I am in your world now, vampires. Look pathetic mortals at the Guardians – your saviors – for it will be the last thing you see!"

Brendel crouched, then rose and rolled his hands outward. Waves of dark blue energy washed over the audience. Shawn and Gwyn huddled together, covering each other, using the energy of The Mother to shield themselves from this power as it moved over them, rolling through the lobby and out onto the street. The audience sat dead in their seats, flesh seared, their eyes burned from their heads. Out on the street, an explosion rose between the buildings, shaking the terrace the theater was built on.

The vampires bolted up. Shawn drew his slayer, and Gwyn formed energy in the palm of her hand and threw it at Brendel. Gwyn's white energy met the demon's blue, colliding in mid-air, and sizzled in the middle. Shawn formed to his most potent supernatural state and flew at the witch with vampire speed driving his slayer through Samil chest. Pushing the witch back and pinning her against the wall.

"We meet again, Samil," Shawn growled at the witch.

"We do Demon Slayer," Samil shot back as she reached out and grabbed Shawn's throat. Heat and dark energy traveled through the witch's hands into his neck. He quickly grabbed her hands, pinning them to the wall while working his sword through the evil creature's chest, trying to cut her heart.

Brendel threw his dark energy over the top of Gwyn's, hitting her in the chest and throwing her back, stunned. Falling to her knees, Gwyn fought off the dark energy, but then the demon lifted his hands and called out, "Father, it's a mother's witch give me more energy for this whore." The second throw of energy hit Gwyn lifting and propelling her out into the lobby. Brendel pivoted around and rolled his hand out, releasing another wave of dark energy. The power that hit Shawn, tore him and his slayer from Samil and threw both to the back of the auditorium.

Shawn still held his slayer, and Samil slumped to the floor, gravely wounded. Flying straight, he hit Brendel with the hilt driving him back. Brendel came at him, then Shawn feigned and shot back, driving his fist into Brendel's face stunning the demon. Brendel, with great strength, swung and drove his fist into Shawn's chest, propelling him up into the stage riggings. Shawn lay dazed and tangled in the wires while Brendel jumped from the stage, floating over the dead humans to Samil. The demon gathered the limp witch with his left arm and flew out the door.

Regaining his senses, Shawn untangled himself, fell to the stage floor, and rolled to his feet. Quickly, he went to the lobby and found Gwyn lying dazed on the floor, blood coming from her mouth and ears, her organs damaged by the force of Brendel's power. Shawn knelt next to her and gathered her into his arms. "Are you all right, love?" Biting his wrist, he dripped his blood into her mouth.

Slowly, Gwyn woke up, and as Shawn held her, she looked around, and out through the doors. "He is out in the street, and he is going to kill more humans. We must stop him!" Gwyn said as she tried to stand.

"You stay here," Shawn said sternly as he laid her back on to the floor. Shawn went toward the entrance door and out onto the boulevard.

Again, the demon pushed out an energy wave that traveled down the street, killing instantly any humans it touched, their charred bodies falling to the pavement.

The demon held Samil, helping her to stand, and he bellowed at Shawn, "See what you have brought meddling in my affairs! What Eos and vampires have brought to this world! Death to these humans! I will kill them by the millions! I will kill them in my father's name. They will tremble at my power, and they will flee this world! This world will be Lucifer's!"

The demon raised his hand, and a blue plasma beam traveled to the terrace above, striking the primary support connection causing a massive explosion that threw parts of the platform and buildings out into the night sky. With a loud screech, the high terrace tore away from the tower and came crashing down, clipping the platform they were on, and then to the ground far below.

Smoke billowed from the destruction, emergency vehicles with their search lights and sirens were flying around the tower and the massive damage on the ground. Two police hovercraft came in for a landing, sirens wailing. The demon fired on them, and they too were sent spiraling to the ground, exploding in a ball of brilliant fire. Brendel then focused his attention on the emergency crafts, destroying as many of those as he could.

Brendel turned again toward Shawn and yelled, "Humans cannot hurt me! They are powerless against me! My father made sure of that! And you will certainly find that out!"

Shawn hurled himself at the demon only to have dark energy strike him full force driving him into the side of a building. His levitating held him there briefly, then it dissipated, and he fell to the pavement below. Regaining his senses, Shawn rose, flew again at Brendel, driving his slayer into the demon. Again, tremendous energy tore him off, crashing him into another building. This time he held on to his consciousness and floated back to the street. He crouched to the ground in his fiercest vampire form, hissed at the demon, and gathered his strength for another attack.

The demon shook his head in disgust and took Samil, lifted into the night sky, and screamed, "We will meet Demon Slayer again. You and your angels have brought this."

Soldiers worked their way down the street, running and crouching behind the fallen debris from the buildings. The hum of their attack flyers rose and lowered in intensity as they landed, allowing more soldiers to disembark. The humans fired their weapons, saturating the area with photon bullets, throwing more debris and smoke into the air. Shawn ducked and rolled then flew into the theater with blinding speed, plucking Gwyn from the floor and back out straight up into the dark sky. Knowing the vampire garrison at Dalton was the closest, Shawn quickly made the trip with Gwyn, and on arrival was met by Katherine, his changeling.

"In here," Katherine called out, as she pointed to the burial building used by the warrior vampires for their wounded. Through a solid steel door with heavens symbols etched into its metal, Shawn brought Gwyn to the cleaning table. She woke and whispered, "Where are we, Shawn?"

"We are in Dalton, my love. I'm going to bury you. I will protect your grave. And you know The Mother will certainly want to speak to you."

"Stay near," Gwyn whispered as she began to fade again.

"I will my love. I promise!"

Shawn buried Gwyn and drew his symbols in the dirt – the symbols of The Demon Slayer given to him by Michael. He drew them so all demons and evil witches would know this vampire was his changeling and beware. He then went outside to meet Katherine.

"You found Brendel?" she asked quickly.

"We did, and he is much more powerful than Malin. He was hiding in the City of York, an actor in a theater. And Brendel swears he will destroy this world."

"The devil certainly likes to have his fun," Katherine said. "I remember the evil that came from that demon child. Something terrible is coming. I can feel it, and the angels whisper it."

Shawn embraced his changeling. "I miss you! We don't see enough of each other." Once Katherine had been queen and had risked everything to save him. He kissed her softly on the lips. "How's retirement going?"

"Quite well, I spend as much time as I can with Julien, we explore, and I enjoy that so much. Unfortunately, it is ending, it has been over a hundred years, and Julien wants to go on his own. And now Brendel has come."

Shawn brushed Katherine's hair from her eyes and whispered, "This world and its vampires have drawn Lucifer's ire. We have attracted his sick, evil attention. That is where The Mother and the angels have gone wrong. Maybe the price to end Malin's evil was too high. When Gwyn comes from the ground, I will go to The Citadel. You and Alexa must be ready. Be careful and watch out for Julien. Do not let him leave yet."

Chapter Two

S hawn sat up in his couch, sensed the day and felt Gwyn's rising consciousness, saw in his mind's eye the dirt pushing up away from her grave, and then a hand breaking the surface. Gwyn had started her awakening. He rose out of his couch, quickly put on a pair of pants and a shirt, went out into the hallway where he met Katherine hurriedly coming down the hall. Both went to the patio railing, floated over, and descended to the ground below. They hurried along the path; the sun was high in the sky, but the sunlight did not affect them. The power of Michael and Eos had made sure of that.

"I was starting to worry," Katherine said. "It has been forty days."

"Gwyn took a hard blow from Brendel. And the demon hates mother's witches."

Shawn and Katherine went through the door into the burial chamber, as Gwyn was breaking the dirt and starting to rise to quench her blood lust. Shawn quickly took hold of her, to keep her from flying away, and wiped the dirt from her eyes.

"I have you, dearest! We have blood for you! There is no need to go anywhere," he whispered in her ear.

Katherine took Gwyn from him, embraced her, brushed her dirt-soaked hair from her face, and kissed her passionately. "I was so worried for you, my love. I am happy you are awake, and you do look much better. A little dirty, though!"

Shawn had realized awhile back that a special bond had grown between Katherine and Gwyn, and a much stronger love had developed between them. They had grown close during the time of his rescue, and it must have been the despair and desperation they shared through dark times.

"Glad you are here," Gwyn whispered hoarsely to Katherine. "You must protect your changeling. The demon has come, and he will come for you. Lucifer demands your death!"

"I always will be here for you," Katherine said softly to Gwyn, as she stroked her face.

Shawn gathered Gwyn and took her to the cleansing table. Katherine again kissed her lips and squeezed her hand. They both cleaned Gwyn, gave her blood, and then Shawn took her to their couch for a needed rest.

Shawn strolled down a large hallway with high white ornate ceilings, lined with crown molding carved in plaster showing white angels, pixy creatures, vampires, and some well-known dark angels. He came to that specific spot and as always looked up to see Malin's face and a sickening feeling and shudder would follow. Lights hovered in mid-air, giving the hall a bright, spacious feel. When Gwyn came from the ground, she told him The Mother had summoned her to the shrine. The mother wanted to meld with her to experience the power of Brendel. She also wanted her to bring the Eagle's Staff.

Shawn had come alone to The Citadel, and tonight he would see his second maker and queen. The Citadel was the home of The Herit Covenant. The first two queens were Herit, and as the Archangel Michael had decreed, all that would rule after would be Herit. Two large white doors flew open, and a crowd of vampires bursts out. They were animated and chattering about their petition to the queen, some grumbling and some smiling as they quickly passed him by. The queen's session was ending for the evening. Peter walked out the high, ornate, white doors, and Shawn smiled remembering when he first met Peter. It was the night Victoria turned him, funny and amusing for Shawn but not so much for poor bewildered Peter. Yet, he had recovered well.

"Shawn—how are?" I'm stilling waiting for that cask of wine you promised me for saving you," Peter laughed and gave him a friendly shove. "I'm sure it's done aging by now."

"Doing well, and I haven't forgotten about the wine."

"You have seen the demon?" Peter asked nervously. "The news has spread. Everybody is talking about it."

"I have seen him and felt his sting."

"Yes, I heard. Is Gwyn okay?"

"She has come through fine. You must prepare our warriors and quickly. We are probably going to need a lot more too. And how is Juliette these days?"

"She is well. I am happy to say. Always looking for something new to do."

"Give her my best. What kind of mood is the queen in tonight?"

"Victoria is always in a good mood when you are near. She waits for you." Peter opened the door and stepped aside. "We will talk more."

"Yes, we will."

Shawn went through the entrance into a large throne room. The Crimmian builders had built the throne room spectacularly with high light blue arched ceilings covered with murals of angels in a blissful realm. They made a large pool in the middle with stairs rising from the water, and at the top was the blue throne, The Throne of Herit. Sitting upon it was his love of a thousand years, Victoria, Queen of the Vampires. The queen rose and spoke to Peter. "Shut the doors; we are not to be disturbed."

Victoria motioned for him to come to her. "Come, Shawn, I want to make sure you are all right."

Shawn flew to Victoria, and they embraced. He kissed her soft, beautiful lips, stroked he silked blonde hair back and kissed her neck. He whispered in her ear, "I miss you! We don't see enough of each other."

"I know," Victoria whispered. "You take too many chances, my love. I worry about you."

"I had no choice. I had to mark the demon. Now I will know where Brendel is and where he is going, and the angels will too. And he is going to Jerusalem."

Victoria kissed him passionately, hurriedly and whispered in his ear,

"Take my blood, and let me feel your lips against my neck!"

Shawn penetrated her neck with his blood teeth, and his mouth flooded with her blood. He tried to pull away, but he was a rider of vampire blood, and this time it held him in its supernatural grip. The blood pulled him over an ocean of time to Victoria's beginnings, her family's old castle on the moor. She was running as a young girl with her cloak flowing behind and dandelions in her hand. Then the blood pulled him into a mist, and he saw the archangel pointing at the demon, but this time he saw himself crumbling before Brendel. He pulled away gasping, blood dripping from his lips, and Victoria's beautiful quizzical face coming into focus.

"You have been traveling again. Take me to my couch, my love. I have a desire for you tonight." Victoria spoke breathlessly.

They made love to each other for the remainder of the night, and when morning came, they held each other, both wondering how much longer they would be together. Would it be years or centuries? Vampires rarely knew. And now he was afraid at what Brendel would bring.

"Shawn, you weren't supposed to fight Brendel."

"He knew we were there, and he drew us in. It was a trap!"

"What did he look like?" Victoria asked quickly.

"Brendel at first looked like me, but as the fight went on, he changed became darker, his facial features changed. The breast was mocking me! I believe he can change his appearance at will. I saw him take on the appearance of a dead human just before he left."

"For the love of Michael, Victoria said, as she pulled him closer. "What has Lucifer sent this time?"

"Brendel is a monster, and he enjoys slaughtering humans. It gives him great pleasure, and he is not afraid of mortals and their weapons. Lucifer has given him great power over this world."

"The Mother has drawn the devil's wrath," Victoria whispered.

Shawn pulled Victoria closer, held her, and stroked her face. "Katherine stays at her house in Dalton now. She stays next to the vampire garrison to protect Julian. Maybe you should send Braden there."

"Braden is safe here at The Citadel. And Julien has Katherine. When she left the throne, Michael left her with most of the power he gave her, and she still has Alexa. How is Gwyn?"

"She is better, but Brendel hurt her. He is pure evil. The demon summoned all his power for Gwyn; he wanted to make an example of her, a mother's witch and took great pleasure in it. She stayed in the ground for forty days, and now she has gone to The Mother."

Victoria sat up, leaned over, and Shawn saw her become serious. "I have something else to say. Drake came to me a few days ago and told me the Gates of Hell did not close after the vampires rescued you. He also told me Brendel is going to Jerusalem. He will gather great power there, enough for him to call on the armies of the dark dimension. Lucifer wants to make this one of his dark worlds. And he mostly wants to kill you then Katherine and me and bring our souls to hell. That is Brendel's purpose. Michael commands us to see what is happening in the city. He wants us to see where the soldiers are coming from, how extensive is the attack to this world."

Brendel

✭✭✭✭

Gwyn walked the trail that led to The Mother's Shrine. She had made this trip many times since Shawn had made her vampire. Taking her time, she used the eagle's staff as a walking stick. Brendel had hurt her, his power was immense, and he was a cruel creature. The demon hated The Mother's witches and took it out on her, but Shawn had saved her, protected her.

Brendel would have killed her if Shawn had not been there. Shawn had become a powerful vampire and warlock of this world. The Mother channeled high power through Shawn; few in this world had such power, and if he had the staff that she now used for a walking stick, Brendel would have found a much different foe. Deep in thought, she climbed higher into the mountains toward The Mother's Shrine.

For two hundred years, she had lived in this world and still could remember when her birth mother came to her and explained what she was. Her mother told Gwyn that she and her sister where Eos witches like her, but The Mother had given her far higher power than most. When she was twelve, The Mother started coming to her, talking of vampires, and she spoke of a particular vampire that had been chosen by the angels to be the champion of the mortals. And he would become the greatest of all Guardians.

The Mother told her to prepare herself, learn all she could about vampires, and someday she would send this vampire to her. Eventually, she would be a vampire of his making. Gwyn had lived her life, wrapping herself in The Mother's power. Living her first hundred years as a mother's witch, learning to harness heavens energy, bend it to do her bidding. Now for over a hundred years, she had been both vampire and mother's witch and teacher of the mother's magic to Shawn.

Gwyn spent her early life preparing for the day the Demon Slayer would come and preparing herself for the battle that vampires and angels would fight for Shawn's soul. They had prevailed, but now Lucifer's anger was unimaginable. Once again, a terrible evil had come, and she would have to fight this evil. The Mother expected this of her as Michael expected it from Shawn; they both knew this, and both wondered if it would always be this way. Gwyn was a powerful witch and vampire, yet when Victoria changed Shawn for the second time, the power The Mother took from him and gave her returned to him.

Over the years, Gwyn had come to terms with the vampire way. Shawn was her only love, and she knew Shawn loved her, but he loved other women too. Shawn and Katherine were the same that way; they looked for love and fell in love easily. Being a witch first, she felt different about this and had learned to accept this though sometimes it hurt her. Gwyn would think of the love she had for Katherine. Maybe Katherine was another vampire she could be with; she had been with women before. Sometimes, she would think of being with Katherine in her couch, tasting her blood, and making love to her. She had kissed Katherine and had felt passion returned to her in the kiss.

Gwyn climbed higher into the mountain, and her thoughts went to Brendel. The creature was much different, far more powerful than anything Lucifer had sent before. The Mother told her to bring the eagles staff and to come to the shrine, where she would tell her of the demon's purpose. Gwyn had been to heaven many times, had spent time with The Mother gathering her power. With a strong feeling of foreboding, Gwyn continued her long climb. Higher she went up the side of the mountain and finally came to the Mother's Shrine. The air was heavy with a wet mist that came from the cascading water off the mountainside, down over the shrine, it fell, rainbows floated in the air, and everything here felt charged with electricity.

Like always when entering the shrine, Gwyn went to the large quartz gem jutting from the floor, and immediately light came from the crystal, swirled, and engulfed her. Feeling the vibrations, she allowed the energy to absorb her and then ride it to heaven. In a flash, she found herself sitting in a rocker holding the staff on a porch of an ancient farmhouse.

Many times, since her beginnings with Shawn, she came to this house to receive guidance and power of The Mother. The farmhouse was where she stayed when in heaven. Suddenly, hearing the squeak of a rocker, she turned and saw a beautiful woman dressed in a white summer dress sitting next to her. The spirit had a smile older and wiser than the earth itself. Her smooth, radiant skin sparkled, golden hair flowed over her bare shoulders, and a man-size eagle stood next to her.

"How are you, Gwyn? It is good to be with you again. Have you missed your house here in heaven?"

"I have missed heaven, and sometimes, I wish I could stay here. Brendel has finally come, and I do not understand why the angels did not see this."

"The beast has come, and all of heaven hoped he would not. The archangel looks at me for this calamity. The future is clouded now. The angels and I did not think Lucifer would go this far. He is going to make the earth a battleground between good and evil. Lucifer has fought this battle on five other worlds. Evil won on four of these worlds, and one repelled Lucifer's evil. This happened because the guardians of that world had a champion, and they prevailed against the horror of Lucifer. The forces the humans will face come from the Dark Universe. This alternate dimension is under total control of Lucifer's evil. All guardians will have to fight. Humans and guardian will have no choice; they will have to fight to save their world—to survive. Brendel will kill or drive the humans from their planet and then he will turn his dark army on guardians. It is time for humans and vampires to unite."

"What does the Archangel say of this?"

"Michael has gone to Lucifer and asked him not to do this. Told him of the power he would squander. Even if Lucifer wins, he will be weak for many years—vulnerable. The dark one mocked Michael told him to send Shawn, and then they would talk. Michael is angry and places much of the blame on me. He expects me to save your world, and to do that, I need the guardians and once more, Shawn."

"What do you want of me?"

"Shawn must be protected through all of this, but that will be hard to accomplish in the physical world. The way he is. But I do have a power which is skilled in handling him."

The staff that Gwyn held brighten. An intense white light rose out of the staff, formed a ball, and entered the eagle's spirit. The eagle spread its wings, climbed into the spiritual sky, and flew away.

"Why are you taking power from the staff?"

"Shawn has been given much of the energy of this staff. The strength is in him, and now I will hide a special power in the staff."

A white light formed around The Mother, part of the energy broke off and grew bigger, much brighter. The intensity of the light and power was too great for Gwyn to be near; she quickly released the staff and retreated from the porch. The light condensed and formed a spirit that was Jessamine. Then a compelling vision came to her, seared its way through her being. It was a vision of Shawn's real purpose, the reason for his existence, but she could not see the outcome. Jessamine smiled at Gwyn, then turned back into the light and traveled into the staff. Gwyn floated back to the porch as the light dissipated. She picked up the staff and felt the vibrations, the tremendous energy of the staff.

"The part of me that is Jessamine is in the staff. Use this power to fight Brendel. I know Shawn does not carry the staff. He prefers his slayer. He has been a guardian far longer than a Mother's witch. That is why I am giving the staff to you. Always keep it near, use the staff to protect Shawn, and when

the time comes, use the staff to deliver Jessamine's blow to Brendel. Also, deliver this message to Shawn; he must come to heaven to see Michael and me."

"I will do as you say."

"We will talk again, Gwyn. Your world must be saved. Michael demands this of me."

Gwyn saw a smile spread over The Mother's spiritual face.

"I know how you enjoy your house. Take some time and rest."

The spirit that was The Mother intensified and rose off the porch traveled out into the bright blue sky, slowly faded, and disappeared.

Gwyn leaned the staff against the porch column, turned, and went through the door into her farmhouse. Feeling weary, she thought, *I think I will stay for a bit. Stay at my house.*

The farmhouse was a safe place for her and had always helped quite her troubled spirit. She went to the kitchen sink, thought of dishes, and they appeared with warm, sudsy water. She began to wash the dishes looking out the window over the sink. She saw a beautiful flowered meadow, birds flying, and the big tree with bright green leaves – Shawn's tree when he came to heaven.

Chapter Three

S hawn and Victoria stood on a bluff, made of thousands of years of blowing sand. Their location was two miles west of Jerusalem, a spot where the vampires could easily see the city. A hot dry breeze blew the abrasive desert sand across the stark landscape, and he felt the bite against his face. They were by a small cave, and Victoria hung back just inside the entrance. A cloak pulled tight around her, only showing the flash of her blue eyes, and Deceida strapped to her back. The sun burned high in the sky. Victoria could handle this sunlight if she had too, but for now, she chose to hide from it, yet Shawn stood outside. The daylight did not affect him.

Brendel and Samil had come to Jerusalem, and then a transparent blue dome grew and formed around the city. High power was gathering in the metropolis as the Dark Dimension made its connection to this world. Now, a sense of evil radiated from its cold light. A human army advanced from the north; their troop transports hovering ten feet above the ground, traveling smoothly over the rough desert surface. Their hovering battle tanks lead the charge. Now they were coming into view, and all-day attack aircraft flew overhead, protecting the multitudes of fleeing humans in their aircars and buses. Earth was plunging into darkness and war again.

Shawn turned and walked to the opening of the cave. "The human army is going to enter the city."

They are," Victoria answered quickly. "But I don't think they know what they are fighting...or how to fight what is in the city."

"Seems to be a lot of humans escaping," Shawn added.

"Luckily, the dome is being penetrated. For now."

"The mortals will enter the city from the north, and then we will enter the city from the south."

"Unfortunately, that is our only choice, but it would have been nice if you had your staff."

"That's what Gwyn always says. The Mother wanted Gwyn to bring the staff to the shrine." Shawn walked back to the opening and searched the desert to the south, but all he saw was heat waves rising from the dry surface. Then he turned and said, "Terrible visions of the future come with the staff. I can form the Mother's energy with my hands, and I have my slayer. And you have Deceida. Come, my queen, let us get some rest."

They went to the back of the small cave and huddled together under their cloaks, waiting for the human army to arrive.

Shawn brushed Victoria's hair back and kissed her gently. "This could be the end of the humans," he whispered.

"Why do you say that?"

"Remember, when I received The Mother's power. When you and Gwyn rescued me in the black castle?"

Shawn felt Victoria's lips against his neck and then his ear. "I remember, my love." Her hand traveled under his shirt to his chest, and he felt her tender caress.

"I went to hell," Shawn whispered. "I saw the horror, and I saw this world burning and Lucifer laughing. The devil wanted me to see it."

"You certainly saw something that I do remember. But maybe the devil was playing with you, letting you see hallucinations. Let's rest. There is still time. All is not lost yet."

"The staff also shows me those visions."

The humans arrived around eight, and their battle tanks hovered firing Photon Pulse Cannons. There were four groups;

each had three long, slightly curved lines of tanks to match the dome's curvature. They used searchlights, moving them over the dome probing for any weakness. The battle tanks hovered at different elevations so they could concentrate their fire on small areas of the dome. Bright orange photon after photon of high energy struck the dome, the power whipping the desert sands into a frenzy, opening sections so troop transports could enter the city.

The transports moved into the city, floated to the ground, and their many doors slid open. The soldiers poured out of the carriers, using the darkness for cover and made their way down the streets. They were traveling dark spots forming on the outside of the dome shooting laser beams, hitting some of the battle tanks, causing them to explode into large balls of fire, propelling smoke and metal pieces out into the desert.

The human attack flyers were now firing their high energy photon missiles and lasers into the city; some penetrated, but most did not. The rockets that seared their way through the dome rocked the city with explosions. Again, lasers came from the dome, striking more of the flyers, and the departure of humans from the city quickened.

"It is time for us to go, my love," Victoria sighed. "The human soldiers have entered the city, and we must too. The Archangel commands us."

"When we enter the city, we will make our way to Brendel and Samil," Shawn advised. "This energy is coming from them. We must stay together. Brendel is powerful and very dangerous, and we do not know what we will find."

Shawn and Victoria left the bluff flying low over the hard-packed sand across the desert toward Jerusalem. Suddenly, the blue dome shifted, grew larger, collapsed back in on itself, and then expanded to its original size pushing out a wave of dark energy. Destroying many of the first waves of aircraft and battle tanks, Shawn saw the wave coming toward them, turned back, and yelled to Victoria, "Take cover!" Victoria took from her back a glowing Deceida, kneeled, and held the slayer in front of her.

"Quick Shawn—kneel behind me!" Victoria yelled.

The dark energy washed over and around them, as Deceida formed a white shield of light protecting them.

"We have to get through the dome," Shawn shouted, "as fast as we can!"

They quickly flew to the dome's edge. Pushing out his hands, Shawn shoved a white ball of energy toward the dome wall. The heat seared an opening, and they both quickly flew through. Hurriedly, they made their way down a street, working their way around the destruction. Shawn heard the booming explosions echoing through the city, felt the ground shaking, the concussions on his body, and the heat assaulting his face. Then he saw the high towers swaying.

They came upon dead humans, some laying and some sitting against the buildings, their arms stretched out or covering their eyes. Mothers were holding their children, their flesh burned and blistered, eyes scorched from their heads.

"I can feel the demon," Victoria called out. Then Victoria's expression changed; heaven had taken hold of her, and she looked out into the night, her eyes briefly burning white light. Shawn heard her whisper, "Feel his power, Michael."

"I feel him, and the witch is with him," Shawn quickly whispered back.

They made their way toward the center of the city. Most of the fighting now was raging in the northern quarters. Loud explosions continued to shake the ground and towers. They followed the main boulevard traveling further into the city, and suddenly a swirl of dark blue energy formed in front of them spiraling into an oscillating tunnel. Six soldiers from some otherworld became visible and walked through. A strange creature followed; they were Valaris Wizards, evil creatures of Lucifer, human-shaped, tall, and slender. They wore no clothes, and their skin was smooth and grey. The wizards had no features on the face or bodies. They held a staff, swirling it in full circles, conjuring the portal, and then cold dark melancholia of evil came through. The unknown soldiers had come from an alternate dimension, a world that long-ago Lucifer turned to darkness.

The soldier's heads were big, with two large black eyes and helmets that held various communication and projecting devices. They, too, were tall and slender, skin red, their extremities long with three fingers and a thumb on their hands. Their knees bent backward than the direction they walked, giving them an unusual gate. The creatures wore dark red battle suits and carried a strange-looking weapon that fired plasma bullets. Strangely, the creatures moved in unison. They immediately opened fire on Shawn and Victoria. Dodging the plasma bullets, Shawn threw white energy that disintegrated three of them. Victoria, in a flash of movement, killed the remaining three with Deceida. The wizard retreated through the opening, and the portal closed.

They continued down the thoroughfare toward the chaos. The terrible violence was spreading throughout the city; the explosions now came one after another. Shawn easily could see the fighting in the high towers, humans and alien soldiers firing at each other and explosions that shook and swayed the sky towers.

Suddenly, a massive explosion echoed through the city, and a high tower tilted and snapped in the middle. The top half took its long plunge to the ground, leaving a fiery trail of swirling smoke and fire. With a horrific roar, the ash and debris billowed down the streets, sending shock waves throughout Jerusalem. Lucifer singles out the city to be his first prize in this world.

Humans must press the attack better. They must stop the portals from opening, Shawn thought. He forced his way through a door, and they took refuge from the waves of debris and ash cascading down the street. A roar as the destruction flew by their building, glass blown in on them, and a deafening sound of wreckage pelting the building.

Huddling in a hallway, Shawn yelled, "Can you sense it, Victoria? Portals are opening all over the city, and alien soldiers are coming through."

"I can feel it. Their numbers are increasing rapidly. We must go forward to find out more about these otherworld solders."

"As you wish, my queen, but we should try to avoid a confrontation with Brendel."

"I am sure he knows we are here."

They left the building and again started down the boulevard toward the center of the city. The air was thick with ash; it covered everything and drifted down like snow. Sirens and alarms sounded as the city rumbled and shook. Scattered along the way were human bodies; many had fallen from the towers.

They traveled further, and again saw a swirl of blue. Valaris Wizard, with a staff, appeared at the entrance of the portal, and this time, many red soldiers came behind him. Some went up side streets, and some came toward them. A squad of human soldiers came from a side street and both laid down a blistering fire of photon and plasma bullets, human soldier after human soldier fell dead. Shawn and Victoria joined the fight swinging their slayers with blinding speed, blocking plasma bullets, cutting many of the red soldiers down. Deceida's metal burned a bright light as the slayer from heaven took the red soldier's heads, and soon, the slayer's enemies laid dead. The wizard again quickly stepped back through and closed the fiery blue portal.

They moved toward the center of the city, and then Shawn sensed the battle had been lost and the desperation of the retreating humans. "The human soldiers are leaving the city," he shouted to Victoria. "They have lost!" Shawn yelled as he slammed his fist against a wall.

"They didn't know what they were fighting," Victoria said.

"We should think of leaving," Shawn gritted out.

"We must go a little farther. Michael wants to see more of this enemy through me."

"It will be risky!"

"We have too. Michael commands me!"

Shawn and Victoria continued down the boulevard penetrating the drifting dark smoke with their vampire's eyes, seeing the wreckage of crashed air cars, steel girders, and other parts of the buildings lying on the boulevard. Craters were blasted into the pavement, and everywhere smoke billowed into the air.

Suddenly Shawn sensed Brendel, and now the dark angel and Samil were showing themselves floating to the ground in front of them. Both were draped in evil and wore swords on their backs. There was no deformity with Brendel. He looked young, handsome—his only giveaway was crookedness to his face and lips that showed his cruelty and evil. As soon as Shawn thought this, Brendel's faced change to a grotesque form, then the demon stared at him, and let out a low dark laugh. "You see what I want you to see, Demon Slayer."

Brendel floated above the boulevard staring at Shawn. "Samil, I have a Demon Slayer following me, meddling in my affairs."

"You do, my lord," Samil hissed.

"What do you think we should do about this?"

"Kill him and the whore queen."

Deceida glowed, and its metal rang as Victoria drew the slayer from heaven, and then an overwhelming power slip in and settled over them. Shawn quickly felt the overpowering presence of the Archangel Michael. By Victoria's look, he had taken over her and was channeling threw her.

"How are you, Michael?" The smirk left the demons face. "I know you are here. Have you come to take a look at me? This world will be my father's. You can thank Eos for that. The Gates of Hell did not close."

Suddenly, Shawn saw Brendel's head snap back, his face became grimace, as if he was being strangled. He saw the demon's neck collapse in, being held helpless. It stopped, and he felt the great power lift as the Archangel left.

Shawn turned to an awakening Victoria and called out, "We should leave and come back with more vampires."

"You will be going nowhere, demon slayer." As soon as the words left Brendel's cruel lips, the demon launched himself at Victoria, sensing her dazed state, trying for a quick kill. Brendel was maddening in his attack on Victoria as if the Archangel was still there.

Samil flew toward Shawn to block him from helping Victoria. Parrying Samil's first strike, he spun and cut the witch across her shoulder. Samil floated back from him, and a sober look spread over the witch's face. Shawn attacked again, bringing his slayer down repeatedly first right then left. Their steel ringing, and he drove Samil back then spun and delivered a cut across her thigh.

Samil raised her hands and yelled, "Beelzebub, give me power!"

Shawn saw her bring her hands down, throwing a ball of burning dark energy at him. Crouching holding his slayer in front of him, he quickly chanted a mother's spell, and the power washed harmlessly over him. He flew at the witch, thrusting his slayer into her chest, driving her to the ground, helpless. The witch got to her knees, and Shawn raised his slayer, preparing to take her head. He heard a scream and saw Brendel drive his sword into Victoria's chest, watched her legs give out, and the queen collapse to the ground. Victoria laid motionless. Seeing the wounds on her body, Shawn knew she had given the demon a fight but was severely hurt.

With blinding speed, Shawn flew at Brendel, sparing Samil. He grabbed Deceida from the ground and the beast kicked him in his stomach, propelling him into the side of a building. Shawn fell to the pavement below. Shaking his head to clear it, he stood, and held Deceida, as it rang in his hand. Quickly feeling the power of the sword, he launched himself at the demon. Dark energy came at him, and he held Deceida in front of him slicing through, propelling himself at Brendel driving the beast against the side of a building, plunging Deceida into him.

Brendel screamed, rose, and with a blow from the hilt of his sword, knocked Shawn back.

"Malin told me about you, Demon Slayer, that you would be the one to watch out for." Brendel drew his sword and flew at Shawn, their blades repeatedly striking as Brendel slowly pushed Shawn back. Sounds of steel ringing echoed down the walkways. Then Shawn felt his body shifted into another realm, darkness pulling at him, and back giving Brendel time to slice him across his stomach with his sword. Backward he fell holding his stomach. Brendel quickly turned, raise his sword to take a struggling Victoria's head. Shawn screamed, flew at Brendel, and as the demon's blade came down, Shawn thrust Deceida to block the blow. The blades collided a loud crack and a bright light shot from Deceida blowing Brendel down the walkway.

Shawn screamed at Brendel, "You dare do such a thing!"

"Your queen killed Malin," the demon raged, as he got to his feet. "Lucifer wants her head."

"I will kill you someday for what you have done here! For what you tried to do to my queen! My maker! Tell Lucifer it was I that killed that piece of shit, Luvon!" He gathered Victoria in his arms and glared his hate at Brendel. Bleeding from her mouth, Victoria clasped her blood-soaked chest and moaned, as Shawn shot straight up toward the dome. Chanting a spell repeatedly, he called on The Mother to help him with their escape. Then an opening appeared in the blue dome, and Shawn with Victoria shot through. Looking back, he saw the dark energy and the burning city. The opening quickly closes, and there was no pursuing Brendel.

Shawn held Victoria tightly, wiping the blood from her face, telling her, "You will be all right, my love. I have you, and I won't let anything happen to you."

He flew faster and strained his energy to reach the Citadel with Victoria. It was morning, and in this part of the world, the sun burned hot.

Victoria moaned and spoke softly to Shawn, "You have to bury me. I cannot take the sun. I am too weak."

"All right. We will go to the ground soon." Shawn used his powerful eyes and senses to search across the water. Eventually, the island of Sicily came into view. Landing on the southern seashore, he brought Victoria to the sea and washed the blood from her wounds. She was a vampire, her wounds were healing, and the bleeding had slowed but the sunlight hampered her healing. Shawn offered his wrist, Victoria bit, and drank his blood until he pulled it from her blood coated lips. He held her in the seawater and brushed her wet hair from her face. "How are you doing, my love?"

"I am doing better, but you should bury me. The sun is hard to take now," Victoria said weakly.

"I will bury us together, and we will wait until you are stronger. There is an orange orchard inland. We will go there."

Holding Victoria, Shawn waded back toward shore. When he came to the beach, a portal began to open, dark blue lights swirled, and then two Valaris wizards sent by Lucifer came through holding spears with yellow tips. Shawn was very familiar with this kind of spear. Long ago, Katherine and Jessamine had saved him from the deadly venom of the yellow tip. He must be careful the tips could cause instant paralysis and then death. And once a yellow tip had made him mortal. Shawn gently laid Victoria on the sand and told her, "Lucifer is not done with us yet."

Shawn changed to his most potent form and drew Deceida. The wizards lowered their spears and sidestepped in opposite directions, to attack from both sides. These were bizarre creatures with no face, and an overwhelming alien sense came with them.

"Go back through the portal if you want to live!" Shawn warned, as he raised Deceida and prepared to attack.

Then a strange broken language came from their blank faces. To his amazement, he understood what they were saying. "Lucifer wants your souls. You two must pay!"

"Then he should have sent more assassins," Shawn shouted back.

Shawn advanced flying into them, parried the first spear that struck at him and swung his slayer, taking the tip from the other. He fell back, and the wizards moved forward, thrusting their spears outward. With stunning speed, he flew over the creatures, came down behind them, and took the head of one. The other wizard thrust and drove the yellow tip threw his shirtsleeve. Shawn flew back; he did not want the yellow tip to pierce him that would mean certain death for him and Victoria.

Circling the wizard, Shawn raised Deceida high, preparing to attack, looking for an opening. The dark wizard swept the yellow tip back and forth, trying to keep Shawn away. Slowly, Shawn side step, suddenly, he pushed out his hand and threw white energy at the beast. The force stunned the wizard, and Shawn quickly moved in, slicing the spear from the warlock's hands, twirling and taking his head.

Feeling desperate, Shawn went to Victoria and gathered her in his arms. "I'm not sure of this place, Victoria! Let's go to the orchard, and we'll see!"

"Brendel knows where we are," Victoria informed weakly. "Be careful!"

Shawn flew inland and landed in the orchard. He immediately went to a shade tree and laid Victoria under it. Turning, he saw another portal opening, and then he muttered, "For the love of heaven, they do know where we are." Samil with a sword and three wizards with yellow tip spears step through. Samil's wicked smile had long left her. The witch still felt the wounds Shawn gave her.

Shawn kissed Victoria's forehead and urgently whispered to her, "It's Samil and three wizards! I am sorry, we cannot stay here. Be ready. I'll be back!"

Shawn rose, holding Deceida; the sword from heaven rang and glowed with a righteous might. He walked toward Samil and the wizards. "You are healing quickly, Samil. Brendel must need you. This time you might not be so lucky. Where's is that pathetic creature?"

Brendel is finishing the job in Jerusalem. Lucifer wants the death of the queen. The slayer of Malin. That is why I am here."

"Then Lucifer will have your death. The queen is with me!"

Another portal opened, and four more wizards of Lucifer's stepped through holding yellow-tipped spears.

"I guess Lucifer's not so sure about this!" Shawn growled at the witch.

Samil immediately formed energy in her hand and threw a ball of blue energy at him. Shawn crouched and held Deceida in front of him, but still, the force threw him back. He landed, rolled, and then rose into the air where he hovered above the ground.

"Looks like Beelzebub gave you a little more power. Unfortunately for you, it won't be enough."

Shawn glared at them, threw the energy of heaven, a white ball of fire, obliterating one of the wizards. Coming back to the ground, Shawn stood square, a force that these evil creatures could not handle. He held Deceida high and advanced for the attack.

Two wizards with yellow-tipped spears came at him. Shawn parried one of the spears, but the second came through and grazed his side. He brought his slayer around, driving the tip away, then turned back around and took the head of the warlock. Falling back, he held his side, dizziness coming over him. He knew he had to get Victoria away from this place, to safety and quickly.

"What is the matter Demon Slayer? You look a little ill." Samil drew her sword and came at Shawn, striking at him their steel ringing. Shawn parried and delivered a powerful blow driving Samil back. Quickly the witch advanced again and struck Shawn across the arm. Shawn retreated, knowing his wound from the yellow tip was already decaying. He waved Deceida in front of him, keeping the evil creatures at bay and projected a powerful psychic message to The Citadel that their queen was in trouble.

Again, advancing on Samil, he drove Deceida into her, she screamed and flew back as the Wizards came forward. Samil cursed at him, formed energy, and threw it at him. Shawn chanted a mother's spell to protect him from the power. The dark energy again washed over him; realizing the situation, he made his way to Victoria, gathered her in his arms while Samil and the wizards surrounded them.

"Can you hear me, Victoria? Try to stay awake."

Victoria opened her eyes. "You are hurt. Fly, escape this place."

"I will never leave you! If we die, we die together!" Shawn took Victoria and shot straight up, turned east, and accelerated to his top vampire speed. Still, Samil and the wizards followed close behind. They were tracking him and knew where he was going, but he could stay ahead of them. Turning north, he flew along the coast of France and felt help rapidly approaching. Katherine, Gwyn, and Peter were approaching from the north, but it would take time for their rescuers to arrive.

Again, he used his compelling vision to scan the countryside. To the east, he saw stones and boulders that humans had stripped from the surrounding farmland and piled high in a long line next to a freshly plowed field, and on the other side was hedge groves. *Finally,* he thought, *the hedge groves will give cover.* He descended, landed, and laid Victoria next to a large boulder and again sent out a powerful psychic message so their help knew where they were.

"Help is coming, Victoria!" he told her as he brushed her bloody hair from her face.

He could see her weakness, saw it in her eyes as she nodded her head. He would fight to the death to protect her. Shawn drew Deceida and called out, "Are you ready, Deceida to protect our queen!" The sword from heaven's metal rang loudly.

Victoria raised her head and said hoarsely, "Help is coming. Wait for them, Shawn. They will be here soon."

"There is no time, my love, evil is here, and I am going to end that witch's life!"

Samil and the wizards came in quickly, landed, and immediately spread out. As always, Shawn felt The Mother's power rise up from deep within him. He pushed his hand out and shot the energy of The Mother at the evil ones. But just as quickly, Samil chanted a spell, and dark energy formed around the evil creatures. The two energies collided with a loud boom. Samil charged in. Shawn swung Deceida connecting with Samil's sword, driving the witch back. The wizards rushed in, and he parried their spears and split one down the middle, and they fell back. Back and forth they went Shawn, parrying their strikes, dodging, driving them back away from Victoria.

Finally, help arrived; Katherine, Gwyn, and Peter landed. Peter immediately went to Victoria, and Shawn yelled to him, "Take the queen to safety, Peter, hurry! Get her to The Citadel!"

Peter gathered Victoria and instantly took to the air. A wizard began to conjure a ball of dark energy, but Gwyn fired her staff and disintegrated the evil creature. Samil again chanted a spell to raise dark energy to protect them from Gwyn's, but the staff was too powerful.

Shawn yelled to the vampires, "Be careful of the yellow tips! They are dangerous!"

Nodding her head in agreement, Katherine with Alexa moved in and quickly took a warlock's head. Shawn was sure that Katherine still remembered that long-ago cave and the yellow tip spears. Samil seeing her numbers dwindling, and her prize had escape took to the air to make her getaway and screamed at the wizards, "Kill them all!"

The remaining three wizards gathered, one began to chant a spell in an attempt to open a portal. The other two faceless creatures stood their ground, pointing the yellow tip spear at them. They were helpless against The Mother's Staff. Gwyn lowered the staff and fired, disintegrating the wizards where they stood.

Immediately Katherines was with him, helping him to steady himself. "Your hurt Shawn!"

"I'm all right, but Jerusalem is lost. Brendel was too strong. I don't think any single vampire can defeat him."

Shawn was glad for Katherine's help, as his head was spinning from the spear tip. His flesh around the wound was starting to rot, and he could smell the evil stench.

"We will mobilize the vampire army," Katherine said. "Lucifer has his foothold in this world. But for now, let us get you back."

Wrinkling her face, Gwyn came to him, lifted his shirt, and placed her staff against the wound. Drawing the evil poison into the staff, so the festering injury could start to heal. "I have a message from The Mother," Gwyn told him. "She has commanded you to go to Heaven and meet with Michael and her. The Mother is aware you have become skilled in avoiding Heaven and your place in it. But this time, she says you must go."

Shawn snorted. "They will want something from me. First, I go to The Citadel and make sure Victoria is all right, drink some wine, and rest."

The vampires floated up and took flight back to The Citadel. Shawn felt the cool air rushing over him, keeping him alert. Brendel was a seriously strong demon and had access to other realms. This world was in trouble. Lucifer was going to kill and subjugate the humans to make The Mother pay for what she did to him. And he was coming after the Herit Covenant. Bad times were coming again, maybe the worst of times.

Chapter Four

S hawn and the others landed on The Citadel grounds. Everywhere there were vampire warriors, brought by Katherine, moving quickly to fortify the compound. Shawn had shaken off the spear wound, walked with purpose with Deceida on his back, and made his way inside, followed by Katherine and Gwyn. They went down the wide spiral stairs into the basement, toward the burial chambers. Shawn met Peter on the way. "How is she, Peter?"

"Brendel hurt her badly, but my maker wanted us to wait for you before we buried her." Peter turned to Katherine. "Some heads of the Covenants are here, wanting to know the condition of the queen."

I will handle them," Katherine said. "I've had some experience with this. Shawn, go check on Victoria."

Shawn hurried to the burial chamber where he saw his love lying on a cleansing table, surrounded by her Crimmian attendances, a white sheet covering her. Victoria's wounds had stained the sheet red. She had always protected the Crimmian Society and now had hundreds serving her faithfully. Throughout the burial chamber, elite vampire guards were placed to protect their queen. With a worried look, Braden stood next to her holding her hand, offering suggestions to the Crimmians attending the queen. He went to her and took hold of her hand, kissed her, and her eyes opened. "You are here. I was afraid for you. For both of us at times. Now you are with me, and I can be buried."

"You will be all right with a little time in the ground."

"Drake came to me and told me the angels had called us both to heaven. You will go, Shawn. That is a command."

"Yes, I have already been informed. I will be buried next to you, and from the grave, we will start our journey. You should know that Samil escaped, and Brendel has control of Jerusalem."

"Drake told me. We must mobilize the reserves. Katherine knows what to do. She will lead until I am well." Victoria then waved at her attendance and commanded, "Dig another grave."

Victoria pulled Shawn close and whispered in his ear, "I must allow the earth to heal me now, grow strong again. We will need more warriors. Tell Katherine for me. Victoria faded, lost consciousness, and her attendants made final preparations and then buried her. Shawn drew the sign of The Demon Slayer on her grave to protect her, and then he undressed. Katherine and Gwyn came into the chamber, and Shawn informed Katherine that Victoria ordered her to take command. Katherine and Gwyn took Shawn to the marble table and began washing the dried blood from his body.

"Shawn, I informed the ancients what has happened and told them I would be in charge until the queen comes from the ground," Katherine said. "As usual, they weren't pleased, but they understood."

Shawn looked up at his two changelings and instructed them, "We will need more warriors. Lucifer's wizards are opening portals, and soldiers from another world are coming through. They are not supernatural killers, and guardians and humans can easily kill them. The wizards are a different story, and they can control dark energy. Most likely, all vampires will have to become warriors to save our world!"

"We will see you when you return," Gwyn told him as she kissed him on his lips, and then she whispered into his ear, "I forgot to tell you The Mother wants me to keep the staff." They were the last words he heard as Katherine and Gwyn took him to the grave.

Shawn felt the cold dirt fall on him, and his spirit leave his body to begin the trip to Heaven. Traveling toward the light, he felt the vibrations in his soul as he passed through the different levels of existence. Finally, he arrived at Heaven. He was by his tree with the large green leaves and the beautiful meadow that surrounded his spot. The sky was a vibrant blue and dotted by small white clouds. The one difference now was a white house off in the distance.

The last time he was in Heaven was when Anne put him in the ground. Two hundred years had passed since then. He remembered the bliss he felt floating in The Mother's energy. Existing in her part of Heaven, how he did not want to leave, how he did not want to feel the pain of losing Anne and Marilyn. Still, eventually, The Mother made him go, told him she had a purpose for him, and that purpose brought horrible Malin.

Off in the distance, Shawn saw The City of Light. Its brightness made him want to look away, to perceive something different. How could he go to that place, it was too bright, too much energy for his earthly spirit. He saw the path that led to the city and started his trip; sure, somebody would come to him, to help him. Then he was alongside the house and noticed a lovely porch attached. He saw the flowers surrounding the house, their colors changing and flowing. He did remember this place never seemed quite solid. The porch held rocking chairs, and then he remembered the house in heaven that Gwyn told him about.

Two lights left the city, traveled toward him, and instantly they were hovering in front of him. He felt a great joy when he saw the lights form into Anne and Marilyn.

He felt Marilyn's words, *"It is good to be with you again, Shawn. To sense your spirit."*

"It is, it has been so long since we were together," Shawn projected. *"I have missed you so!"*

And then he heard Anne's voice, a remembrance of a voice he had heard long ago. *"Greetings Shawn, it has been a long time since you have come to heaven."*

"I haven't felt a need. The Mother got what she wanted, and Malin is gone."

He felt Anne come near. So, near her essence brushed against his, and then he heard her whisper, *"Prepare yourself, dark days are coming for the earth and you."*

"I am becoming weary of all this, living on earth and fighting the angel's battles. It has become too much for me. Too much darkness."

"Michael and Eos are aware of this, Shawn, but they need you again. Of all the vampires, you are the one that knows the humans the best. You have always loved them. They don't deserve you."

"When I was being rescued, the devil showed me this would never end, and their will all ways be darkness."

"Try to calm your spirit. Someday the angels will allow you to rest, to escape the darkness. Now Marilyn and I will take you to The City of Light."

Shawn's reality fell away from him, and then he found himself floating in bright light. He could feel Anne and Marilyn near, heard their voices reassuring him.

Again, he heard Anne's voice, *"Try to remain calm as you get used to the brightness. Slowly, the intensity and energy will increase until you are ready to enter The City of Light."*

"Will you stay with me while I am there?" Shawn thought, and then he heard Marilyn's reassuring voice. *"We will be with you when you are in The City of Light and when you meet Michael and The Mother."*

"Then, I am ready!"

Light engulfed Shawn, so intense it was all he knew. Slowly, he faded away, losing all awareness except for the light. His consciousness became a small point lost in the light, and then his awareness grew as he became used to the light. That was when he heard the reassuring voices of Anne and Marilyn. That was when the energy would intensify, and he would again lose himself. This process repeated until finally, he woke to The City of Light. Herit once told him you must die many times to reach Heaven.

Shawn stood on a sidewalk next to a street lined with shops of all kinds. Here spirits had a more solid appearance. He saw Anne and Marilyn standing next to him, looking the way they did when they were on earth. There was no technology, only a simple way of life. Spirits were walking or floating overhead. A shop across the street caught his attention. He stopped in front and watched the bladesmith pound a long sliver of glowing metal into a slayer blade. Then he heard Anne's voice, *"Swords from heaven."*

A spirit of a long-dead warrior vampire from some other world landed next to the blacksmith, and a small, bright light came from the apparition and entered the sword. *Amazing,* Shawn thought. Now he understood Deceida.

"Michael wanted you to see this reality the way it truly is, he thought it would give you comfort," he heard Anne say. *"He knows how upset it made you seeing Lucifer's world."*

And then he heard Marilyn's voice, *"Follow us, Shawn; we have something to show you."*

Marilyn and Anne rose over the city, and Shawn followed. He flew over the city, and soon they came to a large arched building made of blocks that looked to be of red sandstone, which radiated a soft light of the same color. They entered a large, arched opening with no door, the inside was enormous, with a high, curved ceiling. Through the large, glassless windows, Shawn saw a beautiful valley unfolding toward the horizon. Books lined the high walls of this vast building.

Marilyn told him, *"This is the hall of souls, and the books bear record to their existence."*

Then Anne told him, *"You have never been listed here. Michael has kept your existence secret. Because of the demons. Recently you have shown up in the hall of souls. Let me show you."*

Shawn, Anne, and Marilyn floated up until they were midway between the floor and ceiling, and then down the hall, on and on they went until finally, they came to a section tuck back in a corner. Anne took a book and showed Shawn his existence.

Then he heard Anne's voice, *"Michael has finally allowed your name to be placed in the hall of souls."*

The book listed him as an earthly warrior and a Guardian of Michael's. Then he heard Anne's words, *"Heaven does await you!"* He followed them out a large, arched window, and they went straight up into the spiritual sky, and again, light engulfed him and soon faded to show a vast palace of light.

"Michael's home," Anne informed him. *"Follow us."*

Shawn followed, and they went down a sizeable arched hallway and then through a massive doorway into a mammoth hall, and at the middle, on a dais sat a man on a golden throne. The man was three times the size of a human, and on his back was large black wings. At his feet laid a sword of heaven. A woman that radiated light stood next to him. They looked wise but looked neither young nor old. Still, Shawn could see they were spirits and that they shone tremendous power.

"Greetings to you, Shawn," he felt the words from the Archangel Michael strongly.

Then a softer kinder voice, *"It is always good to be with you, Shawn."* It was Eos.

"I have come here as you both have command. My world is collapsing, and Lucifer showed me what would happen. Mother, you should have seen this, and Michael, you certainly know what Lucifer is capable of."

"You have always done as we have asked," he heard The Mother say. *"We must call on you one more time."*

"We know the Dark Angel quite well, Shawn," the Archangel told him sternly. *"His pride and arrogance are immense, and now we will give his evil a terrible blow. We have asked him not to do this, but he must have his revenge. Mortals will be the first to attack. Brendel's armies come from the dark*

dimension; they are the Kargarians and Tarragons, and their numbers are immense. The humans will weaken these armies, and then all warrior vampires will finish Brendel. We have informed Victoria that all vampires must become warriors, all must fight and sacrifice. It is a time when humans will come to know guardians. You must contact the humans, meet with them, explain to them, and give them leadership in this battle. The mortals have never fought this kind of enemy. They have already discussed amongst themselves the possibility of finding the Guardians. Their science has started to probe into our realm."

"Maybe we should not have killed Malin," Shawn projected strongly toward Eos.

He felt The Mother penetrate his spirit. *"You might be right, Shawn, but we must always challenge evil. No matter who or what the evil is. The likes of you and I will always confront evil. The dark energy of this universe always tries to absorb the light. This energy creates evil beings like Malin, Brendel, and Lucifer. And now you must face it again. Heaven has given you the power and made you are champion. Again, heaven prays for your victory. From this time forward, you will always be known as The Guardian of Earth."*

The Archangel then commanded him. *"Kneel before me, Shawn, and receive my power and a sword of heaven."* Shawn saw the Archangel take the sword, stand, and his wings spread. Michael brought the sword down to touch his spirit, and he felt great power travel into him. *"The power and glory of heaven are with you. Use the sword of Adeen, the sword of fire, use it wisely, or the sword will burn you to ash."*

"All heaven and I pray for you," Eos said. *"I have put considerable power in the staff to protect you. I have given the staff to Gwyn for her to use. Keep Gwyn near when you approach the demon and remember the staff has tremendous power. Go, Shawn, and one more time, fight for heaven."*

Shawn followed Anne and Marilyn out of the throne room. Across the hall, he saw Erdin Kenmare, Victoria's maker, the man with the silver chest armor. Victoria stood next to him and would be the next to go before Michael and Eos, to receive their commands. He smiled at her or thought he smiled, who could tell in this reality. He followed Anne and Marilyn out of the hall, and back over the forests, and the green, flowered fields to The City of Light. Shawn stayed for a time, how long he could not know here, discussing the events unfolding on earth with them. He asked Anne and Marilyn if he could stay here with them, but they said he could not. Finally, they wished him well and told him it was time to leave, to go back to his destiny once more.

Chapter Five

S hawn stood over Victoria's grave. He had been back from heaven for two months and left the ground as soon as he had returned. Victoria stayed buried, her wounds were far more severe than his. Finally, he had felt Victoria returning, becoming aware of this world. Now, he stood over the grave with Katherine, Gwyn, Braden, and Peter. Katherine had started the process of mobilizing all vampires for the fight to save earth from Brendel's dark forces. Recently, a blue dome began to form over Rome, Brendel was launching another attack on a city of earth. The demon was going to conquer earth's major cities one by one.

The dirt pushed up slowly, and he watched Victoria's hands thrust upward through the ground, then she rose, wounds healed, young and pristine again. Shawn grabbed hold of her, keeping her from flying out into the world to look for badly needed blood. When a vampire came from the ground, the need for blood boiled in them. Mortals, no matter who they were, would be in danger if they were near.

"I am here, my love and your family," Shawn whispered in her ear.

"I saw you there," Victoria spoke hoarsely as she struggled to break his grip.

"I know. Calm yourself; we have blood for you!"

"How intense that place was!"

"I told you!"

"Shawn, you must be my ambassador to the mortals."

43

"I know Victoria. Michael and Eos spoke of it. Brendel has attacked Rome, and I must go there and contact humans. You must rest, and we will talk when you are ready."

Peter came and took Victoria from Shawn. He and Braden took her to the cleansing table, washed the dirt from her, Pete showing Braden what to do. Then they both gave her blood, and Shawn and Katherine also gave her blood. After Peter and Braden had bathed her, they took Victoria to her living quarters for a needed sleep.

Shawn and Gwyn had come to Rome and stood on the northwest side of the River Tiber. Across the river, the dome began its rise to enclose the city. Victoria and Katherine had stayed at The Citadel making plans to make all vampires part of a massive army. It was midday, a day humans would call hot, but there was no sound of insects or birds flying this close to the dome. No creature of the earth would come this close to the evil felt here. The air was still, and the burning sun high in the sky; both of them could easily withstand the sunlight for they were vampires and Mother's witches. Shawn had brought Adeen, and Gwyn had The Mother's Staff. They were not here to fight but to observe and, most importantly, try to contact the mortals.

This time, a much larger human army approached from the northwest and had just entered the Plain of LaStorta. Their battle tanks, transports, and assault flyers were again preparing to punch holes through the blue dome. They had been successful at Jerusalem gaining entrance to the city, and Shawn hoped the vast firepower of the humans would have the same success here. Thousands of troop transports were also preparing to attack, to begin their assault through the openings.

Loud explosions quickly rose in tempo as the humans' high energy photon missiles started their assault on the dome. Firing platforms by the hundreds moved into position shooting high-temperature pulsars with ionized gas plasma beams, trying to sear holes through the dome wall. The humans repeatedly fired at the dome, kept up their onslaught, and finally, the dome sputtered and wavered. The dome shrunk in then expanded outward, sending out waves of dark energy, striking the incoming assault flyers and the first line of assault vehicles of the humans, destroying the pulsars. The dome reformed but was ragged with many holes punched through.

Portals opened just outside the breaches in the dome, and tens of thousands of red soldiers from the dark realm poured through, riding their battle platforms. The red soldiers stood row upon row on the platforms; across their backs worn smartly were their blasters. Their battle vehicles came first, large hovering battle tanks shaped like hockey pucks, made of dull grey metal and strange red markings on their sides. Red lights would form on the side metal, circle around the outside surface, come together in a large red circle then fire an intense red laser at the humans. The war vehicles moved across the river, and when they reached the middle, the humans fired on them. The alien creatures shot back, the ground shook, and the noise became deafening from the massive explosions.

Photons of high energy began to fly over their heads, and Shawn said, "I believe it is time for us to find someplace else to observe."

"I believe you are right."

The vampires floated into the air and flew west to find high ground to watch the fighting. All afternoon the armies fired on each other. The humans would deplete the red soldiers ranks only to have more come from the portals. The human military fought gallantly, but there were too many alien soldiers coming through the openings. The humans fought on destroying their battle vehicles, but more would come to replace them. Swarms of attack fliers went through the portals like bees from a hive. The alien army seemed to have an endless supply of war equipment and soldiers. Eventually, the invaders started to push back the human army.

Evening came, and the two armies separated. The humans set up a military camp on the flatlands ten miles to the east by the seashore. Shawn and Gwyn made their way to the camp and approached cautiously using the shadows, as vampires had for thousands of years. Their first encounter was human battle tanks dug into the earth for protection. They moved around the tanks and saw the human numbers were many, and the mortals represented a tremendous fighting force. Still, they did not know what they were fighting. They did not know about the parallel dimension that long ago had succumbed to the darkness of Lucifer. The mortals could not comprehend the power of dark energy and the numbers they faced on the other side of these portals. A plan started to form in Shawn's mind, a way to defend this world, and that meant he would have to kill Brendel.

Shawn floated to the ground, and Gwyn followed. They were close to the main human encampment and hid by one of the troop transports. Shawn heard rumbles of explosions in the distance. Human pulsar cannons would answer the fire of the enemy and blast their deadly photons of energy, sending them streaking through the night to their destinations.

Looking around the vehicle, Shawn saw two recon soldiers in the distance. They were out scouting their strange enemy and now were returning, approaching the human's outer defenses. A light flashed twice, then a return of two flashes of light. Soon Shawn's vampire ears could hear the personal greetings as the soldier moved through the outer defenses.

"They're coming this way. I think the best way to make contact is overpower those two humans," Shawn advised.

"You can't be serious!" Gwyn answered.

"We subdue them and then explain to them who we are. And then ask the men to take us to the higher-ups."

"That's a lot of *thens*, Shawn."

"Have a better idea?

"Not really."

"Come on, we'll approach those two," Shawn said with a slight smirk, as he started toward the two soldiers. Then with blinding speed, Shawn and Gwyn moved and stopped carefully behind them. The men turned startled, and Shawn spoke. "Don't be afraid. We mean you no harm!"

"Identify yourselves," one of the soldiers stuttered as he fumbled for his blaster.

"You can't be here, and you certainly aren't one of us!" the other human shouted as he drew his weapon.

Shawn was quickly on him, ripped the weapon from his hand, held him by his arm, and Gwyn quickly disarmed the other human.

"Please," Shawn pleaded. "You're right; we aren't supposed to be here! We aren't like you! But we aren't your enemy, and we do come from this world, not from the other side of the portals."

Shawn let the man go. He tried to run to make his escape, but Shawn was on him again and held him.

"You cannot escape me!" Shawn said. "That is impossible for you, and your weapons will do you no good. We are what you call the guardians or vampires."

"This is all I need!" the man stammered.

The man wiggled in Shawn's grasp and was becoming extremely uncomfortable being this close to him.

"You are making me feel strange!" mumbled the man.

Shawn pushed the man away. "It's natural; it's what the angels wanted. But if you are good men, we can't hurt you."

The men stood, staring at them, and Shawn easily saw the fear on their faces, sensed that these two had resigned themselves to the fact they probably would never make it home to their families, and it would be useless to try an escape.

Then one of the men asked, "Why are you here?"

"Humans need to know what they are facing. And knowing your kind, I'm sure you have information for us."

"We need for you to take us to your superiors," Gwyn told them.

"We would like to speak to your leaders tell them what they are fighting," Shawn added. "Help if we can! Do you understand?"

"We understand!" one of the men said, turned, and nodded his agreement to the other man and told him, "I don't think we have much of choice at this point."

The other man said, "Come with us; we will get you as close as we can."

Shawn and Gwyn followed the soldiers to a small hover vehicle. They soon found themselves riding in the back, air blowing against their faces. The vehicle hovered two feet from the ground, traveled at a good clip down a road that led to the center of the camp. They went through the encampment and came to a heavily guarded area. Past that checkpoint was the headquarters of the humans that commanded this army.

The man that was driving was a lieutenant, and sitting next to him was a sergeant. The lieutenant pulled the vehicle to the side of the road, turned and said, "We can't take you any farther. The guards would stop us, and something bad could happen. We will go on foot and try to contact our general, bring a representative to you. Please, stay here and wait for us!"

Sure thing," Shawn said. "Know this, human, we will know if your kind has ill will toward us, if they mean us harm. Understand?"

"I understand, wait here." The men got out and walked down the road.

Shawn quickly chanted a mother's spell that would make them appear like soldiers sitting in a transport.

"The humans are nervous with us," Gwyn told him. "We must be careful."

"Project friendship to them. We are an alien presence to them, creatures that have hunted them. That is why they have an innate fear of us. Especially now. Shawn turned to Gwyn, with a wide grin, and chuckled, "Don't spook them."

Gwyn laughed. "I won't spook them. It wasn't that long ago that I lived amongst the humans. I know how to be with them."

Troop transports started to pass them on the road. At first, it was a few, but then it became a long line of them. The air became thick with dust from the vehicle's levitators.

"How do they stand this?" Shawn said.

"I think they are used to it."

"The humans will do no more fighting here," he said disappointedly. "They are retreating again."

"The mortals are going to have to make a stand somewhere."

"Sooner or later, look, they're coming." Shawn spotted the two men walking back down the road. They came to the side of the transport.

"We are to take you to the command center. The people who lead this army will meet you there. Is that acceptable to you?"

Shawn searched the lieutenants' mind and saw he was truthful. "That is fine with us. Let's go meet your generals."

The soldiers slid in, and this time the sergeant took the wheel. They waited for the troop transports to pass and then pulled out onto the road. They followed the long line of war vehicles, sometimes winding their way around the slower battle vehicles. As they went, they passed many humans with looks of bewilderment and fear. Shawn sensed their human minds and saw the fear of the unknown; they had known peace for so long, but now they faced a force that they did not know or understand, and now they must fight again for their very existence.

The transports went left on to another road, and they continued straight. They traveled for an hour until they went through a heavily guarded checkpoint and came up to a large camouflaged tan dome. The dome was made of a modern material that resembled a lightweight plastic but could change its camouflage look at will. Shawn also sensed and heard the hum of a strong energy field surrounding and protecting the area known as central command.

They pulled to a stop in front of a man, and behind him was a heavily armed contingent of soldiers. A flyer landed, and Shawn watched a woman quickly disembark and approach them. She seemed a little harried as if her superiors had just informed her of the situation. Shawn and Gwyn stepped out of the vehicle as the wide eyes humans looked on.

The man wore a tan jumpsuit with black boots, various insignias on his sleeves, and a small blaster strapped to his side. The woman wore a dark blue jumpsuit and had a strange purple patch on her shoulders with a red letter "V" in the middle. She, too, had a small blaster strapped to her side. The man was tall and slim, around fifty years, with dark hair and streaks of grey at the side. Shawn sensed he was not in command but on the general's staff and nervous. He was there for his commander to evaluate them and the situation before bringing them inside.

The woman was mid-thirties with long fiery red hair pulled back and braided into a wide tress. She was attractive with sharp features, radiant complexion with a hint of freckles splashed about her face. Yet, there was something different about this woman.

Then Shawn felt a brush on his mind from the woman, a weak attempt to see into him. The woman had the gift. With a smile, he turned, stared into the woman's eyes, and told her mind to be careful, or she might see something she would not want to see. The woman gave him a quick, nervous smile and then looked to the ground. Regaining herself, she raised her head, met his gaze, stepped forward, and looked him square in the eyes, offering her hand for a shake. Shawn sensed her anxiety and saw slight perspiration on her upper lip. This woman knew about his kind. That was her purpose here; she brought knowledge of vampires to this meeting.

"The human race extends its salutations to the vampires, guardians of our world. I am Colonel Rachael Bonnet, honored to be here on this important and historical event, and this is General John Richter. Rachael then shook Gwyn's hand and stepped back.

Shawn's gaze went to the nervous general. The general nodded, quickly shook both their hands, and stammered, "A great honor to meet you." A lie Shawn certainly was aware of. "Please, come with me, and I will take you to the commander."

Shawn and Gwyn followed the general, and the squad of armed humans surrounding them.

The woman walked next to Shawn, and she would repeatedly glance at him, make weak darting probes at his mind, and finally spoke. "You're Shawn Bryce! Aren't you?" Rachael then looked at Gwyn. "I am sorry I don't recognize you."

"That's quite all right," Gwyn snapped. "I don't recognize you."

Shawn again sensed the woman and realized she knew plenty about vampires and thought herself skilled in the forces of the universe. Yet, she did not understand the courtesy that came with this ability. He made a quick decision on what to do with this human. "Tell me, Ms. Bonnet, how do you know about me?" Shawn then turned toward her, looked in her eyes, capturing them, and took over her mind. The woman froze in mid-stride, he sent her a message to her very core; it was not proper to try to read his thoughts and told her guardians could not allow this. Shawn wanted her to know the power she was dealing with, what it was like having mastery over the light. He held her body and mind. Feeling panic starting to rise in her, he flooded her soul with the energies of heaven. *Do not be afraid of me! I will not hurt you. Do you see what power you deal with? You must ask permission to see into my mind.*

Shawn released her allowed her to gather herself, and then he asked again. "Tell me what you know, Rachael. As you see, I will find out anyway."

"I am a member of the government that studies and catalogs the verifiable events that vampires such as yourself have participated in. I am also part of the military trained in techniques to fight vampires if humans ever had to. You see, Shawn, humans, know more about vampires than you think."

Shawn chuckled to himself and thought, *Vampires could never fight the human race, at least the good ones. The angels would never allow it. It probably would be a good idea the mortals did know that. At least not now.*

Rachael shook her head to clear it. "I will tell you, vampire, how we got so much information on your kind. We have relied on what you call Crimmians and their Crimmian Society. Some came on their own, and some Crimmians we took into custody. From what they told us and what we could be sure of by wreckage left behind when you had your fights with others like you and all the missing bad guys, we then knew there was a high probability it was true."

"The creatures you fight are not like us," Shawn warned. "They are Kargarians."

"We know what energy they are using against us," Rachael said as they walked along. "This is dark energy that comes from dark matter that fills the voids of our universe. We always thought it to be trash energy of the universe, but as you can see, we are finding out differently. Who is using this energy and where they are coming from is under great study right now! Now that you have contacted us, we hope to find out."

"I ask again how you know of me."

"Your name has come up many times over the last couple of centuries."

"I see!"

They came to the energy field, and that quickly disappeared. Soon they arrived at the entrance of the headquarters guarded by soldiers and a dense energy field. The energy field went, and the door slid open. Upon entering, they saw many guards at their stations and human military officers of all ranks standing in groups talking, waiting to get a glimpse of the vampires.

Rachael nodded to the guards, and they quickly waved them through. Shawn could see the unease spread through the group; the pained looks come to their faces.

Shawn spoke to ease their anxiety. "Greetings to you, humans. We will not harm you! We are here as friends! To help you!"

Rachael led Shawn and Gwyn to another energy door and that to disappeared. They went into a large room with many workstations, maps, and diagrams floating in the air. The humans would study them and then with a wave of their hands, brush them aside, banishing them to the ether and causing more to appear. The constant crackle of communications between the leaders and the soldiers in the field, the sounds of explosions told that small firefights were still going on with Brendel's forces.

A hush traveled over the room, and all turned to stare at them. A bald man with a slight scruff of grey hair on the sides stepped out and offered his hand. He wore a dark blue jumpsuit with a silver star on each lapel. Life and responsibility had weathered his face, and now he found himself in the fight of his existence. Shawn and Gwyn shook the man's hand, and then the man spoke. "I am Commander Hahn, leader of the European Federation Army, and I am delighted to see you two. As you can see, the battle isn't going our way."

"You are withdrawing," Shawn said.

"This is not going to get any easier, Commander," Gwyn added.

The Commander then answered, "My orders are to cede the Italian Peninsula to this enemy. Whoever it is."

"You are dealing with the dark forces of an alternate dimension," Shawn told them. "You are dealing with The Dark Angel, Lucifer, and his demon Brendel. They have tremendous power. The red soldiers come from a world and a dimension that only breeds soldiers for the devil, and their numbers are unimaginable. Soon you are going to have to make a stand, or the human race will be loss!"

"My superiors have ordered me to move the army to Munich and wait for the American and Russian Federation armies.

"We have fought Brendel, and he is a strong demon, stronger than any that have come before, and Lucifer has sent him for your world."

Anxiety spread over the commanders face. "A flyer is waiting to take you to Brussels," the commander told them. "We have contacted the leaders of this world. They want to meet with you and discuss this calamity. Colonel Bonnet will take you there. I pray your kind can help us. "

Colonel Bonnet escorted Shawn and Gwyn to the flyer, and soon they found themselves on their way to Brussels.

Shawn turned to the colonel. "I think I will call you Rachael. I hope you don't mind. I never had much like for military titles." He then became lost in his thoughts, vaguely remembering the horrors of when he was a soldier. He knew the darkness was descending on this world; heaven was going to allow the humans to be the first wave against Brendel, and as in all first waves, they very well might perish. But, these noble creatures would buy the time vampires needed to organize.

Chapter Six

S hawn and Gwyn stood with Rachael in a courtyard just outside a reinforced government building. They were waiting to meet the now arriving leaders of this world. Copper statues filled the yard that celebrated great people or significant events of the human race. Beautiful fountains sprayed water high into the air, causing rainbows that sparkled and drifted in the sunlight, birds frolicking in the pools oblivious to the pending doom. One human after another came through the doors to peer at them, some stood in groups, most went back inside, and Shawn quickly heard their nervous talk. The government complex he found himself in was not on a high tower. Humans had built the compound on and into the ground with a bunker mentality from modern blocks of extremely harden materials.

Rachael stood in front of him, at her usual three-foot distance, and he saw the apprehension that would come and go, the hairs standing up on her arms. He saw the slight freckles on her nose and decided she was a woman any man would want. He would ever so often brush her mind, look into her, reassure her; usually, Rachael was aware and smiled back at him. This time Shawn sent a message into her mind, *"Why do humans look at us so?"* She smiled at him, and with great effort, sent a message back to his mind, *"Because you are vampires and Heaven has given you so many gifts."*

"That is what they think?"

"Yes, that is what we think!"

Shawn smiled at her and became quizzical. "Where are you from, Rachael?"

"I am from Montreal. I have a beautiful apartment there, and I love the city. I go there when I can to be with my friends to escape what I do.

"And what are you escaping?" Shawn asked.

"My job. Studying vampires."

"Are we that bad?" Gwyn asked sarcastically.

"No, you're not! My apologies!" Rachael quickly answered. "Most of us know if we follow the golden rule, we should be on the good side of your kind."

"That is why we are here; remember that," Gwyn answered as she pointed to red-letter on Rachael's lapel. "You are a member of this army."

"I am a soldier of the Army of the Americas on loan to the European Army. Woken up in the dead of night and flown across the ocean in a ramjet to meet with you. I assure you it was a very unpleasant flight. I also know about mother's witches," Rachael said with a smile that was slowly changing to a stern look. "I know Heaven has given your kind everything and mine so little. We have been studying this other realm that keeps our babies from us! Even our scientists have finally realized who is responsible!"

"And who is that?" Gwyn asked.

Rachael turned to Gwyn, looked her in the eyes, her face becoming even more serious, and he felt a flash of anger. "The Mother, maybe?"

There it is, Shawn thought, *why humans might never trust us.*

"We are from the same place," Shawn quickly added, trying to soothe her angry mind. "We both come from Heaven. We have indeed been given a greater life force than you. The angels have their reasons; try to be patient with them. I know it is hard. It is hard for me, too sometimes."

Shawn watched Rachael's head rise and look toward the building. Something had stolen her attention. She had received a message through her nanochip, and a symbol appeared in front of her then quickly dissipated. Rachael's government had told her they were ready for them.

"Please follow me they are waiting for you," Rachael said. "You will be meeting with the heads of the six earth federations."

Shawn and Gwyn followed Rachael through an arched doorway into a large atrium; this was the control center for the government complex. They followed a large hallway at a downward slant until they came to another doorway made of shiny silver metal. Cast on the center of the door was the symbol for Earth. The blast door broke in the middle and swung inward. They followed a walkway running along the side of a sizeable busy control room. For now, this was the center of the fight against Brendel's army. Hanging in midair was a map of the city of Rome and the map of the Italian peninsula. On the far side of the room, humans were monitoring live feeds from the city. *Humans have hidden Nano cameras throughout the city. Brendel must not be aware of this,* Shawn surmised.

They continued through another doorway and into a room with four men and two women sitting at a large round, glass table, and behind them were their secretaries and aids. They all stop what they were doing, turned a hard gaze, a bewildered gaze, their way. Symbols formed around the aid's heads, one was the bright red letter "V," but none around the leaders that sat at the table. The leaders were the elders of this race, grey-haired, their faces showing years of leadership and responsibility. Shawn quickly felt the tension coming from them.

"Are you sure about this," Gwyn mumbled to him. "They don't seem too sure!"

"We have to do this. We have to save this world," Shawn whispered back. "And Michael and The Mother commands us to do this."

"You will get used to us," Shawn said in his friendliest and most reassuring voice. "What you are feeling will go away—

eventually. I know this is new for you, but we have been in your world for thousands of years. And you all are still here." Shawn said this jokingly, but the humans weren't smiling. "We have kept this type of evil at bay until now. Once again, the time has come for us to show ourselves to you. Our Queen has sent me to be an ambassador to you. And, this is my companion Gwyn."

One of the women rose, straightened her grey pantsuit jacket, clasped her hands together, took a deep breath, and walked toward them.

Shawn gave his friendliest smile. "You have nothing to fear from us. Heaven has sent us to help you."

"Welcome, Shawn Bryce and Gwyn Bryce; it is an honor to greet you. I am Ester Brune, Head Chair of the European Federation and Madame Chair Pro Tempore of the World Federation's Council." The Madame Chairwoman then introduced the other five heads of the federations of earth. "Please, come sit, we have some questions for you. We have three seats next to Head Chairwoman Mary Fitzgerald of the American Federation.

The woman wearing a black pantsuit stood and nervously extended her hand. "Welcome, Guardians! I come from Seattle, and I can tell you the weather is dreadful this week."

Shawn looked at Gwyn to see what she was thinking; he always wanted to know what Gwyn was feeling and knew she would undoubtedly ponder this statement.

"Well, you know where we live. Care to tell us how?" Gwyn demanded.

Rachael quickly interrupted to smooth the way. "We had many sightings of the Bryces in Seattle. We surmised that you must stay there a lot. We do not know your address or where you stay, and we wouldn't want to. My organization knows quite well the dangers of tracking vampires."

"Well, we certainly do spend a lot of time in Seattle," Shawn chuckled and gave Gwyn a look. "And I certainly sense your apprehension. We are here to help you and to answer your questions!"

The Madame Chair then spoke. "Can you tell us where this red army comes from and the size of the army that comes through the portals."

"The army you face comes from another parallel dimension to our own, a dark reality that has succumbed to evil. A place Lucifer rules!" Shawn's gaze fell over the leaders, and he sensed their resolve. They would fight for their world, but they also feared this red army. "There is more bad news. The soldiers you face are Kargarians and come from a large planet that is many times larger than earth. Their numbers are vast. You could see as many armed soldiers as there are people in this world come through the portals. War machines by the millions."

Shawn then heard the humans gasp and saw the fear on their faces.

"You must immediately attack the portals when they open," Shawn told them. "Try to limit how many red soldiers come through. The wizards can only keep the portal open for so long."

"You will have to fight the Kargarian army," Gwyn added. "They are coming for you. You have no choice. I am also a mother's witch. The Mother or a powerful angel known as Eos controls your world; she has crossed Lucifer to many times, and now he wants it from her."

"A demon commands this army, and his name is Brendel," Shawn added. "To rid yourself of the red army and Lucifer, the demon must be killed. He has unimaginable power, and we have to kill him to save your world."

"How can we do that?" the Madame Chair asked.

"You don't! That is for the Guardians to accomplish!" Shawn told them.

A man sitting at the table rose, the leader of the Russian Federation. "I have been informed that Rome has been lost, and a dome is starting to form over Moscow. The Russian Federation Army will not be going to Munich."

The Madam Chair then spoke, "I have just received the same message! The European army will go north to Moscow! We must make a stand. Guardians, can you tell us more about their energy source?"

"What you experience is dark energy that holds dark matter together, that you already know," Shawn told them. "This matter also fills the empty spaces of the various dimensions, the spaces that light does not penetrate. There are dimensions that this is the dominant force, and creatures can come to other dimensions carrying this energy."

The Head Chair of the African Federation looked around at the other council members then she spoke, "We know of these creatures. Many people from our lands have seen this energy. It comes with the creatures that appear in our jungles, only during the hottest of summers, and they bring this energy. They come for our people and kill them in the most hideous of ways."

The American Federation Head Chairwoman added, "We also have isolated this energy – and we have isolated your kind of energy, Shawn. We call it high energy and have begun studies to understand it and where it comes from."

The council called out their agreement to this latest statement. Again, the Madame Chair spoke, "There is another matter. I do not like to think about it, but we must discuss it. The building of the space transports. If humanity needs to escape this world, we must be ready."

Shawn listened to the human's plans of building thousands of space transports to remove most of the human population. The humans would rather leave than succumb to this evil. Construction of the carriers would begin at all of the hundred spaceports scattered over this world. Sitting at the glass table, Shawn learned of space cities built inside large asteroids in the Asteroid Belt. The earthiers had been secretly building these cities for the last hundred years. They had developed many space cities on the dwarf planet Ceres and now readied and fortified them just in case humanity needed them for its next home. Now the Earthers' battleships were moving into the belt, securing it for the people of Earth. Lucifer's and Brendel's evil had moved out into the solar system forcing the Earthers to be the aggressors.

"Can you negotiate with the spacers?" Shawn asked. "Avoid any kind of hostilities? Brendel's army must be defeated here, or Lucifer will just follow you out into space."

He could see the sudden change of the leaders' faces. Shawn had struck a nerve. He had known a spacer once, and his name was Drake, Katherine's changeling and vampires had killed him. The act that had unleashed such change in the way vampires were ruled.

The Madame Chair spoke her voice, becoming emotional. "We have studied your realm. Have known since the apocalypse about your kind. We now know it is your so-called angels that have kept our population low. Now they have picked a fight with the devil, and we again have to suffer. Keeping our population low is what's going to doom this world. Our army has killed them by the thousands coming through the portals and still more come--more war machines."

"The angels make pawns of us all," Shawn assured the chairwoman. "They have made a pawn of me. Mortals are no different. The Mother cares for this world and all creatures of this world. Not just you and you mortals almost destroyed this world. That is why the angels keep your numbers low. Humans are not completely innocent in this."

"We will fight this red army," the Madame Chair replied. "We have no choice, but we will make other plans just in case. The Martian Federation does not want Earthers in the belt. If we have to, we will fight for the belt too."

Shawn turned his sharp senses on the Madame Chair and told her, "You have to hold the red army back, make a stand, and we will try to kill Brendel."

The chairwoman met his gaze. "The federations would like Rachael Bonnet to stay with you. If we are to have an alliance, we must know what schemes your angels come up with."

"Madam Chairwoman, they are your angels too! I am tired. Gwyn and I will go to our quarters and rest. We will consider your request and let you know."

Gwyn stood and looked at each council member one by one, then pointed to Shawn and told them, "I was a mortal for a hundred years and now a vampire for more than a hundred. I still remember quite well what it is like to be human with your hopes, fears, and treacheries. This vampire that our queen has chosen to be our ambassador to you is twelve hundred years old. Throughout that time he has always has been your champion and has always defended you. I would not betray him! That is my warning to every one of you! For your kind to survive, you will need to trust this vampire, and you will need him."

"Well, I see we have some ways to go," Shawn said. "You must fight the red army, and we will do what we can with Brendel. We will discuss this more at a later time. Rachael, will you show us to our accommodations?"

They had taken a transport and stood outside of what was a twenty-story high upscale hotel, located deep inside this massive government complex. They entered and followed Rachael past a guard station and then took the lift to the top floor. Leaving the elevator, a guard station with a large contingent of armed soldiers met them.

Rachael explained to Shawn and Gwyn, "This floor and the garden roof above is for your use, we know vampires like access to the sky. My quarters are on the floor below. I am your liaison to humans. I am aware you don't have nanochips, so I had old communicators located in your quarters. There is no need for humans to use them anymore. I also have one in my quarters. Before I go, I have a question for you. Our research told us vampire were sensitive to light, yet you both seemed unaffected by it."

"We are both mother's witches," Gwyn answered. "Light does not affect us."

Rachael said her goodbyes, headed for the door, and Shawn called after her, "Thank the federation council for us."

Shawn and Gwyn laid in a large bed, feeling sleep starting to take hold. They had just made love and now held each other in the dark. He would run his fingertips lightly over Gwyn's soft buttocks and up the small of her back. He had known Gwyn for more than a hundred years and loved her deeply. Gwyn was always in command of her surroundings and had been instrumental in teaching him The Mother's magic. He knew Gwyn wanted more from him, but he was a vampire and gave her as much love as he could. He also told her he could never stop loving Victoria or the others, and she must understand.

Stroking Gwyn's silky hair, dreading what he was going to say, he whispered to her, "I want you to go back to the council and report on what has happened here, what you have observed. Tell them I believe we have an alliance with the humans. For now, anyway. They could turn very quickly."

"No, Shawn, I do not want to leave you here alone with the mortals."

"I will be all right. Do as I say; I am your maker."

"I don't think the humans trust us. They have resentment toward Heaven and us. Humans can be dangerous if they think they have been crossed!"

"Anything in this world these days can be dangerous." Shawn yawned.

"They are mad at the angels about population control."

"Can you blame them? Their emotions run high on the subject. I am tired," Shawn whispered. "Let's get some rest."

Shawn knew he had to be careful with the humans; they could act irrationally sometimes, especially when they were afraid and fighting for their survival. He had to stay close to humans. To see what resolve they had for pursuing this war. He welcomed the sleep that was now slowly overtaking him.

Chapter Seven

V ictoria sat on the blue throne, watching the last of the vampires leave the throne room. A session was now ending. She had sat patiently listening to the various partitions and complaints of the vampires. She then informed them that soon this would not matter, and they were to report for warrior training. Recently, she had come from the ground healed from Brendel's brutal attack and a visit with The Archangel Michael in Heaven. Shawn had saved her, fought desperately for her, the same as she had done for him in the past. The Archangel told her to prepare for a terrible war, prepare for Lucifer's attack on this world, and to ready herself to lead the vampires of earth. Michael told her Shawn would press the attack on Brendel, but he was vague about the outcome. She had a foreboding for Shawn that grew each passing day. Some blamed the angels for unleashing Lucifer's wrath on this world. Victoria could not argue with them.

Drake came in her sleep and told her a blue dome now covered Moscow, and portals were opening everywhere in and around the city. The messenger angel told her Brendel and Lucifer were moving quickly to subjugate this world. He also told her Prodasa head of the Parfeev Covenant was leading a band of vampires fighting in the city. His covenant had pleaded with him to leave, save himself, but Prodasa would not abandon the city. Katherine had always warned her about Prodasa's arrogance, and now Victoria had to go after him.

Gwyn had just arrived back from a significant first contact with the mortals and was entering the throne room with Katherine. Many of the departing vampires still would give slight bows to Katherine as they passed her. Katherine was the first queen, the hundred-year queen that had taken an army of vampires to the black castle by the Gates of Hell and rescued Shawn. The Mother had planned all of it and probably brought this misery to this world. Katherine had immense respect throughout the vampire world, but not too much with the covenant leaders because of the losses they suffered rescuing Shawn. At the end of all that business, Victoria was the one to kill Malin, and now Lucifer wanted her soul for it.

Victoria watched Katherine and Gwyn make their way to her throne. The two were always at ease with each other, and over the years, they have developed a close bond. Sometimes she thought the relationship was more than just sharing the same maker. She had once glimpsed in Gwyn the desire to be intimate with Katherine, but Gwyn quickly sensing her and hid the thoughts.

"And how was the pity session?" Katherine laughed loudly as she and Gwyn floated over the pool and walked up the steps. As expected, Katherine embraced her and kissed her on the lips. That was Katherine's way. Gwyn also smiled and greeted her.

Victoria laughed at what Katherine called these sessions. "The same as you remember. One grievance after another," Victoria said as she took a step back. "You are well, I see. Gwyn, I am anxious to hear your report. I hope you did not leave Shawn in danger."

Victoria was an old vampire of more than two-thousand years, and she could not begin to remember what it was like being human. But she knew the fickleness of mortals and how they could turn in an instance on you. And they indeed could devise ways to kill vampires. Victoria did not get close to humans, as Shawn did. Humans fascinated Shawn, and he always liked being near them, interacting with them.

"Shawn is safe for now," Gwyn shot back. "Shawn is my maker, and I must do what he asks of me."

"Of course, you must," Victoria agreed. "I do not trust humans, especially with Shawn. How did the first meeting go?"

"We made contact easily and was taken to the commander of the human military outside of Rome. There we met a Colonel Rachael Bonnet, who will be the human's liaison to us."

Victoria sat listening to Gwyn, explaining what had transpired. She saw the admiring glance that Katherine gave Gwyn as she spoke. Victoria tried to view into her mind, but quickly Katherine's eyes darted toward her, threw her defenses up, and ever so slightly a mischief smile spread over her face. Many times, she had seen this smile over the years, the smile when she was hiding something from her. And Katherine knew what Victoria was searching for.

Victoria was not surprised to hear that Shawn was already making the humans feel somewhat at ease. Neither was she surprised to understand how much information humans had gathered about her kind. Humans had always tried to know whatever they could about their world. Mortals had reached great heights with their technology. They were now starting to use this science to glimpse into other realities. They had found out what The Mother has done with their babies. She had lived many centuries and knew this did not bode well for their relationship with the humans.

Always in the back of Victoria's mind was her worry for Shawn. The angels tasked Shawn so, and they were still putting him in terrible danger. She would inform Katherine of Prodasa plight, and they would go after him. She also would send Gwyn back with The Mother's Staff to protect Shawn, to watch for any human treachery.

The following eve, Victoria and Katherine, flew east. As they approached Moscow, this time, the blue dome only covered the inner part of the city. Portals had opened on the outside of the dome, and the heavy fighting was going on there. Towers lay toppled, and thick dust and smoke hung in the air.

In the eastern parts of the city, the carnage was widespread. Now the fighting had subsided for the night. The portals had closed, and the humans were fortifying their positions while moving heavy weapons into place.

The Russian Federation and European Federation armies were locked in a desperate struggle with the red soldiers for survival. Fires burned, and plumes of smoke rose into the sky, blocking what light coming from the moon and stars. Many emergency medical fliers were traveling amongst the dead, securing the wounded, and taking them to the rear. Thousands of dead red soldiers also littered the area, left behind when the portals closed. Their putrid stench hung heavy in the night air. Many of the red soldier's war machines also lay destroyed mixed with the carnage of the city.

Victoria and Katherine landed amongst the destruction, their swords from Heaven at the ready, and heard the cries and moans of agony of the wounded mortals yelling out for water, for any kind of help. They met dazed humans stumbling along, trying to make their way through the rubble and out of the city. Their wails drifted through the smoked air.

Then streaks of white and yellow flew all around and over their heads, hitting and digging into the chunks of concrete, pelting them with debris. Victoria and Katherine ran and took shelter. Diving and rolling, Victoria ended squatting against a large steel beam from a fallen tower and found herself looking into the face of a dying human soldier. He pleaded to her in a ragged voice for water. Victoria looked toward Katherine to see what she would do. Katherine pointed to a dead soldier that had a canteen of water and stared back at her. Victoria saw Katherine's glare and knew she wanted her to show more compassion for humans. Katherine was like Shawn when it came to humans.

Crawling, she retrieved the canteen of water and held the human's head to give him water. Her mind drifted to other long-ago wars; it did not matter what age it was, dying soldiers always looked the same. Whether it was a time of swords or a time of lasers, they all had the same fear in their eyes just before death. Victoria looked on the soldier and told him, "Do not be afraid, Heaven awaits you. I promise, human!"

Then she quickly broke his neck to end his misery. Victoria and Katherine went amongst the dying, giving water or what help they could. Some were near death, and the pair ended their suffering. The scent of death hung heavy in this place. Later, the sun rose above the horizon, and they took shelter.

"New portals will open," Victoria warned. "The fighting will start again. We must wait for an opening in the dome. Make our way through and find Prodasa."

"I know Prodasa, and it will be hard to change his mind," Katherine said. "Even if we can get to him."

Soon a hum rose in intensity, and portals opened. The Valaris Wizards of the evil worlds swirled their shafts, and the fiery blue portals formed and grew. Then thousands upon thousands of red soldiers came through to reinforce their crumbling ranks. The humans fired their photon cannons, streaks of light energy flew over Victoria and Katherine's heads, booming explosion filled the air, and shook the ground. The inferno had started again. The humans repeatedly fired their deadly weapons, and slowly they advanced on the portals and the red army. They were quickly met with the horrific fire of the red soldiers and their war machines. Human remote-controlled fliers flew in overhead and fired on the dome. More and more, the fliers fired their missiles and pulsars, the intense pace quicken until finally, openings started to appear in the dome.

"Now Victoria, this is our chance!" Katherine yelled.

"Let's go then!" Victoria commanded.

The two flew with vampire speed, dodging a laser beam that came up from the ground and making it through an opening. They landed quickly and took shelter behind a fallen aircar.

"Can you sense the demon, Katherine?" Victoria asked.

"Yes, I can, and I can sense Samil too. They're in the middle of the city probably hold up in a government building."

Prodasa is about a half-mile to the south of Brendel," Victoria said. "His feel is fragile, though. We will try to make our way to him. We must avoid Brendel. Cloak ourselves; we do not want to have a conflict with him."

They traveled amongst the destruction and the human dead. Sometimes come upon dazed groups of mortals wandering trying to make their way out of the city. Victoria would advance take cover, and then Katherine would follow, one covering for the other as they moved forward. They ran into red soldiers and used their speed and slayers to take their heads and send them to the devil. Crashed air cars and burning fires littered the inside of the dome. Victoria and Katherine made their way building to building then came upon red soldiers herding groups of mortals.

"We should help them," Katherine whispered.

"No, we must keep our cloak up and our presence a secret as long as we can! Brendel is too powerful to face now! We will take cover in this building, it looks sturdy enough, and wait for dusk."

They did not wait long before darkness moved over the city. Victoria and Katherine left their shelter and continued toward the center of the city, finally, coming to an area where they could sense Prodasa.

"He is below us," Victoria told Katherine.

"He is, but there is something not right with him," Katherine said.

"He is hurt. We must find a way to get to him," Victoria then froze and spoke. "Can you sense it? Brendel and Shamil are moving!"

They both stopped and stood still; Brendel's was leaving his lair.

"They are going to the edge of the dome," Katherine said with relief. "The humans are coming through the openings and pushing the Kargarians back."

"They are going to terrorize the red soldiers into holding their positions until the portals reopen and reinforcements come."

Victoria and Katherine left their cover and began searching through the rubble, lifting large chunks of debris and tossing them aside. Eventually, they found the shelter doorway, forced it open, and peered down a dark stairwell. The smell of a moist decay and burnt electrical wiring was strong.

Victoria turned to Katherine and gritted out, "He is down there."

She watched Katherine shake her head, and her face turns grimace. Katherine had many rough times with Prodasa during her reign.

"Figures," Katherine said through clenched teeth.

"Let's go…he's hurt."

Slowly Victoria and Katherine made their way down the stairs moving debris and bodies aside as they went, deeper and deeper into the ground until they came to an underground concrete tunnel.

"He's close; we'll follow this tunnel," Victoria whispered. They proceeded down the dank tunnel their senses at the highest level.

"Vampires are coming!" Katherine whispered.

Soon they saw three shadowy figures coming toward them. Two men and one woman, and they were older vampires.

One of the vampires yelled forward, "My queen, you should not have come to this place! It is too dangerous!"

"Then Prodasa should learn how to follow the orders of the Archangel," Victoria yelled back. "Where is Prodasa?"

"Down this tunnel…follow us," one of the vampires said. "He's hurt my queen, and says he can't leave the city."

"We'll see about that!" Victoria muttered.

Down a steep incline, Victoria and Katherine followed the vampires. Deeper, they went into the earth and finally came to another metal door. They approached the door, and the vampires slid it aside as it squeaked its protest. They went into a large room with smooth painted green concrete walls, an old Russian dialect stenciled on them, musty cots, and ancient electronics used in a time long gone. On the far green wall, a group of vampires huddled around a figure lying on one of the cots. The only sound whispered from the vampires and drips of water seeping through the ceiling forming small mineral stalactites and then falling to the floor. An old government bomb shelter, Victoria realized, leftover from the last apocalypse.

Victoria walked to the group and saw Prodasa lying severely wounded. The ancient vampire had a small hole in his chest where Brendel had tried to capture his heart. He also had a deep cut to his neck. Prodasa was missing his left hand; certainly, they would have to bring him back to The Citadel and bury him. His covenant slayer, one of the five originals, lay next to him.

Victoria looked down on Prodasa. "Well, it looks like you have yourself in a bad situation."

"My queen," Prodasa said hoarsely. "We fought the demon and his witch. Brendel also had many wizards with him. This is all that is left of us."

Victoria looked around the room, counted only ten vampires, and then said, "You should have left the city! Followed orders! The vampires that you lost were needed for a future fight. Are you sure you escaped Brendel's detection?"

"I am my queen," Prodasa spoke, as he avoided Victoria's gaze. "Brendel briefly lost track of us, and we came here. I remembered this hidden place from the last war."

"I am sorry to see you like this," Katherine said. "But it seems you still have a hard time taking orders."

"And you, Katherine, still don't know your place!" Prodasa snarled. "I had to defend my city and my honor against this demon and his horde!"

As soon as Prodasa had finished talking, a hum started and increased into a piercing whine. The sound came from above and penetrated the earth down to where they were, then a loud, hard thump, and the ground above them shook. Brendel knew where they were and had brought a flying war machine, a pulsar. He placed it above them, repeatedly firing a plasma wave that would pound and tear at the ground and eventually blast its way to them. Regularly, the rising hum, the thump, and a blast that sent intense vibration down to their shelter. Dirt filtered through the cracks above, and the stalactites started to break loose and fall.

"We need to escape this place. You vampires grab hold of Prodasa and follow me," Victoria commanded.

"I sense Brendel, Vic!" Katherine called out.

"That doesn't matter! We have to get out of here! And quick!"

The vampires made their way back through the tunnel while the pounding from above continued. Brendel was driving them to the surface. Explosions and fire roared down the shaft and washed over the vampires; parts of the tunnel had collapsed, so they used their vampire strength and dug their way through. As Victoria dug, she looked back at Prodasa sitting against the tunnel wall and saw him motion her to him.

She kneeled next to him, and Prodasa spoke in a low, hoarse voice, "I must tell you this, my queen. When I was fighting Brendel, a strangeness occurred. My slayer grazed his chest, and then I swung it in an arc catching him off guard, and it cut his neck. Listen to what I say! The demon fell back, clutching his neck, and for the first time, I saw fear come over his face. Only briefly, though. But I caught a glimpse of his dark mind. Maybe it was the fear, but his defense lowered for a moment. I don't think he knows I saw this. Listen to me, my queen. I saw a fear of death, a fear of losing his head, and not being able to come back to this world. Take the demons head, and that is the way to kill him. He is of the flesh!"

"Are you sure, Prodasa!"

Prodasa grabbed at her jacket with hands shaking hands and choked out, "Yes! You must let others know!"

Eventually, they came to the surface and went out into the open. Hovering above them was a large flier producing a dark energy plasma beam and shooting it to the surface, blasting dirt away, and an opening to the bunker. Suddenly, the flier moved off toward the west, as Brendel and Shamil approached with ten-warrior wizards and landed twenty feet from them.

"Spread out!" Victoria ordered.

"Like rats from their hole," Brendel hissed. "Look what we have, Samil! The queens! Can you believe are luck. And you don't look so good, Prodasa."

Prodasa shook his handlers off and drew his covenants slayer. With one of the five original swords from Heaven, he raged at Brendel. "This time, demon, it will be you that won't look so good!"

Victoria watched the severely wounded Prodasa launch himself at Brendel. They clashed, and Brendel parried with his dark blue steel, swung around and struck the ancient vampire across the back. Prodasa flew back and again prepared to attack.

Victoria charged at Samil while Katherine led the vampires in the attack on the wizards. Repeatedly she brought Deceida around driving the witch back. Victoria saw Prodasa again advancing on Brendel, and still, the demon feign and this time drove his sword through Prodasa. The vampire was too weak from his wounds. Brendel shoved Prodasa off his sword with his foot, and the ancient vampire stumbled back, and the demon brought his sword around and took the head of Prodasa. The vampires fell back in shock and watched Prodasa crumble to the ground as dirt.

Brendel screamed at them, "This is what will happen to all vampires on this earth. Powerful Prodasa, leader of the Parfeev Covenant, is no more. And it was easy! You're next Victoria come for me!"

Victoria wiped the dirt from her face and eyes then looked to the west sensing the calamity unfolding. The red army numbers were too great as they poured from the portals, and the human army had started their retreat.

Prodasa's fallen sword suddenly burst into a giant ball of bright light. The light shot upward like a laser beam, piercing a hole through the energy dome above and continued to travel into the blue sky, back to where it had come from.

"Katherine screamed to the vampires, "Quickly, through the hole!"

Victoria raised Deceida, and its metal rang and glowed a white light that would burn a human's eyes. Staring at the demon, remembering what Prodasa had told her, Victoria sidestepped, looking for an opening, a chance to strike and take his head. To maybe save Shawn and end this tragedy. Then Katherine grabbed her arm and shouted, "Not now, Victoria, his time will come. We have to get through the opening."

Victoria woke from her battle trance, her deep desire to kill this demon, and mumbled, "You are right."

"Now, Victoria, follow me!" Katherine screamed.

Victoria and Katherine, with the vampires, flew through the opening, turned east, and made their way back to The Citadel.

Chapter Eight

S hawn found himself flying inside a military transport and sitting in a comfortable cushioned seat. Usually, he did his flying differently, but this time he was with Rachael. He also gained a travel bag and had strapped Adeen to its side. Humans became nervous when he carried his slayer on his back. He had agreed to allow Rachael to travel with him and report to the federations. Still, for now, he was following her to the American federation government buildings in New Chicago. Shawn wanted to be near her to learn more about the federation's plans.

The dark forces had defeated the mortals at Moscow; eventually, the Kargarians overwhelmed them with their numbers. Humans with great foreboding started to transfer the world government to New Chicago. The European and Russian Federations armies would stay in Europe for now. Still, the other federations would not come to their rescue. They wanted to keep their armies' home to protect their territory. As usual, during times of great trouble, humans were becoming divided.

Rachael sat in a seat across the aisle from him, and he turned his head to find her staring at him. She still suffered slightly from the aversion humans developed over the centuries to vampires. They had always thought vampires hunted them for their blood. To Rachael, he was a significant curiosity, something unique, and would stay close for more extended periods. Sometimes she would even touch him.

Shawn had reconnected with Gwyn in Brussels, but soon word came from Victoria for Gwyn to bring The Mother's Staff back to The Citadel. Poor Gwyn was trapped between The Mother and the Archangel. The Kargarians started building a military camp close to The Citadel, and Victoria thought Brendel might be preparing to attack.

Gwyn was puzzled and wanted to know why he was staying, why he wanted to travel with Rachael, and he must know vampires could not stay in Brussels anymore. Humans were going to abandon Brussels. Shawn could see that Gwyn was troubled and tried to peer into her mind, but she was a powerful witch. Sometimes deep down when she became jealous, she would easily brush him out of her mind, hiding her thoughts become closed off to him.

She then implied that he was attracted to Rachael. Shawn did like interacting with humans, and Rachael did interest him. He told Gwyn that he knew because of her age, being a mother's witch first, and how much power The Mother gave her, she still looked at love like a mortal. He held her and explained to her that he could not begin to remember what it was like being mortal. What it was like loving only one. All he knew what it was like for him to love. And how he has loved for over a thousand years. He could not love just one because he had the blood of the angels in him, so he must love many. He saw Gwyn's frown leave her, and then she teased that she had found someone else to love, but she would always love him the most. They held each other and fell asleep, and the next day Gwyn left for The Citadel.

The sound of Rachael's voice brought him back to the here and now. "You are so deep in thought Shawn other than our war problems what troubles a creature like you."

"Many of the same problems that trouble mortals. We are still susceptible to the trials of love and life like mortals."

The cabin door opened, and one of the pilots motioned Rachael to come forward. Shawn quickly heard what the pilot whispered to Rachael. A dome had appeared over Paris, and the two battered federation armies had surrounded the city. Rachael came back to her seat with a worried frown on her face. "A dome has appeared over Paris!"

I heard," Shawn replied. "And they desperately need reinforcements, but knowing humans, none will come."

"I fear Europe and Russia will be lost."

"That part of the world is lost, and America could be next," Shawn added. "Europe and Russia must hold out as long as they can. Their armies are the biggest in this world. They must allow the rest of humanity to prepare some kind of defense."

Then fear spread over Rachael's face, a terrible look of despair, and she looked at Shawn as her eyes filled with tears. "Do you think we will survive?"

He knew that tears did not come easy to this woman and didn't want to lie to this mortal, but he couldn't say what he really thought. "I don't know, Rachael! Brendel must be destroyed. And you humans aren't capable."

Then his powerful hearing heard the two whooshes of photon missiles. Even before this flying crafts sensor knew, he saw in his mind's eye, the Kargarian attack flier and the missiles traveling toward them. Then an alarm went off, and the lights turned red. The transport banked sharply left and dove downwards, but defensive maneuvers were too late. One of the photons hit the craft, then a flash and explosion as the fire consumed the cockpit and rushed back through the cabin toward them. In an instant, Shawn grabbed Adeen, flew, and covered Rachael with his body, as the flames washed over him. He chanted a mother's spell for a surrounding shield against the fire, as the craft started to come apart.

Making his escape, he flew out into the sky away from the flaming flier and its lethal debris. Watching the fiery ball that was the aircraft plunged toward the sea, he held Rachael, protecting her from the unmerciful assault on her body. The warcraft turned came at them and fired its laser, again Shawn chanted, and a force field formed around them, deflecting the laser harmlessly away. Shawn flew straight up, turned, and shot downward, throwing Rachael away from him. He spoke another mother's spell for protection and plunged through the Warcraft, causing it to explode into a ball of fire, and it too took its fiery trip to the ocean. He flew around and, with blinding speed, dove downward catching Rachael as she fell. Looking into her eyes, Shawn saw she was in shock. Holding Rachael, he flew toward the American Federation coast. Entering her mind, he gently went deep to soothe her to let her know she was safe.

I have you, Rachael! I will protect you! Be strong!

Shawn looked at her stunned face, her red hair whipping from the wind. Soon he saw her eyes blink open, and her arms tighten around his neck. He squeezed her close to reassure her and whispered in her ear, "You are all right. We are flying!"

"My God, I see that! Amazing!"

"We have to make it to the coast. Probably another hour."

Shawn traveled on through the night, holding Rachael tight. They ran into bad weather, and Shawn chanted a spell to form a shield in front to divert driving rain around them.

Shawn had just flown through the bad weather when he felt the evil coming from behind. It was Samil.

"I am going to have to fly faster," he said. "We are being followed."

"The red army," Rachael whispered.

"No, I am afraid it's worst. It is Samil!"

"A witch!"

"Yes, you are about to see a true Lucifer's witch!"

Shawn increased his speed to fly as fast as he could to make the coast where he could better defend Rachael. The witch followed, keeping her distance. Shawn wondered what she was up to and projected his powerful senses only to have Samil shut him out. Only a glimpse he stole, but it was enough to see that the witch had a message.

"When we get to the coast, I am going to land," he told Rachael. "Stay behind me. Try not to stare into her eyes. She will try to get to you mentally, so be prepared."

"Shawn, I can't handle the witch in my head."

"If she tries, I will attack her! It won't last long! You are going to have to be strong now! You wanted to stay with me!"

"I did!"

Shawn reached the east coast of the Americas in the area that was once known as New Jersey. He landed on a wide beach and at the shoreline were two giant, old copper statues buried in the sand their busts breaking the surface. Two faces of long-ago humans now captured by the sands of this beach. The waves crashed into and washed around these two heads and then pulled the sand back out. Drawing Adeen, he pushed Rachael behind him. Adeen's metal grew bright and rang in anticipation of the witch.

"The witch must be near," Rachael said. "Even I can sense her."

"She will be here soon, but surprisingly she is still alone."

Shawn watched Samil fly in and land on top of one of the heads. She stood looking at him and then crouched, resting her arms on her knees.

Shawn raised Adeen. "I am ready for you, witch."

Samil smiled. "I am not here to fight you, Demon Slayer. I know I would lose. Brendel will take care of you in time."

"Then what do you want, Samil!"

"The Demon Slayer now stays with humans. You cannot save them. They are part of the price that Lucifer has set for The Mother's deceit."

"If you try to harm this woman in any way, you will not leave here alive."

"Settle yourself, Demon Slayer! I am here to deliver a message to her," Samil spat, as she pointed her finger at Rachael. "Hear me, human! Lucifer wants only this world this planet. He also wants the vampires of this world. He will allow mortals to leave if they choose. If humans stay, they will be his slaves to do his bidding. Leave and live!"

"Negotiating already, Samil?" Shawn became suspicious, for this was not Lucifer's way. Sensing and feeling the energies of this world, he allowed his mind to expand outward, to detect the ether. In this medium, all that has happened flowed, and he found what he was looking for. "Brendel has suffered his first setback at Paris."

Samil stood and hissed. "He has not been defeated, only temporarily halted. You cannot imagine the numbers that will come through the portals, the destruction that is coming. Leave humans! Leave this world and save yourselves."

"Soon, you will be fighting all the creatures of this world," Shawn told Samil as he raised Adeen. "Not just the humans!"

"Can the human speak?"

"I can speak, Samil! My kind will not run from you! This is our world!"

"Mortals cannot stop us. You will leave, or you will be Lucifer's. These vampires will not save you, ask him, human. Ask him if his queen will save you!" Samil rose into the air laughing and said as she left, "Lucifer will have this world."

Shawn shouted after Samil, "You are wrong; the angels will not let you!"

Quickly Rachael turned, stone-faced, and stared at him, reached out, touched his face, and tensely spoke, "No warmth from you. Are the angels using my kind again, vampire?"

"As I said, the angels use us all! Vampires will fight for this world that I can promise! And while you are with me, I will fight for you."

"Vampires will fight for this world. But will they save us?"

Shawn did not answer. "Are you ready to fly again?"

"You are the only ride I have! Give me a minute!"

"Take a minute, but we should leave this place. It is a couple of hours of flight to New Chicago."

They flew on to New Chicago. Rachael had finally got used to him, and they chatted about her early years, how she grew up in Quebec. What started her interest in vampires?

A couple of generations back, a very prominent member of her family had helped a vampire named Louis. The man's name was Robert and had stumbled on a vampire and witch fighting.

Robert, who had studied vampire lore, recognized the situation for what it was and did what he could to help the vampire. Unfortunately for Robert, he sustained some severe injuries in the process. The vampire brought him to a hospital, and Robert would survive his injuries. Eventually, the vampire returned, thanked him, and took some of his blood. The vampire gave him blood in return. My uncle wrote in his memoirs what a magical experience it had been, Rachael told him. He wrote the vampire told him now because of the blood he would always know where my uncle was and if he was in danger. Rachael said to him that her Great Uncle Robert became president of the Canadian Province. He rarely became sick and lived well into his thirteenth decade. Because of this she became fascinated with vampires, their immortality, and their power.

Shawn walked with Rachael across a large courtyard on a massive government complex known as Freedom Hall. On arrival, Rachael had given her government Samil's message. They had been here for two days before the council had summoned them to appear. The humans had placed photon pulse cannons and laser batteries on every strategic location on the complex. Large numbers of soldiers prowled the walkways. Everybody had a stoic look, a quick walk, a purpose; this was a world at war fighting for its survival. On arrival, Shawn had learned the humans had been successful in collapsing the dome that surrounded the city. Their armies had fought their way into Paris, pushing the Red Army back and now had set up a defensive line across the city. Brendel did not have control of the city just yet.

Shawn had spent most of this time with Rachael. She was interested in his long life and asked him endless questions about it. He knew she found this aspect of his existence fascinating. She had asked him about his early years before the first apocalypse. There was much he didn't remember, but he would try to tell her how humans lived at that time. He told her there were no air cars. The cars of that time had wheels and traveled on roads. She would give him a quizzical look so he would explain what roads and tires were and other aspects of the old technology. He told her humans had no high towers, only tall buildings. In that age, more people lived in the countryside than in the cities. The world was a dirtier place because of the type of power the people of that time used.

Shawn explained how humans divided themselves into countries that did not get along, how the world's great powers divided the people, and the cruelty they showed each other. This is what allowed the Esmanaa Demons to start the Great War, he told her. What allowed the demons to turn humans against each other and divide the human race because of their different religions and cultures.

Shawn told her how the humans worshipped Heaven but had little knowledge of the real purpose of angels and Heaven. They thought Heaven had only one purpose and only one supreme being. In Heaven, Shawn told her there is no one god, only angels. Mortals knew nothing of the other creatures that occupied their world. They believed they were the only ones. Arrogance is what allowed humans to destroy their world so easily. This attitude is what angered the angels and why they keep mortal numbers low in this world.

Rachael asked him what life was like during the Great Dark Age. He told her of the terrible despair after the war, how humans separated and did not trust each other, how the human race almost perished. That's when guardians step in to protect them against themselves and the demons. The dark forces were trying to deliver that fatal blow to their existence, and this is when humans finally began to realize they weren't alone in this world.

Shawn entered the large government building with Rachael at his side. An energy beam came from somewhere by the ceiling and scanned them both. The force fields that were the doors in this building opened as he came near. He followed Rachael down long corridors and finally came to an assembly room with the heads of the America and South American Federation. Holograms of the busts of the European, Russian,

African, and Asian Federations hung in the air. A loud booming voice came from some hidden source overhead. "The American Federation welcomes the vampire, Shawn!" And then another energy beam appeared out of nowhere and scanned Rachael.

The head chair of the America Federation left her conversation and walked toward them. Shawn felt quiet despair in the room. He sensed that the European and Russian Federations armies had left Paris and now were in retreat to the Normandy Coast. In the center of the room, tacticians and military generals gathered around a large curved table and overhead floated screens that showed the retweeting army and the advancing red army. The general would point to locations explaining information to the federation leaders and then wave the screen away, and another would appear. The head chair approached, and Shawn extended his hand. "Good to see you again, Head Chair Fitzgerald."

The chairwoman reluctantly took his hand. "Good to see you, Shawn and you, Colonel. "Come, let us sit and talk. I have the authority to represent earth in all matters."

"As you wish."

Shawn followed Head Chair Fitzgerald to a lounging area with plush chairs and a sofa.

"Let's talk here," the chairwoman said, as she motioned to the furniture.

Shawn slid into the comfortable chair and watched chairwoman and Rachael sit on the sofa. A seriousness had come over Head Chair Fitzgerald.

The army had to abandon Paris. There was no end to the red army and their war machines. Our military is now headed to the Normandy coast and from there to London.

"I am sorry to hear that," Shawn replied with a tense voice. His disappointment was hard to hide and his anger at their loss. It was becoming clear to him that the humans were not going to stop the Kargarian Army.

"Unfortunately, a dome is starting to form over London. If we lose London, wc will lose control of Europe and the Russian Federation."

"Humans must stop the red army, and you must make a stand somewhere," Shawn urged. "Already, you divide yourselves. You must unite the armies and make a stand! Forget London! Draw them out into the open and concentrate on their portals!"

"We are doing the best we can. We do not have the insights of the angels like you do! Heaven does not hold us in such high favor."

"Madame, I'm getting tired of hearing that!"

Shawn watched the Head Chair look him directly in the eyes and then glanced at Rachael and back to him. He easily could see what chairwoman was thinking. Looking at Rachael, she asked, "What do you think, Colonel? Will the vampires fight? Will they fight for us?"

Shawn watched the two human women. The chairwoman caught Rachael off guard, and he saw her pondering, searching, wrestling with her loyalties. Then Rachael looked at him a sorrowful look came over her face, and he saw in her mind, *sorry Shawn.* Then she spoke, "What I know is the vampires will fight, and they will fight to keep Lucifer from taking over this world. I am not sure, though, if they will fight for us."

Shawn smiled at Rachael and placed a thought in her mind; *It's ok, Rachael.*

"I'm sorry, Shawn," Head Chair Fitzgerald said as she gathered her courage. "I think it is time for your kind to show mortals your loyalty. We need vampires, to help protect the transports bringing our army across the channel."

Shawn looked at the chairwoman and then caught Rachael's gaze, *did they understand what they were asking for,* he pondered. *Did they realize the affect vampires would have on them when changed and ready for battle? Maybe he should show them.* "I'm not sure Head Chair Fitzgerald that you realize what you are asking. Humans are uncomfortable around us when we aren't changed to our vampire form. What do you think will happen when there are around thousands of us?"

Shawn allowed himself to change to his vampire form. He was letting his full kind to be on display his burning blue eyes, fangs white, long and sharp, his size almost double. He was displaying his vampire state for them. A look of shock came over Head Chair Fitzgerald's face and a glimpse of fascination from Rachael. He stared at them and then spoke, "Will humans accept our kind amongst them? Next to them? Vampires are killers when we are in our vampire form. Humans will see this. I see the disgust on your face and feel your need to get away. This is how we look when we are in battle or when we feed on your blood. When we are like this, we are dangerous killers; even now, I can smell your blood. When vampires turn humans, it takes a hundred years for them to control this lust. That is why changelings stay with their makers for so long."

Shawn moved faster than any human eye could see. To the human eye, he disappeared and then reappeared next to Rachael. He put his arm around her, pulled her close, smelled her, and sensed the thrill she was feeling, felt her breath quicken. He saw her staring out into the room; eyes fixated a look of anticipation. Rachael wasn't afraid; it excited her.

"I smell your blood, Rachael. The sweetness of it! This is what we are! Look at me!" Then he gently turned her head and looked into her eyes, passed through them, entered her mind, and told her, *if you stay with me, someday, I will take your blood!*

Shawn again moved with blinding speed back to his original seat. He allowed himself to change back to his mortal look. Head Chair Fitzgerald regained her composer and mumbled, "We will adapt. We have to. The colonel just showed me that it is possible."

"I will go to my queen and inform her of your request, and maybe I can persuade her. Vampires are still gathering their numbers. She takes a harder stand with humans."

"What do you mean still gathering?"

"We are gathering an army, but we need time."

"You are just now gathering an army when you knew about this before us?"

"All vampires will have to fight to save this world, and that will take time," Shawn said plainly.

"Vampire, I would like Rachael to go with you. To meet your queen."

"I don't think Rachael would like that."

"I will go," Rachael said quickly. "You told me once, Shawn, you wouldn't let anything happen to me. I assume that is with vampires too."

"You have nothing to fear from vampires, but all of them aren't as friendly to humans like me."

"I know! I did meet Gwyn!"

"Chairwoman Fitzgerald, I will leave for the citadel next eve. And if Rachael wants, she can come."

Chapter Nine

S hawn sat next to Rachael, sensing her turmoil, her mood, and knew she was thinking of vampire blood. Rachael flew the high-speed aircraft that he found himself in, and she came aboard with her combat gear and weapon. Shawn now realized this woman was a widely trained, top-shelf, government agent, and her superiors regarded her highly. They were currently located mid-Atlantic, heading toward Amsterdam and The Citadel.

Shawn swiveled his seat to look at Rachael to get her attention and break the trance she was in. "So deep in thought."

"I am sure you know what I am thinking."

"I do, vampires and blood. You can ask me about these things. I will tell you what you want to know."

"Will you take mine?"

"Only if you ask. I need your trust. Vampires do not feed on the pure. But, sometimes, we sneak a taste. Innocent blood is much sweeter than evil blood."

"Do vampires ask before they change humans?"

"That is different. When we decide, the angels allow us to take the humans we want. And of course, few humans would allow this. You must understand, if I did decide to change you, there would be no choice for you. That is your danger being with me."

Shawn watched her again go deep in thought. "I don't think I like you always in my mind."

"I am not always in your mind. Only when I need to know what you are thinking. I will try to give you a warning from now on."

"Is your blood that different from humans? I have always wondered what vampire blood is like."

Should I, he thought, *she does seem interested in vampire blood. The queen would undoubtedly be upset with me if I did.* "My blood is much different than yours. In some ways, it is like yours, but the angels infuse it with different energies of Heaven. Would you like a small taste? Maybe a small taste of yours? Just a little nick of your wrist. No teeth!"

Again, Rachael went into deep thought, and then to Shawn's surprise, she agreed. Rachael was a clever girl, and her great uncle did tell her about the blood. Her need to understand vampirism had finally led her to this, to take a chance. Now, she would be linked to him and more easily drawn to him. He would always know where she was, what she was feeling without entering her mind.

Shawn watched Rachael lick her lips, then turn with a nervous smile and extend her wrist to him. "Are you sure, Rachael?"

"Yes, go ahead!" Rachael told him as she wrinkled her face and pursed her lips. "I can't let this chance go by. I am in the vampire corps."

Shawn could see her desire to taste vampire blood. All her life, she had studied vampires and their magical blood. He decided to press his luck, especially with a human as attractive as Rachael. "It would be better if I could take the blood from your neck. It would be more realistic for you. Being in the vampire corps."

Shawn watched for her gaze, and it came to a look of excitement, and to his surprise, he sensed a sexual feeling. He sensed her efforts to hide the thought quickly. "Okay, No teeth!"

"No teeth," Shawn whispered, and then in an instant, he was next to her, his face next to her neck, taking in her essence. He felt her heart speed up. Then just as quick with a flick of his finger, he cut her just below the ear. It was a small cut, slightly deep to get a good taste, and then he allowed his lips to brush her ear as he placed his mouth over the wound. He pulled a small amount from her, swallowed, and then took a little more. Her hand gently came to his face, and he felt a slight push, and he immediately backed away.

"How sweet your blood is, Rachael. How pure it is. I couldn't help myself."

Shawn could sense the thrill Rachael was feeling, and then she whispered, "It's my turn."

"Put the craft on automatic pilot and sit back. You will feel tingling energy travel through you. If you take a couple of mouthfuls, it will cure ills, make your physical form stronger, and you might see Heaven."

He changed to his vampire form, then bit his wrist and made a small opening to allow his blood to flow, coating his lips red. "Drink my blood, Rachael, and you will never be afraid of me again."

"I won't become a vampire?"

"No, you will not. Not yet."

Shawn extended his wrist, and slowly Rachael brought her mouth to it, tasted the blood with her tongue, and then looked at him. "It doesn't taste like blood. It made my tongue tingle."

"Drink my blood so that you will know me!"

Rachael brought his wrist to her mouth and took a mouthful, swallowed, and then took another. Shawn saw her shudder, bring her head back, moan, and as she went into a trance, she slumped forward. A few minutes went by, she came back, opened her eyes, and they glowed briefly. Rachael was radiant and even more beautiful.

Shawn held her. She reached and touched his cheek. "I am not afraid of you anymore. I am drawn to you."

Shawn smiled and brushed her hair from her face and asked, "Where did you go?"

"I went to a green meadow with a vivid bright blue sky. I never saw a blue like that. I found myself next to a tree with large bright green leaves, and off in the distance was a white house. The colors there radiated from the surfaces as if the different colors had their own texture. Then a bright ball of light came from the horizon and traveled toward me. The light came near and then just hovered in the sky. An apparition appeared forming into a human shape with features of a woman. She said she was Anne and you knew her. Then she said the Archangel welcomes me and told me to make sure you knew that. I didn't get the feeling she was welcoming me, though; it was something else more like worry. Then the apparition floated back to the bright light at the horizon, and I came back here."

"Anne was my maker. Of all vampires, I loved her the most. And I have spent centuries missing her!"

"Do you know what she meant?"

"No!" Shawn lied. "I'm sure you will find out someday."

Amazing, Shawn thought. He knew what Michael meant; Rachael would be a vampire.

"Did you know your blood would have this effect on me? Did you trick me, Shawn?"

"I was aware of some of the effects it would have on you. Like your uncle said, it would bring us closer, and I will always know where you are if you are okay. In Heaven, there is no way for me to know what will happen there. I thought you might get a glimpse, but the angels wanted to contact you. I do know you will probably hear from them again. Now you must decide if you want to do this—to be with me. The results might not be what you want."

"Did you know it would change how I feel about you?"

"You have always felt that way about me. The blood just made it clear to you."

"All this from only a small amount!"

"It was you that became attracted to vampires and their blood. I had nothing to do with it. Maybe the angels did. I don't know."

Traveling on in silence, Shawn looked out at the night stars and watch the dark clouds quickly pass them. Toward morning, Rachael took control of the flier, bank left, and then descended. The sun was rising over the horizon, painting the sky and the tops of the clouds a soft pink.

They pierced the cloud cover, and Rachael exclaimed, "How pretty it is. I love flying in the morning. Especially now that my senses are so heightened."

They came down through the clouds, and Rachael yelled, "Holy Shit!"

She banked the flier sharply right and then brought the nose up to gain altitude. Shawn felt the acceleration pull at his body. Off in the distance was a Kargarian Army camp and only thirty miles from The Citadel. Rachael had occupied his attention, and he had not sensed the danger. He should have been more aware of his surroundings, yet they were far enough away, so he didn't think the Kargarians had detected them. This was new, the Kargarians had left the domes, and now were spreading throughout the countryside.

"Swing wide around the camp," Shawn said. "When you reach The Citadel, land in the field behind the building."

"How do I contact them to let them know who we are?"

"The vampires will know who we are. I would hurry, though."

They descended again, Rachael flew over the palace and quickly brought the aircraft to a landing. The soft hum of the turbos fell silent as Rachael powered off the craft. Rachael turned her head, and Shawn could see the worried look on her face. Shawn knew she could sense the many vampires at The Citadel.

"You will be all right. You are with me. No one will harm you," Shawn laughed and teased her, "You should be glad you tasted my blood. It will be easier for you."

"There is a lot of vampires here," Rachael gulped. "Even I can sense them."

"There certainly is, but you will only have to meet a few. You will have to meet the queen. You said you wanted too."

"Victoria?" Rachael asked.

"Yes, the queen. She is indifferent to humans. Not like me. Also, some will get very close to you. They smell you to judge you, and a few will enter your mind. Remember, vampires can't hurt the innocent."

"I remember," Rachael hopefully mumbled.

A smile came to Shawn's face, as he saw the approaching vampires. He had missed his kind. "Come on, let's go! Katherine and Gwyn are coming!"

They left the aircraft, walked across the field, and Katherine and Gwyn approached them, both with slayers on their backs.

I see Gwyn," Rachael said. The other is Katherine?"

"That is my changeling, Katherine."

"The first queen!" Rachael said excitedly.

"That is correct, and she will have some questions for you."

Shawn noticed Rachael had slowed and felt her anxiety. The doubt starting to enter her mind and the thought, *what am I doing here?* "You will be all right," Shawn assured as he took her hand.

They went to the vampires. Katherine embraced him, and kissed him passionately, as Gwyn waited, then she did the same.

"Shawn, you brought a mortal home with you," Katherine teased. "What have we told you about bringing strays home?"

"Funny! Rachael, this is Katherine, and of course, you know Gwyn."

"How are you, Rachael?" Gwyn greeted with a smile.

"I am fine," a nervous Rachael responded. "It is an honor to meet you, Katherine Bryce."

Shawn watched Katherine capture Rachael's gaze and enter her mind. He had hoped she wouldn't do this, but Katherine had led an army, and she wanted to know whom she was dealing with. And then she let her go and said, "A spy but a known spy you are. And she fancies my maker. The mortal does have a little of the gift."

"She does," Gwyn agreed.

Katherine, in an instant, was next to Rachael, embraced her, and Rachael squirmed, trying to free herself, but Katherine's strength was no match for her. Shawn saw Katherine place her lips against Rachael's neck, take in her essence, and then kissed her on the lips. He should have known Katherine would give Rachael the full vampire treatment.

"I smell vampire blood in you, human. Care to explain?" Katherine said as she released Rachael and took a step back.

"Enough, Katherine!" Shawn commanded. "She was curious, and I let her taste my blood."

Katherine bowed slightly to Shawn and said, "As you wish."

"The queen awaits you, Shawn," Gwyn said. "And she says to bring the mortal."

Shawn certainly wished the greetings had gone better. At times Katherine could be a little feisty and Gwyn a little cold. They proceeded into The Citadel, then into a large common area where Shawn saw vampires watching screens that showed the Red Army camp. All vampires had slayers on their backs ready for an attack that could come at any time and something new blasters at their sides. Down a long corridor, they walked and then through large double doors into the throne room.

Two covenant leaders passed them, as they went out the door and gave Rachael a good look up and down. Victoria ended her conversation with Peter, looked, and smiled at him. Peter turned, took a step, and floated across the pool of water and greeted Shawn as he left. "Good to see you, Shawn. The queen is worried about you. And I am off to keep an eye on those pesky Kargarians."

"Good to see you, Peter, and keep your head down."

Victoria floated over the pool and gently landed in front of him. He welcomed her embrace and passionate kiss. "How are you? My love. I worry about you these days. Being with humans."

"I'm fine, Victoria. This is Rachael."

Shawn saw her loving look go to a stern gaze that landed on Rachael. He sensed Victoria quickly overcome Rachael's mind, brushing her will aside, searching her thoughts, learning who she was, what she was.

"So, you have come to visit. To spy on us and tell all to your superiors."

"Greetings to you, Queen Victoria. It is an honor. That was our agreement with Shawn, who I believe represents you."

"He does represent me to humans."

"Humans, as you say with disdain, will need to know what guardians are up to. What schemes your angels are coming up with. If we are to be allies."

"Well, you certainly are not afraid to speak your mind! I also see you are angry with the angels, yet you want our help! As you see, we have the enemy at our gates too."

"Humans need your help, Queen Victoria. This is your world too."

"That is where you are wrong," Victoria answered tensely. "This is your world and nobody else's. Vampires are here to protect you; it is not our world. You see, the angels don't treat you that bad. For millennia, you have fought amongst each other, poisoned the world, and almost brought this planet to its end. That is why The Mother is upset with you, why she tasks you. But in your favor, The Archangel has seen you progress over the last few centuries, and he is pleased with you. He has directed vampires to help you, but humans must fight for this world, or you will perish. You and Shawn will go back to your leaders and tell them to move their armies to the Americas. Do not move them to the British Isles. Unite your armies. When your army crosses the Atlantic, we will protect your retreat."

Victoria turned to Shawn. "Gwyn will stay here with The Mother's Staff. I need her and the staff to take Braden and

94

Juliane to Washington. I know that is not what The Mother wants, but that is what Michael and I want."

Shawn recognized this command for what it was, a striking difference between the Archangel and The Mother. Michael was showing his annoyance with The Mother.

"I will deliver your message, Queen Victoria," Rachael promised.

"This continent is a loss, and humans must make their stand in the Americas. Do not trap what is left of your armies on the British Isles. You may leave human; Peter is outside waiting to take you to your quarters. I wish to spend some time with Shawn."

As Rachael turned to leave, Victoria warned, "There is another message you can deliver to your superiors. I have loved Shawn for over a thousand years and do not betray him. I will hold your leadership responsible!"

"It's okay, Rachael," Shawn assured. "I will meet you later."

"Come, Shawn, walk with me," Victoria said.

Later Shawn laid with Victoria in her couch. They had made love, now held, and caressed each other. He had loved this woman for twelve hundred years. He could even remember when he had first saw her. A blood tear came to his eye. He had been with Marilyn his first love of this world when he was mortal, and now a long-lost love.

Victoria wiped it from his cheek, placed it in her mouth, and whispered, "So sentimental."

He thought back on his long life, and sometimes he felt tired of this world. Especially when he remembered vampires, he had lost. And the responsibilities angels put on him living a life as a guardian.

"You must be careful with the humans," Victoria told him. "And with this human woman."

"I do not fear humans!"

"I know you don't," Victoria replied. "Already you allow this woman to close to you. It is always the same with you. You and Katherine are the same when it comes to love. You cannot turn this woman. I need her as a mortal. She will work for us. Do you understand?"

"I understand."

"Drake came to me with a message from Michael. Guardians must kill Brendel if the humans are to be saved. You are the only one in this world that has the capabilities. Again, the angels look to you. When you meet with the human's leadership, you must make sure they understand that Michael wants them to unite to fight Brendel's army. Instead of going to Britain, they must move their armies to the Americas. This continent is lost. The Citadel will stay here to be the beacon of light."

"When will you attack the Kargarian army's camp?"

"When humans move their army. We will attack the camp to provide cover for them. You and warrior vampires will escort them across the ocean. Oh, I have some other news you might be interested in."

"And what is that?"

"Katherine and Gwyn have been spending time together in their couches."

"Really!"

New Chicago was coming into view as Rachael bank the flyer left and started their descent. A human-generated dome now covered the city. Mortals, he thought, had learned a great deal about these types of domes – how to destroy them and now how to create them. Distortions and a loud hum would rise to a crescendo, travel off and dissipate. They still had some work to do on the functioning of the dome. A small hologram of a human head appeared off to the side and said, "Welcome, Colonel Bonnet. The top of the dome will recede to make an opening. When you have entered, follow all protocols for traveling in the city and proceed directly to Freedom Hall."

"Command, I copy that," Rachael said, then banked the craft right and headed to the top of the dome.

The summit of the dome wavered, and then a large opening appeared. Rachael dropped the nose of the aircraft, flew through the opening, bank left, and then traveled true toward the government complex of the city. Rachael flew low, mingling with the traffic, and to Shawn's surprise followed all traffic laws. They wound their way around the high towers over the many green parks of the city. Shawn saw a broad base of a sky tower under construction. These were the new towers that would rise a mile into the sky. He wondered if the humans would last long enough to complete these new towers.

Around another tower, they went, and then Freedom Hall came into view. The humans built the complex like a fortress with hardened material that could withstand tremendous forces. There were many buildings, and in the middle was Freedom Hall, where the governments of this world had gathered. Rachael lowered the nose and traveled toward a landing area that held many different types of military aircraft. Shawn felt the flier touch down and saw a small delegation hurrying to greet them. Two military men by their dress and a woman in a modern pantsuit. The door slid open, and Shawn and Rachael stepped onto the tarmac.

"Welcome, Colonel," said one of the officers while both exchanged salutes with Rachael.

"Welcome," the woman said politely. "Please follow me. The federations want to see you immediately."

Shawn followed the woman's brisk pace. It was easy for him to see the government complex had turned into a heavily armed fortification. Every human carried a weapon or had a sidearm strapped to their hip. Soon he found himself standing in front of the representatives of four federations. The Madame Chair informed him the African and Asian federation were staying put and preparing to defend their homelands.

The Madame Chair from the European Federation spoke first. "Greetings to you guardian."

"Greetings, Madame Chair and Chair Heads."

"We have had a turn of events over the last eight hours. The Kargarian army has left Paris, and now it is in the countryside pursuing our two armies. Also, a red army is coming from the north. It seems they have an encampment outside of Amsterdam City. And something has kept this army from entering Amsterdam." Madame Chair turned her gaze to Shawn. "Europe will be a loss if we don't save London."

"From my intelligence, London is already a loss, Madame Chair," Head Chair Fitzgerald said.

A door slid open, and a military officer came through, and Shawn quickly saw he carried a framed document. The document was a letter he had written centuries ago to the newly forming government of the Americas. He had penned the letter at the end of the Great Dark Age. Madame Chair Brune slid a piece of paper that had an unfinished note he had left behind.

"We found this note in the quarters you occupied in Brussels. Unusual to find writing like that in this age," Madame Chair said. "Of course, we sent it to be analyzed. And that is when an observant tech drew the connection between the handwriting on the note and this letter. So happens he was also a scholar of history."

"That letter is an important and famous document of the Americas Federation," Head Chair Fitzgerald added. "It is the ideas that our government was formed. We keep the letter at our government complex and display it on a pedestal in Freedom Hall. The handwriting is the same. You, Shawn, wrote that letter!"

"It is hard for me to remember that far back. I believe I did write a couple of letters back then. The letters seemed appropriate at the time. I always have cared about mortals and always have done what I could to help the human race. After all, I came from the human race."

"It is an honor for me to meet the guardian that wrote this letter," Head Chair Fitzgerald said, as she stood with a smile that was unusual for this woman and extended her hand for a handshake.

Madam Chair Brune then spoke. "Sorry to interrupt, but I have to ask. What do you say, Shawn? What did your queen say about joining the fight?"

"Europe and the Russian Federations are a loss. My queen and the Archangel want you to move all of your world's armies to the Americas. That is where you must make your stand. Queen Victoria will send vampires to cover your armies crossing of the Atlantic."

The chairs conferred amongst themselves with their sporadic waving of hands and whispering with symbols appearing and disappearing all around their heads. Eventually, Madame Chair spoke. "Asian and African Federations will not bring their armies to the Americas. We realize what we have lost in this part of the world. The European and Russian Federations will move their armies across the Atlantic. We will wait for your queen's answer."

Shawn and Rachael went back to their quarters, and a day later, Queen Victoria's answer came. The vampires would help the European and Russian Armies cross the Atlantic. Shawn now stood with Rachael on the balcony of his living quarters at the government complex. The humans had given him a living area, told him he would always be welcome here. He had told Rachael that she could not go with him this time. It was too dangerous for her. The federation had not taken the news well. They insisted she was a soldier and could take care of herself. Shawn realized that to them, she was a soldier and expendable, but not to him, and again he said no. He had strapped Adeen to his back, turned, and smiled at Rachael, as he prepared to leave.

"I wish you would let me go with you!" Rachael pleaded one more time.

"I will be moving very quickly, and it would be too dangerous for you. I explained all of that to you, and some of the older vampires would not appreciate it if you were there."

Rachael hesitantly drew close, gave Shawn a light kiss on his cheek, and said, "Be careful! Until we meet again, vampire."

Shawn smiled as he lifted into the air, and he replied, "Until we meet again, my dear Rachael."

Chapter Ten

B rendel sat on his throne at the top of a high tower in the recently conquered Jerusalem. This top platform was made of a thick, black marble and set out in the open. No walls or dome enclosed it. Nothing of this world could hurt him. He could see the dark energies of the universe swirl around him. Because of his father Lucifer, he could manipulate this energy and make it do his bidding. Everywhere the surfaces held a frost. In hell, his father's evil was hot here; a demon's darkness was frigid. He would look out from his perch take in the world, directed his army in its methodical takeover of this planet. Soon he would control a large part of this world, and soon, this world would join the four dark realms of this galaxy, and another dimension would begin its fall and become Lucifer's.

Now he would turn his attention to the Americas. Still, there was one nagging question, one detail that had not been played out yet. The vampires had not committed to the battle. Brendel knew they would be formidable. He also knew that to control this world, he would have to kill the vampire, Shawn Bryce. The Archangel and Eos channeled great power through him, and he was the key to this planet. Brendel knew his chance would come with Shawn. The good always let their guard down; that is when he would strike and rid this world of The Demon Slayer.

Vampires lived a long time in this world, but these earthly guardians of Michaels had one life in this world, unlike humans that had many. He would kill Shawn, and he would be another warrior angel of Heaven, never able to bring his power back to this world. The power Eos hid in him would leave this world and go back to her. The Archangel must hold Shawn in high regard to rescue him from Malin. And Malin indeed had warned him about Shawn. Not to underestimate his courage and the power he held.

He watched Samil appear out of the darkness and land on his platform. A powerful witch full of his father's hate for the light, loyal, and his only companion in this world.

"So deep in thought my lord," Samil said.

"Shawn must be killed to win this war!"

"Killing Shawn will not be easy, my lord. He is a powerful vampire and mother's witch. He gathered great power and respect when Malin failed to kill him."

"I will kill Shawn. He will let his guard down; his pitiful love for this world will allow me to send him to our father. What do you have to say about London?"

"London will fall. Humans cannot match the Kargarians in number."

"Have you begun the expanse outside the cities?"

The Kargarian forces have left Rome and have the human army caught with its backs against the sea. It will only be a matter of time before our army destroys them."

"I have a reminder for you, my lord."

"What is that?"

Away from the cities and out in the open, humans can kill more Kargarians. Already their casualties are in the millions."

"That doesn't matter. What have you learned about Amsterdam?"

"That is where the vampires gather, and we have heard very little from them since Moscow, my lord!"

"They have not committed their forces yet. When they do, we must be ready. They will be formidable."

"We will be ready. Our numbers are vast. We also know Shawn is with the humans and stays with one of their military operatives. She is the human Colonel Rachael Bonnet."

"Is she a desirable woman?"

"Yes, my lord."

Brendel raised his head, a wicked smiled spread over his face, and a dark laugh echoed out into the night. "Really! Maybe it is true what Malin says. Shawn is always looking for love—a fool for it. That is his great weakness. Maybe the human woman is the way to kill The Demon Slayer. Learn more of this woman and see how much The Demon Slayer cares for this mortal woman."

☆☆☆☆

The day had been stormy and windy, and Shawn sat on the beach, looking out at the angry ocean. The sun rode the sky low and projected its twilight through the scattered grey clouds. All day, he watched the rockets boosting the large space transports filled with the European people into space to make the trip to their new home in the belt. Humans were abandoning the continent by going to space or making the dangerous trip to the Americas.

The waves rushed ashore, crashing onto the beach, and the foaming seawater quickly flowed over the sand, stopping its advance a small distance from his feet. The roar from the ocean filled the salt air. Gloom filled him. At his back was the village known as Le Havre, mostly deserted now. The people of the town harvested the seafood from the ocean and delivered it inland to Rouen, were the humans distributed the food to the cities. Their bounty had been plentiful, and then Brendel had come.

Farmland stretched west surrounding and moving past Rouen, where the European and Russian federation armies had settled. The humans had fortified their camp with photon pulse cannons, lasers, and now air transports and attack fliers filled the fields around the city. The European and Russian federations had finally agreed to move their armies to the Americas.

He raised his head and sensed what he did not want to. It was Rachael, and she was to the west in Rouen. He hoped she wouldn't come here, but the human had a warrior's mind, and he supposed had to follow orders. Later, when darkness came, Victoria would bring five thousand vampires to Le Havre and occupy the town. There they would wait for the humans to start their Atlantic crossing.

He looked down the beach and watched Katherine and Gwyn stroll along the foaming sea. Laughing and holding hands, then they'd stop kissed each other and looked to him. He smiled back and brought his eyes to the sand. The world was coming apart, and you wouldn't know it by those two. Shaking his head, he looked up as they strolled toward him. He and Gwyn had come two days ago to this area. Katherine had come from Amsterdam the following day. Gwyn, one of his changelings, spent most of her time with him. She was no longer bound to stay with him, but The Mother had different ideas. Surprisingly to him, Gwyn and Katherine had fallen in love with each other. The intimate kind of love. They always had a special bond. Katherine did not surprise him, but he had never known Gwyn to be with a woman. Gwyn recently mentioned that when she was young, she had been with a few. At that time, he had wondered why she was telling him this, but now he knew.

"You should ask my permission for that," Shawn teased and wagged his finger at them.

"I suppose," Katherine responded, "but we are both your changelings."

"I told you, I had found somebody else to love," Gwyn added. "I was going to tell you, but Katherine wanted to show you."

Suddenly, the sky dimmed as five thousand vampires flew between the fading sunlight and the shoreline. One vampire, the queen, broke off from the formation came and landed in front of them.

"Greetings, Queen Victoria," Katherine and Gwyn said with an exaggerated bow.

"You two are flattering this eve. And what about you, changeling?" Victoria eyed him and laughed. "Don't you know how to greet your queen?"

"You know I am always glad to see you," Shawn said as he stood and embraced Victoria, kissed her, and stepped back. "What have you brought?"

"The mortals sent Rachael to The Citadel to deliver a message. Their evacuation will start four eves from now. Rachael is a brave one, that is for sure. She inquired about your health, asked if you were well."

"She is in Rouen?" Shawn asked in disbelief.

"She did say she was going south to Rouen."

"Damn, I was hoping she would not go there."

Shawn saw Victoria's eyes turn the blue of sapphire as she flashed them at him and felt the penetration into his mind. Then he heard in his head plainly, "Again, I tell you, I need the human as a human!"

"I am aware of that, Victoria!" Shawn snapped. "But we also need her alive."

"Walk with me, Shawn!" Victoria commanded.

Shawn walked with the woman he had loved all his vampire life, looked on her beautiful neck and face wetted from moist sea air, and her long blonde hair blowing in the salty wind. He had always seen Victoria's beauty. Victoria had always walked like a queen, always was comfortable in commanding others. She had come from nobles when she was human, and now she was Queen of the Vampires.

"The humans are starting to leave the planet," Victoria scoffed.

"I know. I have been watching their spaceships leave all day."

"They are not staying to fight, they are leaving," Victoria harshly said as she turned her gaze on him. "They are going to lose this war. My decisions on helping humans must include that fact!"

"They are afraid, Victoria! You can't blame them! Heaven and Hell hide from them! This is new to them! They will prevail!"

"Be careful, Shawn, your beloved humans, could get you killed. I am leaving to go back to The Citadel. The vampires have finished gathering. Forty thousand are in Amsterdam, and twenty thousand are at Dalton in the Americas training for war. That is most of the vampires of this world. I am leaving you in charge of the vampires I brought with me. Protect the humans in their crossing. Heavens knows they will need it."

"I don't like leaving Rachael in Rouen. She works with us, and that leaves her vulnerable to the evil forces trying to take over this world."

Shawn saw Victoria look to the sand and whisper, "I have asked Drake about Rachael, and he told me the angels would not speak of her. Michael has warned me of bad times to come, and I am afraid for you."

"I will be fine, my love. I always am!" Shawn laughed. "The angels aren't finished with me. Who would do their dirty work."

Shawn laid in a soft bed with his racing thoughts, and sleep eluded him. He looked on a sleeping Katherine and Gwyn. They had coaxed him into bed to make love to them; he was their maker, and like all vampires, they needed from time to time to be with the one that had turned them to this life. Stroking their soft bare skin, he thought of the love he had for them. How strange that they had fallen so deeply in love with each other. But in a way it didn't surprise him, they had spent many desperate years together saving him, and now they wanted to be with each other. They enjoyed each other's company, and he sometimes knew they sought each other out.

Victoria had left earlier to go back to The Citadel. He worried about the humans, would they lose this world. Certainly, they would rally in the Americas. After the crossing, he would go to the queen and convince her to commit the vampires to the fight. Victoria always was hard on humans, had little faith in them. She expected more resolve from them, and as usual, Michael and Eos had a different idea on how to handle the mortals. He wrestled with his thoughts and then felt that sting to his mind, raised his head to sense the night, rode the light, and knew something was wrong in Rouen. He felt a powerful evil stealing its way toward Rachael. Lifting out of bed, he landed with a thud on the hardwood floor and pulled his clothes on quickly, turned and reached for Adeen.

"What is it, Shawn?" Katherine asked sleepily.

"It's Rachael. Evil is rising around her. You and Gwyn are in charge until I get back."

"Maybe you should wait!" Gwyn warned. "Let us go with you. I have the staff."

"No, stay and take care of the vampires here."

Shawn took two steps, flew through the open window throwing the curtains outward. The wind rushed against his face as he opened his throttle and flew as fast as he could toward Rouen. Landing on the outskirts of the city, he used his great speed and stealth to avoid the perimeter guards. His senses were on high, as he scanned the area to find the miniature surveillance cameras scattered throughout the city. Few lights burned, and the humans had hunkered down behind their defenses. Military vehicles were parked everywhere between the buildings on the sides of all the streets. Rouen was a small city with no towers, only a few high-rise buildings. It was an agriculture and seafood hub full of large cold warehouses to store their harvest before sending it on to the people.

Shawn made his way through the alleys sensing many soldiers. A mist covered the ground like a grey blanket in what little light there was. He rounded a corner of a building and, with stealth, ended standing behind three soldiers. He startled the soldiers, and one raised his weapon at him.

The leader placed his hand on the barrel and lowered the gun. "Vampire," he whispered. "They are our allies now."

"Greetings to you. How goes it?" Shawn said as he extended his hand for a shake, but their apprehension was high, and there were no takers.

"Badly!" one of the men said. "Will vampires be at the crossing?"

"Vampires will be at the crossing," Shawn quickly replied. "Rest assured, human. Have a good evening."

Then the wide-eyed humans stared, as he slowly drifted up the side of the building. Landing on the roof of the four-story building, he crouched and sensed what was ahead. Five Valaris wizards were a half-mile to the north. They were moving with stealth, but he knew they were there, and then he sensed Rachael sleeping in a hotel room below where the wizards stood. They had opened a portal from their dark dimension, and they were after Rachael.

Shawn accelerated running from roof to roof. A memory flashed through his mind when he was a young vampire running the roofs with Anne. He came to the hotel, flew to its high top, crouched, and then it struck him, Brendel was near, but he could not tell where. Adeen vibrated and rang on his back. "Quiet Adeen!" He whispered.

He sensed the wizards ahead, and then they step out from a small power giving fusion reactor set on the roof. The wizards were tall and faceless, like all that came from their realm. They spread out, and one threw dark energy at him. Shawn grabbed Adeen and reflected the energy. In return, he pushed The Mother's power at the wizards, but as quickly one drew a circle with his staff and absorbed the white energy. Changing tactics, he shot high into the sky, turned and dropped like a rock into the wizards, and took the head of one. Dark energy struck him in the back, and The Mother's energy instantly surrounded him, protecting him from the blast. The force threw him out into the dark, where he hovered raising Adeen and flew back into the wizards taking another's head.

A strange dialect came from the remaining three, and then all of the wizards drew one large circle with their staffs, and a giant ball of dark energy came from the swirling blue portal. Chanting a mother's spell, he drew a circle with Adeen, and white energy absorbed the dark energy. Then he felt Brendel's evil near, and to his surprise, the remaining three wizards turned, step back through the portal and disappeared.

Brendel came and landed on the roof, bringing his darkness with him. Raising Adeen, he felt the energy, the vibrations of the blade as his sword from Heaven rang its displeasure at this demon. He felt The Mother's energy course and built-in his body, and his blue vampire eyes turned to a brilliant white light as Heaven's energy filled him. Everything turned cold, and the demon came with the harsh grinding sound of a million insects and maggots covering all surfaces. The monster looked down on him, and an evil smile spread across his face.

"How powerful you have become, Demon Slayer. I will not fight you tonight, but our time is coming. I wanted to see how far you would go for this woman. Your precious mortal woman is safe, for now. Do you think you will always be there to protect her?" A loud, deep laugh echoed in the night. "Will you change her, vampire?" Again, a deep chuckle as the demon turned and faded into the night.

Shawn rose and floated just above the surface of the roof, went by four dead human guards, their eyes burned from their heads. Then over the edge and down the side of the building until he came to Rachael's window. Sensing her, he knew Rachael was in the next room, hiding in a closet. Certainly, a closet was no protection against a demon. Shawn allowed his psychic energies to enter her mind, give her a feeling of safety, and then a whisper to her; *the evil is gone, come to the window. I will help you.*

The door between the rooms opened slightly, and Rachael peeked through. Shawn tapped on the window and got her attention. Rachael quickly came and opened the window.

"Thank the Heavens you came. The evil surrounded me, and then I saw in my mind a horrible creature. A coldness filled my body, and darkness pulled at me. Was it the devil Shawn?"

Shawn guided her shaking body to the bed and sat with her. "That was Brendel."

He wrapped his arm around her, pulling her close and slowly kissed her quivering lips. Then he felt her shaking stop, and her last fear of him leave. He pulled her onto the bed and made love to her gently, for she was mortal. He felt her warmth as he kissed and caressed her. Then he felt her give herself to him completely.

Chapter Eleven

B rendel stood deep in thought, looking out into the night, stroking his chin, and then slowly an evil grin spread over his face. "Father, I now know how to kill the Demon Slayer. This world will be yours!" To him, the way was clear Shawn would go to any lengths to save the mortal woman, and his love for these humans was strong. The Demon Slayer cared for the woman, and with that thought, he gave an evil laugh. Love was a feeling only the good could afford. That was Malin's downfall. He had no idea about love only that he could use the emotion to destroy the good. Shawn's feelings for this mortal woman would be his end. He would see to that.

Samil had arrived with her report on the human army in Rouen.

"My lord, we have a great victory; the humans are abandoning this continent. Their army is preparing to cross the Atlantic."

"We will destroy them! Send them to the bottom of their sea. I will contact the dark realm to open the portals and send their flyers."

"There is another development. Five thousand vampires have gathered a short distance from the humans."

Finally, Brendel thought and then turned to Samil. "The vampires are showing themselves. Now we can destroy them along with the humans."

"The time has come to rid this world of those filthy vampires," Samil said.

"We must be vigilant, Samil, who knows what The Demon Slayer will do."

⋆⋆⋆⋆

Shawn took Rachael to The Citadel and brought her to his living quarters to allow her to rest. Brendel had shown an interest in her. He would try to use her in some way. He must be more careful with Rachael and now knew he had to keep her safe. A slight yawn came from her as he watched her sleep, and he smiled at the innocents on her face. Humans needed more rest than vampires; such a short life filled with sleep, he mused. How pretty she looked in sleep and how frail she was in life. But all humans were fragile, limited strength and abilities with little life given to them by Heaven, doomed to live over and over again. Eventually, when they finally get it right, they could become the lowest of angels. This had never seemed fair to him.

Rachael had many abilities for a human, a scholar of vampire lore, an ambassador, a soldier, spy, and she was psychic. He now cared for her that was always the way for him, she was a unique human, and he liked falling in love; the newness of love was what he craved. His long life made him that way and was the reason vampires always were looking for love. Looking down on Rachael, he watched her stir awake. Sending his senses outward, he found Victoria and whispered to her mind, *Come, Rachael is waking up*, and then the return touch to his mind *soon*.

He walked to the window and looked out over the large courtyard of The Citadel. The twilight of the evening was turning to the dark of night. Looking up, he watched the fire trails of the spaceships, as more humans started their trip to their new home in the belt. Everywhere he saw vampires with their slayers, more vampires than he had ever seen together.

Then he heard the rustling of the bedding, as Rachael sat up. He turned to greet her. "Good eve, my love, how are you feeling tonight?" He had given her some of his blood earlier to help her with the fear.

"I am feeling better. Come and hold me for a moment; it makes me feel safe."

Shawn slid into bed next to her, put his arm around her, and pulled her close. Brushing her hair from her face, he smiled and whispered, "My dear Rachael, someday you will be mine, but unfortunately, that time is not here."

He felt her warm lips touch him, and then the whisper in his ear, "I can't imagine being a vampire. When I was a child, I wanted to be a vampire, but now I am not sure."

"For guardians, my love, it doesn't matter what a mortal wants when it comes to that."

"I know! When I was young, that was the one part that made me dislike vampires."

"The angels will always have their way. Remember that!

"Our dance will continue for my immortality?" Rachael asked.

"It will. Go wash up The Queen will be here shortly."

"Will you join me in the shower?" Rachael asked as she gave him a look of desire.

"Not this time. I'm sorry to say. Victoria is not a fan of vampires being with mortals."

Another seductive look from Rachael and a quick brush of his cheek with her fingers. "I think The Queens sees little in me that she is a fan of."

"She will someday."

"If I live that long."

"Nothing will happen to you as long as you're with me."

He knew many vampires frowned on his kind being with mortals. It was something most thought would not be in the best interest of humans. But he would never use Rachael for her blood, though it tasted delicious, or allow harm to her. Raising his head, he sensed Victoria coming down the corridor. So he floated to the door, waved his hand, and the door slid open to reveal Victoria standing with a look of displeasure on her beautiful face.

"Come in Victoria, and please don't start."

"I am your queen, and I will start. You are staying with the mortal now. Are you sleeping with her?"

"You know I am!" Victoria always made him confess his sins even though she was aware of the truth.

"Many times, over the years, we have talked of this, and you know how I feel about it!"

"I will make Rachael a vampire when the time comes. And all of you must accept it."

"She has attracted Brendel, and she will get you killed before you can change her."

"Then, I will tell Katherine to do it."

"Well, Gwyn certainly won't."

Rachael came from the other room and was greeted with a smile from Shawn and a puzzled look from Victoria.

"Be careful what you wish for Rachael," Victoria warned.

At least she is calling her by her name, Shawn thought.

"I am glad to see you again, Queen Victoria," Rachael said. "I have a message from General Purdue, the supreme commander of the army in Rouen. I was going to travel back and use the code you gave me to make contact, but I became surrounded by evil entities. At first, I didn't know what it was, but Shawn came and rescued me."

Shawn saw Rachael trying her best to be friendly, but Victoria kept her stern look for all to see. Shawn knew she must maintain her authority in front of Rachael; it was her way. Victoria was an ancient vampire, and he knew she had developed her views of humans over thousands of years and would not change in a day.

"And the message?" Victoria asked sharply.

"In two days, our army will cross the Atlantic. It should take six hours for the entire army to make landfall on the old Virginian coast. At that point, the Army of the Americas also will help provide cover."

"I see," Victoria answered.

"The general very much hopes he sees vampires at the crossing. He also wanted me to inform you that he will begin his crossing at night. We do want to work with your kind."

"At this time, I am sure you do. He will see more vampires than he probably cares too. Five thousand are on the coast and will cover your crossing. Also, when the Kargarian flyers attack your army, vampires will leave the Citadel and attack their camp to the west. That should draw many of them away from your army and give you a better chance."

"Then I will return to Rouen as soon as possible," Rachael said.

"No, you will not! You will stay here under my protection until the crossing is over and Shawn returns. We need you, human, and Shawn should be there not saving you!"

"I will watch out for Rachael!" Shawn quickly replied. "There is no need for her to stay here!"

"I am Queen, and she will stay at the Citadel for now. You will go back to Le Have and lead the vampires. Do you understand?"

"I understand," Shawn said reluctantly. Rarely did Victoria get stern with him, but this was one of those times, and he knew it was probably safer for Rachael at The Citadel. "I will be back for her!"

"I am sure you will."

Shawn had said his goodbyes to Rachael and now stood on the beach at Le Have with Katherine and Gwyn. Five thousand vampires also lined the beach with their slayers, and for the first time, they carried pulse blasters. The stars and the moon broke through the gray of the evening. He felt Gwyn's displeasure at him for sleeping with Rachael, and Katherine was not happy about it either.

He kicked at the ground sending a spray of sand into the water. Looking down the beach, he could see the vampires preparing themselves for the attack. They wore their armor, and their slayers were strap to their back. In this time, all vampires were warriors, and the weak among the vampires, the ones selected for other reasons, would probably perish before this war was over. Shawn knew that vampires also would pay a heavy price for this world.

He glanced to his side and saw Gwyn staring at him. "Gwyn, please! I am a vampire, not a witch!"

"Shawn likes mortal women. He always has," Katherine added.

"I'm surprised he changed us!" Gwyn said sarcastically.

"You both are wrong! I care for Rachael! She has many good qualities, and when this war is over, I will make her my changeling, and she will be a part of our family. You two should start getting used to the idea!"

Then came the roar in the distance of a thousand upon thousands of transports protected by even more fighter aircraft. They traveled overhead, blocking out the night stars and spreading complete darkness over the sky.

Shawn turned and yelled to the vampires. "We must make sure as many as these transports make it to the Americas. Harden yourselves when you strike. The Kargarian aircraft are easily penetrated. Destroy as many as you can. Use your blasters!"

Rachael had told him that in their studies of the Kargarians, they learned their metal was not as dense as ours. The dark realm that held their world had a different gravity pull that left their matter less dense than on Earth's. They also learned their sun burnt red. These were the reason the red soldiers were tall and lean. Shawn step forward lifted into the air, and yelled, "It is time for vampires to join the fight! For our Queen! For our world!"

A loud rallying cry came from the vampires, their voices echoing across the water. "For the Queen!" We are with you, Demon Slayer!"

Lifting and accelerating high into the night, the vampires flew amongst the formation, preparing themselves for the attack. Shawn flew with Katherine and Gwyn between two transports. He gave them a reassuring look, and they smiled back then nodded. Soldiers stared out the windows with fear etched on their faces. They knew many of them would not survive the crossing. On top of the transports was a clear dome where humans manned rapid repeating pulsars, and they too stared out at their new companions, not quite believing what they saw.

Onward, the vampires flew amongst the armada. The clear night turned to clouds then rain and ice, lighting flashed in the distance, and Shawn felt sleet pelting his face. Gwyn cast a spell diverting the rain and ice around them. They continued, and soon the night sky cleared. When they reached a point where the humans could not turn back, a massive hum rose in the night as hundreds of the blue portals opened. Kargarian aircraft streamed out of the portals by the thousands. Thousands of human pulsars opened up on the Kargarian aircraft, and the night sky lit up and became as bright as day. Everywhere the evil flyers darted and flew in and out of the formations. By the thousands, they swarmed like mad bees into the horrific fire of the humans. Kargarian flyers burst into flames and plunged into the ocean below. Human transports and aircraft also erupted into flames and fell from their formations.

Shawn saw the anxiety on Katherine and Gwyn's faces as burning aircraft fell all around them. He then sent the psychic signal to the vampires to begin their attack. The vampires left the formation and dove into the Kargarian aircraft. Hardening themselves, the vampires swarmed the Kargarians. They flew into the Kargarian aircraft, dodging their laser fire, piercing their thin hulls with their blasters blowing them apart. Their fiery remains were plunging to the sea below.

He caught chunks of falling debris and threw them into their thrusters, causing the fliers to explode in mid-air. Kargarian flyers by the hundreds were falling from the sky. Human transport after transport would veer off and start their flaming descent to the ocean—pilots, humans, and Kargarians blown from their cockpits spiraling to the sea below. The warplanes hit the surface of the sea, spreading their burning fuel over the water. The water was covered with flames for miles and glowed a bright green from the wreckage of the flyers. Thousands upon thousands of humans were dying tonight, and he felt their many souls leaving this world.

Shawn again sent a psychic signal urging the vampires to hurry the attack to save as many mortals as possible. The terrible journey went on and left a path of wreckage across the Atlantic. And for the second time in human history, the radiation levels rose to dangerous levels in this part of the world.

Shawn repeatedly attacked the enemy warcraft, but there were too many. And just when he thought the humans were not going to make it, a large part of the Kargarians broke off the assault and headed back toward Europe. Victoria had started her raid on the Kargarian outpost by Amsterdam. Vampires and humans flew on together for an hour, and then Shawn saw the coast. He turned and gave a look of relief to Katherine and Gwyn, and they nodded back at him. The Richmond spaceport was now in sight.

Sirens wailed, and photon missiles streak through the sky out over the ocean, destroying the remaining Kargarian fliers. Many crippled transports came in low and crashed-landed, skidding to a stop, bursting into flames and the emergency crews quickly moving them aside. Smoke and fire billowed into the air as the sirens continued to sound. Shawn had seen nothing like this since the apocalypse. Shawn sent another psychic message, *quickly vampires; we must try to get as many humans out of the burning aircraft.*

Vampires flew among the wreckage saving many of the humans. Shawn pulled badly burned humans from the debris and knew for most what was left of their lives would undoubtedly be of agony. He would end their suffering. Some humans became alarmed by his actions, but he just told them to calm themselves, he was showing mercy and sending them to a better place.

The generals came and thanked him, told him they would not forget what vampires had done for them. The generals knew their army would not have made it without the vampires. Shawn bid them farewell, gathered the vampires, and started the trip back across the Atlantic toward Amsterdam. The Citadel was under attack by the Kargarians, and the vampires still had half a night left.

He accelerated, and Gwyn and Katherine matched him. Most vampires kept up, but some straggled behind. Two hours later, they came overland, exhausted, and flew directly toward Amsterdam. The west wing of The Citadel was on fire, and smoke billowed into the early morning sky. Shawn adjusted his flight speed turned west and flew toward the fighting. The Kargarians were in full retreat. The ground below him was covered with their corpses and their flyers. Kargarians were not a physically strong race because of their gravity and were no match for the vampires.

Shawn and most of his vampires arrived when wizards and witches by the hundreds were franticly opening portals, trying to save as many of the badly beaten red soldiers as they could. The Kargarians were desperate to escape the vampires. Vampires blanketed the sky, swarming and killing the Kargarians by the thousands. Forty thousand vampires were taking a terrible toll on the red soldiers and their war machines. Vampires had destroyed the Kargarian camp and now went after the red soldiers hiding amongst the wreckage. Then a strong psychic message from the queen telling the vampires to break off the attack and return to The Citadel to guard the only fortress left in this hemisphere to resist Brendel and his evil. Shawn and his forces circled and started the trip back to The Citadel. The sun was beginning to rise, and if the vampires had to come out and fight in the daylight, it would be to defend their lair.

Chapter Twelve

B rendel stood at the top of his high tower at the edge of the platform, arms across his chest, looking down on deserted Jerusalem. No humans now lived in the city. The fires had finally gone out, and all that remained was the burnt ash of the city. A frown spread over his face; the vampires had shown themselves and their might. Much of Heaven's energy had come to this world over the centuries, a direct result of his father's constant attacks upon it, another fact he had not realized. The vampires were powerful because of this, and they had given the Kargarian a terrible beating. The Kargarians were physically too weak to deal with vampires of this world, and their losses against the humans were far higher than he had expected. The human weapons were formidable, and they, too, were putting up a good fight. The mortals were good at killing, and they killed the Kargarians by the millions.

He was behind in his takeover of this world, and Lucifer was impatient with him. He would have to bring many more wizards and witches into the battle against the vampires. Maybe he would also use the Tarragons, the lizard race, in the fight. They were a hardier breed than the Kargarians. Lucifer wanted to use the Kargarians, though; he believed them to be more expendable, and this did not sit well with the Kargarians. They were starting to complain about their losses.

The alternate dimension that was the dark realm held many races that had succumbed to the dark forces. In this reality, only four worlds had fallen to the Lucifer's evil. Malin was responsible for those worlds, but she was no longer able to come to the physical planes thanks to Eos and The Demon Slayer. He turned back around and saw Samil land on the platform.

"What news do you have of the vampires?" Brendel quickly demanded. "How many are there!"

"They have an army of sixty thousand. Forty thousand commanded by Queen Victoria in Amsterdam, and the first queen, Katherine, commands twenty thousand in a place called Dalton in the District of New England."

Another mistake Malin had made. She had led him to believe there were far few vampires in this world. Now with the vampires in the fight, he must destroy the humans and as fast as possible.

"We will bring more Valaris Wizards from the dark realm to handle the vampires. The Demon Slayer must die! Leave me now! I want to be alone!"

☆☆☆☆☆☆

Shawn had retrieved Rachael at the Citadel and brought her and Gwyn to the house at Washington. Victoria and Peter had stayed at The Citadel. Still, they sent Braden with Katherine to be with Julien at the garrison in Dalton. Victoria wanted to remain in Europe for now. Shawn knew she didn't want to succeed Europe to Brendel and would stay as long as possible.

Shawn now walked the lowest streets of Seattle. It was a dark night, no moon, and there was little light filtering down through the haze from the towers above. Most cities in the Americas were under light restrictions at night. He listened to his steps echo off the walls of the buildings. Fog had rolled in from the bay and now carpeted the lower areas of the walkway.

He had not fed in a month, and it was making him tired, irritable, and now he had no choice but to find blood. Finally, the first time came when he had to leave Rachael for blood. She had wanted to go with him to observe, but he told her not yet. Humans thought the sight of vampires taking blood was a gruesome act. Rachael was with Gwyn at the Washington house, and Gwyn had The Mother's Staff. There still was no fighting in this part of the world, but Shawn felt a melancholy tonight. Maybe it was a lack of blood. Would it always be this way one fight after another?

He floated six stories up and settled on the roof of the building. He looked skyward and watched the waves of aircraft passing overhead, preparing for the attack from Brendel that certainly would come. Also, in the distance, he saw the endless fire trails that were the spaceships, arcing into the night sky. Day and night, the human transports were leaving the Seattle Spaceport. He squatted and searched the night for that familiar sense of evil. These days it was not hard to find. Darkness was on the rise again in this world and trying to consume it, while the decent folk were leaving the planet.

He wished Gwyn was more accepting of Rachael, but she was coming around thanks to Katherine. Changing Rachael was what he wanted; it would avoid the stigma of vampire and human being together. Falling in love with Rachael had been easy for him. She was an exceptional human, a human that was worthy of being a vampire. Still, for now, Rachael would be a vampire's conduit to the mortals. He knew in her way, Victoria admired Rachael and found her talents valuable for her plans.

Looking toward the bay, Shawn sensed what he had come to Seattle for, evil was to the west, and his vampire's ears heard the screams of the woman that these two men tormented. He floated up into the night air and proceeded west until he saw the men chasing the woman. They were on the deserted walkway next to the bay. The men were playing with the woman, taunting her as they closed in on her. Then she would stumble and fall, and they would pull her up, push her, and urge her to run on.

Shawn swooped in faster than a human eye could see and took the first man by the collar, flew straight up with the man kicking and screaming. Reaching the zenith, he sunk his blood teeth into the man's neck, rolled him over, and looked at the beautiful night as he feasted, felt the warm blood fill, and soothe his blood sac. He drained the blood from him, dropped the man and watched him fall back to earth, saw the splash he made when he hit the water. Again, he flew earthward, arced, and took the second man by his hair, flying him out over the water. This time, he took little blood, then broke the man's neck and released him into the bay.

He felt the rush of the blood in his veins, the burst of energy that made him shoot up toward the stars. Higher and higher he rose until the air thinned, and he reached the boundary that no vampire could cross, where his kind must turn back to their earthly home or feel their life force leave them. Down he fell, tumbling and turning, stopping a foot above the dark water of the bay, scooping the water with his hands, and washing the blood from his lips and chin.

Remembering the woman, he flew back toward shore, skimming the water. When he got back, the woman had made her escape, and only the sounds of the water lapping at the beach and the hum of the cargo transports coming ashore to moor could be heard.

"Well, how do you like that," Shawn chuckled. "You're welcome."

Suddenly, the mist moved until it formed a funnel, and points of light appeared, growing in number and swirling with the fog. Shawn knew an angel was coming to see him, but which one. Usually, it was Herit, but as the light formed, he sensed it was Anne. A smile came to his face; it had been awhile sensed she had come to visit. The spirit formed, and he saw a smile on her translucent face. Anne had gathered her power in Heaven, and the light coming from her was intense.

"How are you, Shawn?"

"As well as can be expected in these troubled times. I wish you would come to see me more often."

"I have limited access to this world, and you can come to Heaven."

"How's Marilyn?"

"Marilyn is an angel, so she is fine."

"What has brought you here?"

"You must listen to Victoria about humans and be careful in your dealings with them. You never see them for what they truly are. The leaders have already agreed to use vampires so they can escape this world. They will sacrifice you if they have too. Humans do not trust vampires. They see you as a danger they must ally with. Humans only know themselves."

"And we use them while vampires gathered their strength. Rachael will not betray me that I know. I have seen her soul."

"She loves you and will not betray you, but the others might. Especially if they think it will save them. There is something else. The Archangel has sent Drake to Victoria. To tell her to prepare for the loss of this world by the humans."

"Has he seen the end?"

"He has not said, but the dark realm vastly outnumbers humans."

"They will rally! Michael will see this, and Eos will never allow this world to fall."

"I hope so, Shawn. Farewell, my love."

Slowly Anne's form faded and disappeared into the darkness of the night. The last Shawn heard was to be careful with the humans, and then she was gone, and he was left looking out over the bay. His memories came rushing back of the times he had spent with Anne, the love he had for her, how he felt he could never go on without her. Even now, well over three centuries, when he thought of her loss, it was still painful for him.

Lifting into the air, he rolled and pointed his right hand to the east, accelerated, and skimmed above the pine forest that led to his home in Washington. Arriving home, he saw Gwyn swimming in the lake, her powerful strokes cutting through the water and mist that clung to the surface. The sun was rising, and a new day was spreading over the forest. He landed by the lawn chairs, stripped his clothes, and dove into the refreshing water. He swam out to Gwyn, and she came to him, wrapping her legs and arms around him. He felt her embrace, the taste of her wet lips, and then guiding him between her legs and making love to him.

"I miss you when you are gone," Gwyn whispered in his ear. "I know you will always look for love, and I will become one more changeling of yours that you love. The Mother wants me to stay with you. She wants the staff to be near you."

"I know, but we must obey our queen. Victoria gets her guidance from the Archangel. He is the one that created vampires. I always will love you, Gwyn, as I do with Katherine, and like I did with Anne and Marilyn. You always will be a part of me, but as vampires, we travel through the ages and find other love. We have too, or we will lose ourselves in time, and we will perish!"

"Katherine tells me that all the time."

"Listen to her," Shawn whispered.

"The Mother wants to meet with me, Gwyn added. "I will be leaving for the shrine."

"The Mother wants to see you again so soon."

"It is unusual. I think it has something to do with the wolves? You will be alone with Rachael. Do not make her a vampire."

"I know! Victoria won't allow it."

"Speaking of the human, here she comes. Katherine thinks highly of her. Isn't that funny! You both do!"

Rachael walked to the shore, stood barefoot, wearing her nightclothes. He quickly saw her form illuminated by the rising sun through her thin nightshirt.

"I must prepare for my trip," Gwyn said, as she swam past him toward the shore. Out of the lake, she strolled, and Shawn watched her walk by Rachael turn, give her a quick smile, and wish her a good morning. *Well*, he thought, *at least that is something.*

Shawn cruised just below the surface of the water, his eyes breaking the surface, and he watched Rachael. She held her hand to her forehead to block the glare, but with her human eyes, she had lost sight of him. Closer and closer he swam just below the surface, like a gator after a fowl. Springing from the water with blinding speed, he grabbed hold of Rachael, swung her back around, and flew over the lake, dropping her in. He then allowed himself to fall next to her. Rising back up, he broke the water surface and heard the shock voice of Rachael. "For the love of God, vampire, this is cold water." Rachael dove under the water removed her nightshirt and surfaced with a look of displeasure, she threw the shirt at him then swam to him and embraced him. He saw her look of wonder a look that often came these days.

"Your eyes draw me in. They make my head swim, especially when you desire me. Sometimes, when I look deep in them, I see a burning white light. You are a strange creature. Caring for most and a killer for some!"

"I am what my maker made me. And of course, what the Archangel wants."

Shawn felt Rachael's touch on his face and heard her say, "You have no warmth. You feel as cool as this water."

Shawn laughed and twirled Rachael through the water and said, "That is because I am the temperature of this water. My metabolism is extremely low. So low my body rejuvenates before it can age—a fact that you must know by now."

"I was watching Gwyn in the water, such a noble creature, but it also made me remember a passage I came across in my studies of vampires. It mentioned the love vampires have for water, but then it said The Mother's Water. Would you explain this?"

"The Mother actually is a lesser god, an ancient angel, who is responsible for this world. Her energy surrounds us. When vampires are in the ground or water, her energy rejuvenates us, heals us; that is why we are buried when our wounds are severe. Even now, I can feel it traveling through me. Michael made us, but vampires couldn't continue to exist without The Mother."

Rachael responded, not expecting an answer, "Why do the angels hide these feelings from us?"

Shawn gave Rachael a sorrowful look and whispered in her ear, "Because you are human and so susceptible to evil."

Rachael pushed Shawn away, glared at him, and he clapped his hands, held them above his head, and chanted a mother's spell. He brought his hands down and drew a circle in the water in front of Rachael. He ended facing Rachael and again clapped his hands and chanted, "Mother of light, Mother of the earth and water, come forth to show this human your truth. Allow her to feel your power! Show this mortal who you are and what Heaven is!"

Points of light appeared below the surface, and soon thousands of them swirled and churned, causing the water to turn into a foaming white ball of light. A woman came from the fire, rose through the water, facing Rachael. The woman's skin was made of water, and it sparkled with white light. The face was of a beautiful woman, and it smiled at Rachael. A hand came from the water holding a small orb of white light, which left The Mother and entered Rachael's forehead. Rachael's eyes brightened, her head snapped back. She stared at the translucent figure of The Mother and moaned. The Mother was showing herself to Rachael and giving her a vision. Slowly the light dissipated, and the figure of the woman sank back into the water and disappeared.

The dazed Rachael rolled onto her side and started to sink below the surface of the water. Shawn went to her, held her, saw her blue lips quivering, and her eyes staring off into space. Knowing she was human, he saw her shock that all this had brought to her. Shawn lifted Rachael and flew her to the house through her bedroom window. He laid her on the bed and wrapped her in the bedding. He sat next to her and brushed the wet hair from her face. Slowly, she came around, and tears streaked down her cheeks. Shawn wiped them, held her close, and kissed her lips. "You will be all right! Sometimes the angels show us what we don't want to see. The Mother showed you something. What was it?"

Rachael sat up and looked at him and whispered, "Briefly, I saw an image of Heaven, angels and felt such bliss. I knew it was real, but then I found myself standing in a ruined city, high towers destroyed, and fallen to the ground. I walked and found no humans. On and on, I walked and found no one, then I was flying, but I wasn't human. City after city, all destroyed or abandoned. No humans were left! Then I saw my family packing, leaving for space."

Shawn stroked her cheek and pulled her close. "This age we live in now will only be a moment in time for you. I know you can't understand that. Two hundred years from now, you will hardly remember this time. A time will come when you won't even remember what it is like to be mortal."

"So, you have decided to turn me."

"It is the angels that have decided. Humans don't fly. They have shown you the future, and me, what needs to be done. When is the question."

"Let me go home one more time. I want to see my family one more time! Before the fighting starts again! Before it is too late!"

"I will take you, but we must travel by stealth. Like my maker use to do with Marilyn and me."

Chapter Thirteen

G wyn had gone to The Mother's shrine and sat on her porch in Heaven. She looked at the small, rippling brook in front of her house. Looking past the stream out at the green meadow that traveled and met the sharp blue of the sky. At the horizon, an intense light radiated outward, almost too bright for her to look at. A testament to the massive energies this reality held.

The world she lived in was changing, coming apart; all she knew, held dear, would soon end. A fear persisted in her these days, a concern for Shawn. How could he possibly accomplish what the angels asked of him? How would he survive Brendel? And now the human woman had proved to be a weakness in his defenses. Gwyn didn't like being away from Shawn, but it was either the queen or The Mother that called her away. She loved him and wanted to keep The Mother's Staff near him. The staff was Shawn's chance to defeat Brendel.

Light gathered at the horizon, and Gwyn watched it travel across the green flowered meadow. The brilliants came to rest in her little front lawn, more substantial than she had ever seen here. Her fiery, wavy red hair fell to her shoulders, and freckles scattered on her milk-white skin. Now she looked like a woman of medium stature, beautiful, and she wore a full skirt and a white blouse that came down and past her shoulders and rested at the start of her arms, clothing of a time long past on earth. The woman, in a way, looked like Rachael; Eos was full of surprises. The angel walked up the steps and then sat on the railing. Gwyn could see the tenderness in her face, the concern for her.

Gwyn heard The Mother, *"Don't despair so! You must remember you are a Mother's Witch, and Shawn is a vampire. He is part of the Archangels Choir, and when they are in the physical plane as guardians, many like Shawn are tasked until eventually, evil kills them. Like his maker, Anne. That is their purpose, and it will be Shawn's fate. Michael brings them to his place in Heaven and bestows great honors on them. Someday, when your end comes on earth, you will come to me in my part of Heaven. You will not always be with Shawn; you need to understand that. I told you once that I was giving you a hard task to accomplish, and now you are finding out some of the reasons why. Rachael will be made a vampire, eventually, but it is not certain who will change her. That is not clear yet."*

"I love Shawn. I didn't think I would love him this much. I hoped I could handle vampire love better."

"I know, Gwyn. I am sorry. I have another message for you. The great witch Pandora who loves to roam the earth as a spirit had an unusual incident. The dark wolves contacted her. They have had little interaction with Lucifer for centuries. Because of the assault on earth, they wanted to contact the vampires. You and Shawn must go and see what they want. Also, the leader of the wolves wants to meet with Shawn. Take Rachael; the wolves have a message for the humans. Pandora has told the wolves to expect you."

"Like always, I will do as you say."

"Gwyn, I have given you the staff. In the end, the staff can save Shawn. That is the way to make the future more certain."

Darkness had descended hours before, and Shawn, Gwyn, and Rachael had stopped fifty miles south of Calgary in the Little River area. They had traveled from their home in Washington, rested at Great Falls, and then moved on to this area. They were by a wide trail in a clearing with dense forest all around them. The path was full and rough and led to the wolf's village. Sometimes they flew, but Rachael was human, and quickly got cold, so they would land and proceed on foot until she warmed, and then again, they would take to the air. Due to Rachael's limitations, it had taken them two days to arrive at the meeting area. They had built a fire and now sat around it, but tonight it was a warm summer's night unusually warm for this part of the world.

Shawn turned his senses outward, rode on the light, and came to a spot, ten miles away, where he could see the two dark wolves, but there were humans with them. *How unusual,* he thought. He traveled again on the light and came to the wolf's settlement. He saw wolves, but also, he saw many humans.

"What is it, Shawn?" He heard Rachael's far off voice say.

The voice brought him back to hear Gwyn's reply, "It's the wolves. They are near."

Shawn's gaze turned to them, and to his surprise, Gwyn was sitting next to Rachael, taking her hand and putting it to her cheek. "Do I feel like Shawn?"

Rachael gave her a quizzical smile, "Yes, no warmth, but you are softer."

"Am I?"

Shawn saw how Gwyn was treating Rachael. On this trip, she was kinder, more understanding, and now wanted to learn about her. Gwyn gave him the message from The Mother to contact the wolves. The Mother had also told Gwyn something, and that had changed her. He would try to see into her mind, but she knew and would toss him out. Gwyn was a young vampire, but a powerful mother's witch and The Mother had given her the ability to hide her thoughts from him. Even angels sometimes aren't what they seem.

"We will rest here and, in the morning, go on."

There is a group some ways off. We will meet, and hopefully, they will bring us to their village. Most unusual, though, there are humans with them!"

"Humans?" a surprised Gwyn said.

"Yes, humans."

A far-off look came over Gwyn as she searched the ether sensing the wolves. "I don't think they want conflict. But something is different about them."

"It should be safe. I haven't had contact for a long time with the dark wolves. You are right. Something happened to them for wolves to meet with our kind this way. And live with humans!"

"We can protect you, Rachael," Gwyn assured. "I have The Mother's Staff."

"If anything goes wrong, Gwyn, you are to fly Rachael out of here. Do not stay! Do not hesitate!"

"The Mother wants the staff near you," Gwyn said.

"You are my changeling. Do as I say!" Shawn saw Gwyn's conflict. She wore it on her face; in the end, she would follow The Mother, that he knew.

"Let's get some sleep," Shawn said. He took a bedroll from his sack and spread it on the ground. They all laid on the blanket, Rachael, in the middle, a human between two vampires. Shawn heard the rustle of the wind blowing through the trees and allowed his supernatural hearing to reach out and hear the noises of the forest. The shrill of the insects rising and falling. The far cry of the wolves. Then sleep spread over him. Shawn spirit left his body and hovered just above riding the rejuvenating light, the way all vampires slept.

Waking to the late morning, Shawn saw Gwyn's body half covering a sleeping Rachael. He shook his head at this sudden turn of events and gave both a shove to wake them. He went and rekindled the fire to make a vampire's morning tea and Rachael's breakfast—oatmeal. His sack was full these days with food and a jacket when he traveled with Rachael. The sun was midway in the sky, so they had slept for a while. It was a pleasant day with billowy white clouds making a speedy trip across the bright blue sky.

They drank their tea, and Rachael ate breakfast. Shawn placed Rachael on his back. They ran a few miles then walked for some ways. It was not long until they came upon two wolves and four humans standing across the path, an advanced greeting party. To his amazement, the humans were almost twice a mortal's size. One was a woman, and she was even more significant than the men. The men glanced at the woman for approval. The humans were nervous, and the wolves agitated as they paced back and forth. Shawn knew their presence made the wolves nervous. The shapeshifters always became unsettled when vampires were near; thousands of years of conflict between vampires and dark wolves assured that.

Rachael quickly went, stood behind him, and whispered, "My god, we heard of them but to see them! Amazing!"

"Stay near," Shawn mumbled softly.

Gwyn shouted to them, "Greetings to you. The Mother has sent us to meet with your leaders."

"We know why you are here," the woman quickly replied. "We are the Saskatch."

The men and women were bare-chested and had no shoes on their feet. The only article of clothing was their leather pants. Also noticeable was their feet; they were unusually large and thick for humans. The wolves stopped their pacing and stared at them with yellow eyes and gave a low guttural growl.

"Quiet!" one of the men yelled.

Shawn and Gwyn gave each other a puzzled look. There was something different about the shapeshifters. Shawn could not detect the evil intelligence that went along with a dark wolf.

"You have brought a human, good," the woman said. "We weren't sure if humans would be with vampires. Can you speak for your people?"

"I represent the governments of the human world."

"Stay with Rachael," Shawn told Gwyn as he stepped forward. "The woman is our contact with the mortals. She is under our protection."

"No one will harm her! Vampire! Follow us," the woman said as she spun around and started back down the path.

Shawn quickly noticed the Saskatch had a strange, awkward-looking walking gate, their large feet, and full stride made them walk at a much faster pace. A few miles later, they came to a path, cleverly hidden by brush made into a large gate that swung open. They traveled on this path up high hills and back down. The day turned dark, and their guides continued to walk the path. All night they went, at times, he would let Rachael ride his back for a rest. Mid-morning, they came to a top of a hill and spread out before them was a massive village that filled the valley below for miles. Off in the distance, sitting amongst the small domed huts, a large domed lodge, built from polished white pine that shone in the sunlight.

The woman pointed to the lodge. "That is where you will meet our king and queen. Most in the village know of your arrival. We have spoken of it for a few weeks in the lodges, and most are prepared for your arrival. But it would be better to keep moving and don't stop. Keep the woman between you. My kind won't hurt you, but I'm not sure about the Woolocks."

"Is it safe?" Gwyn asked harshly. "Whoever you are—wolf or human! I won't take kindly to trickery! I carry The Mother's Staff and will use it to strike down any who attack us!"

"It is safe. Let's go," the woman answered.

The trail they followed wound its way down to the valley, and they soon entered the settlement. There were large circular huts constructed of woven vine over a wooden frame, and some living areas were built into small earthen mounds that spread out over the valley. The wolves or Woolocks lived in the earthly living areas. Something had befallen the wolves, that became quickly obvious, most living in the village were large humans, barely dressed. Their women were slightly larger, bare-chested, and wore leather britches. The inhabitants of the town would stare with quizzical looks on their faces. The wolves would pace and snarl, and every so often, one of the humans would yell for them to settle down.

Shawn watched the little children scurry around the huts playing, oblivious to the strangers in their village. Their children were almost the size of a grown mortal. He probed their minds. In the Saskatch, he could still detect some supernatural force, but in the wolves, nothing. The new shapeshifter's skin was light brown, hair long blond or light brown, and their noses were longer than average but thin. Most noticeable about these shapeshifters, besides their size, were their eyes. They were bright yellow or light green and set wide apart on their faces. They still were the eyes of a wolf. Many of them would be considered good looking.

"Something has happened to our wolf friends. Hasn't it?" Rachael whispered.

"It appears that way," Shawn answered.

"What do you think it is?" Gwyn asked.

"I don't know, but I'm sure we will find out. Let's keep walking."

They followed their escorts and soon came to the lodge. It rose four stories into the hazy summer sky. They went through an arched entrance and scattered about a large common area were groups of humans gathering, discussing the governing of the city. Across from this area was a circular wall with arches that led into other rooms and, in the center, was a large arch to the throne room.

The woman led them into the room and announced with a booming voice, "Almighty queen, vampires, and a human have arrived!"

A short distance away, Shawn saw two polished grey granite thrones with a large man and woman sitting on them.

The man stood and announced, "Greetings to the vampires. I am King Ulrich, King of the City in the Woods." The huge man stepped down from his throne and walked toward them. Shawn sensed an intelligent man as he came near, but surprisingly his thoughts were hard to read. The king stopped and bent over, and a smile spread over his large prominent face as he stood back up.

"I sense you have questions, Demon Slayer. You must save them for our queen."

Shawn then noticed the queen and a boy and a girl walking their way. And again, the boom of the king's voice. "My wife Queen Silva, ruler of the City in the Woods, and my two children."

The large woman had gold designs painted on her arms, and she wore polished leather britches and a leather vest with leather frills swaying with her strides. She had an older, more weathered face than the king. Her eyes burnt a bright yellow, still the eyes of a wolf. The two children were as big as they were. When she passed the other Saskatch gave her a slight bow, she was the ruler of this place. And was becoming apparent women were the dominant sex in this society.

"A pleasure to meet you, Queen Silva, and your two children," Shawn said as Silva took hold of his hand and shook it vigorously, and then displeasure came to her face and glare to her eyes.

"A pleasure to meet you, Shawn Bryce. I am sure you do not recognize me!"

"I do not! Have we met?" Shawn asked as he took a step back.

"We met some centuries back when I was a wolf."

Shawn saw the displeasure leave her face, and a wave of anger come. Her eyes narrowed and became cold. "We did!" Shawn started to get nervous. If it was a few centuries back and it had to do with wolves, it probably wasn't good.

He looked into the queen's eyes. He tried to read her mind, but she closed it off to him. The queen had great control of the supernatural of this world. She continued to stare at him, waiting for a response, but Shawn couldn't think of one.

Finally, the queen spoke, "North of here. It was a cold winter that year. The year The Tempter brought the vampire to us. The year of the witch and the last year, we felt Lucifer's darkness. This so-called guardian was crazed, with tremendous strength and under the evil witch's spell. Unmercifully, he killed us by the hundreds. Many wolves fled west, and the ones that stayed hid from the vampire. I was in a group of wolves that this monster attacked. I saw the vampire's face, and I remember what he looked like. How could I ever forget! Only by pure luck did I escape with my life. He hit me and knocked me down a riverbank into a river. So maddened the vampire was he went onto the next closes wolf and forgot about me, allowing me to float down the freezing water and make my escape. The creature wore no clothes, only a bear's head and its skin for a cloak. The vampire had a mask of berry juice, and ice and snow caked his feet. That vampire was you, Shawn Bryce."

"Well!" Shawn stammered. "That was a long time ago. I mean, I know wolves live long lives, and I'm glad to see you have retained that." He could feel the stare of Rachael's eyes on him, knew her mouth was open in disbelieve.

"I was under Malin's spell! Malin and Lucifer are responsible for the killings. You know Lucifer always used your kind for vampire fodder."

"Enough, King Ulrich thundered. "That was a long time ago, and I am sure the vampire was under a spell. We have more important things to discuss."

Silva turned her cold look onto the king and commanded, "I will decide what is enough." She then turned her look on

Shawn. "That is in the past, and we will start a new beginning. The council awaits us."

"What has happened to you?" Shawn blurted out.

The queen took a few steps, turned back, and boomed out in laughter. "The devil abandoned us centuries ago as I said, and this is how we have changed. Lucifer tired of us and no longer needed us. The evil one cut us off from the dark energy of this universe. So, we sought out the light. We who looked like humans have maintained the wolf's speed and strength, but now we know of the light and know how to use it. The wolves you see are another matter. They still have some of their old minds but cannot speak. Shut off from communicating. Why the few wolves you see didn't change like us, we don't know. Beware though they still have their hatred for vampires. What you see now is known as the Woolocks."

Shawn then noticed with a broad smile the king winking at Rachael.

"Protect you pretty human female while you are here," the queen said as she gave the king a sharp look. "I am afraid our men can be crude. Some of our old ways are still with us."

"She is well-protected," Shawn assured.

"That I know, Demon Slayer!"

"Follow me," the queen said. "We have much to discuss with the council."

The children went off, and the king took his place behind the queen's right shoulder. Shawn, Gwyn, and Rachael walked behind them, following the curved wall to another room. Two rather fierce-looking guards swung the doors open. They entered, but the king did not, and he continued on his way. In the center of the room, five women sat at a long table; a large ornate chair meant for the queen was at the head. A woman followed them into the conference room and set a small electronic device on the table in front of where the queen would sit and then stood behind her chair. Queen Silva took her place at the head of the table, and they sat at the three chairs placed to her right. The queen nodded her acceptance at the five females that gave her their proper acknowledgments.

The queen then spoke in a loud and commanding voice. "These are the members of the council that rule The Saskatch. We had a male, but the people replaced him with a female. I hope this is all right for you, Demon Slayer. The queen sent a mischievous look Shawn's way, and he returned with a shrug and then said, "Fine by me."

"Good," the queen said as she reached and activated the electronic device.

The machine projected a map above the table and showed a highlighted area. Most of the marked land was once known as the Saskatchewan and Alberta Provinces.

The queen's voice rose, and she commanded, "Saskatch, claim this parcel of land for our own. This is the land of our ancestors and is ours."

Shawn gave Gwyn and Rachael a puzzled look. Then Gwyn leaned over and said, "This is a matter for Rachael...I believe."

Shawn said to the council and queen, "You should deal with the humans on this matter."

The queen laughed and mocked, "Lucifer is coming for the humans. Soon humans won't matter. It will be Brendel and vampires we must deal with. We desire and prefer to ally with vampires. We will even be willing to fight in your war. Fifty thousand Saskatch soldiers will be at your disposal. They will be mighty soldiers much stronger than those puny red soldiers that come through the portals, but we keep this land."

"I will deliver your terms to Queen Victoria. She certainly will be very interested in what has gone on here."

"Tell her we want to fight with her!" Silva replied as she glanced at an increasingly agitated Rachael.

Shawn heard the screech of Rachael chair legs as she bolted up, turned to the queen, and shouted. "It is the humans you will have to deal with on this matter! We will survive this calamity and prevail! This is our world, always has, and always will be! A day will come when we will retake control of this world!

That I promise you, Queen Silva! I will also make my government aware of this!"

"We will see! I don't think you know Lucifer, human. I will do your kind favor, though. Remember this, only vampires can defeat Brendel and his forces! And maybe with a little help from us."

"You will have to deal with humans for their territory," Shawn said. "If what you say is true and not a Lucifer's trick. I am sure Queen Victoria will welcome you as allies and speak on your behalf."

Shawn knew humans. They would not go quietly into Lucifer's abyss of darkness. They would fight, and if needed, go to their places in space, regroup, and come back for their world. Mortals always found away. For more than twelve centuries, Shawn had lived as a vampire, but still, he had a connection to the humans. Other vampires lost that connection, but he had not. Michael had given him that gift, knowledge to understand the humans no matter what age it was.

Chapter Fourteen

B rendel sat on his throne, looking out over the flat arid lands of Jerusalem. The sun was high in the sky, and the heat radiated from the desert sands. In this age, the deserts were blistering hot and would be unlivable if not for human technology. Throughout the centuries, more than any other on earth, this was an area known for war and strife. Even the angels had an aversion to this place. He had chosen to start his war here to gain his foothold in this world because humans thought little of this part of the world and would not fight hard to defend it. A smile came to his face, with all their science, they understood little about religion.

His father, Lucifer, was becoming impatient with him at the speed this world was succumbing to his evil. Once the vampires became active, it had slowed his advance. The Kargarians had performed poorly against the vampires, so he had gone to the Tarragon's home world and before the cast of creatures known as the Valaris wizards. He had asked for more wizards, and they had reluctantly agreed. Not all of his father's allies were happy with this war.

New and curious development had happened. A Valaris wizard had sent a message that he had seen the two queen's changelings patrolling with other vampires. The wizard said this was becoming common to see the two north of the vampire outpost in the Americas.

Brendel sat on his throne through the day and night, thinking how to use this surprising development to his advantage.

Suddenly, it came to him; he would capture them — not kill them — use them, even though it would give him great pleasure to kill the queen's changelings. He would build a prison of dark energy to hold them. Then he would make terms with the Queens, barter for their changelings' lives and demand they turn themselves and The Demon Slayer over to him. He would need a lot of energy to keep the vampires out of this prison. He would use the Valaris wizards to create the dome.

✯✯✯✯

Shawn was leading Gwyn and Rachael down the Susquehanna, now a pristine river, much cleaner than when he was human. They had left the land of the Saskatch two days earlier, traveled southeast until they came to Lake Glimmerglass, and then southwest to Dalton and Katherine. They followed the river bank and were coming close to Dalton and the vampire garrison. The bridge columns that were used by the ancient cars in a time of roads and tires lay crumbled, almost submerged now by the river water. Now it was a home for the nesting river birds, and soon that would disappear. He strained his memory to remember the bridge that once crossed this river into Dalton.

Gwyn and Rachael had been talkative, were finally getting to know each other, and now were becoming friends. He would eavesdrop on Rachael asking Gwyn about mother's witches and listened to Gwyn tell her about her kind, the differences between them and vampires. Mother's witches came from a different choir of angels than vampires. They are more like mortals than vampires and receive their power through supernatural spells and incantations drawn from Eos vast power that penetrates and surrounds the planet. This energy comes from the positive energies used to build all you see, feel, or hear in the universe. Lucifer's witches use dark energy, the energy that fills the voids were nothing exist only emptiness and darkness. Mother's witches use their spells to extend their lifespans on earth. Unlike vampires that angels changed at the cellular level by supernatural powers stored in high concentration in human blood. This is what brings out great strength, psychic abilities, and their immortality. He heard Gwyn chuckle and say for all the good it does them, and then Gwyn told Rachael never has a vampire lived forever it would be impossible for them to bear.

He listened to her talk of the great witch Pandora The Mother had sent to Shawn to begin his learning of witches. Gwyn told Rachael how Shawn and Pandora made love in the bottom of a swamp boat. This brought abought the birth of the white witch Jessamine that was more mother than a witch. Some believe it was The Mother herself that had taken over Pandora's body in the bottom of the boat.

Shawn listened until the melancholy of his long life started to creep into his thoughts. He remembered all he had loved, and all he had lost to Lucifer's evil. Now he realized his life on earth would always be this way, on and on. These days he took comfort in long ago knowledge passed on to him by Anne, his maker. Heaven was different; a spirit can find times of relieve from all the evil, take moments of rest, unlike his reality here on earth.

They had just started up the trail that led to the vampire garrison at Dalton and quickly came to the area where the old town once stood. In this age, all that was left were remnants of ancient roads and crumbing foundations barely jutting from the ground. Dalton was a town long gone and forgotten by humanity. A vampire garrison of twenty thousand now occupied the area. And the first queen Katherine's home, built atop a fifty-foot tower, was just down the river.

They quickly entered the garrison and saw vampires training with their slayers trying to best their opponent to impress the first queen that stood nearby. He saw vampires practicing with their new blasters, pulsing small balls of high velocity condensed matter that tore their wooden targets to pieces. These were small, lightweight assault rifles that made their bullets from the atoms of the air and had much more firing capabilities than the gunpowder weapons of the past. The vampires could easily strap the blasters to their backs along with their slayers. Everywhere, vampires were preparing for battle.

Shawn worked through the handshakes and slaps on the back by the training vampires on his way to Katherine. She was talking with some of her commanders. They made their greetings, and then Katherine's smile left her face, and she turned to Rachael.

"I see you brought the human. How have you been, Rachael?"

"I have been well, Queen Katherine."

"I am no longer queen, and now the humans will know where our garrison is," Katherine said as she turned to Shawn.

"The humans have known the whereabouts of the garrison for some time," Shawn said sternly. "If they didn't, I wouldn't have brought her."

Katherine softened and returned her gaze to Rachael. "Come on; we will go to the house. You can stay there."

"How do you feel about sleeping with a bunch of vampires, Rachael?" Katherine chuckled.

"I have slept close to a couple for a few nights already."

Katherine laughed and replied, "Well, I think we can give you a private room. You have nothing to fear while you are in my home, human!"

Shawn took Rachael, put her on his back, and flew to the open terrace of the house. They talked until dawn. Katherine told him that Brendel had stopped his attacks. She thought they were regrouping, preparing for their final assault. Katherine informed Shawn that they had detected brief portal openings north of the garrison. She believed it was Brendel's wizards, looking for a weakness in their defenses. Shawn learned to his surprise that Julien and Braden had been going north with scouting parties.

"I am surprised you let them go. Does Victoria know of this?"

"I have had discussions with Victoria about our changelings. They are over a hundred years old now and want to go out on their own."

"I see," Shawn quickly replied. "But is this the time?"

"I have tried to talk to them," Katherine responded, and Shawn could see that she was becoming emotional. "They have minds of their own. Swordsmiths have trained them well in the use of a slayer, and they are exceptional at swordplay. They both know evil, living with Victoria and me, and I have sent my best soldiers with them. They want to give to the cause. Shawn, I don't know what else to do."

"Well, when I was that age, I did almost get myself killed a couple of times."

"I don't think that is what she wanted to hear," Gwyn said as she went and put her arms around Katherine. "These are hard times, that is for sure! But you have to let go too!"

Shawn had slept through the day and into the early night. Quietly, he rose from the couch, not to disturb Katherine and Gwyn. He had bunked with his changelings, and Rachael had gone to her private room. A strong cup of tea was on his mind, so he made his way to the kitchen and steeped a big pot. He took his warm, soothing tea and went out onto the terrace. Hot tea on awakening was soothing and warmed a cold vampire's blood sac. The night was clear with a slight chill, and the bright full moon hung low. He watched the vampires come to the river for their nightly swim to draw strength through the water. Many vampires carried slayers, and a few had blasters.

Using his vampire's eyes, he looked west into the sky. He saw the fireballs arcing into the darkness leaving the boundaries of earth and then disappearing into the blackness of space. Humans were continuing their exodus from the planet, and that made him feel uneasy. Suddenly, he turned his attention north; something wasn't right. Dark energy was gathering to the north, and he felt evil wizards. He heard the swoosh of the glass door to the terrace open, and Katherine and Gwyn came through.

"Tea in the kitchen," he said sleepily.

I don't want tea!" Katherine shouted. "I can't feel Julien! Something is wrong; we need to go!"

Hurrying back to his room, Shawn quickly pulled his pants and shirt on, grabbed Adeen, and went back to the terrace. Shawn was not surprised at this turn of events; he had felt the dark energy. The vampires took to the air and followed Katherine north at a considerable speed. They flew over the Mohawk River continued north into The Adirondack Wilderness, where they landed and continued on foot, traveling by ground, cloaking themselves to the evil ahead. Sometimes they would run at speeds faster than the human eye could see, or times they slowed due to the field grass and water-soaked ground.

He had left Rachael behind but was sure she would be fine as long as she stayed in Dalton and did not go off on her own. He never knew what Rachael would do when he wasn't with her; most likely, she did the human's work. They continued until they came twenty miles from where the St. Lawrence River met the Ontario Sea. Long ago, the five great lakes had formed the Ontario Sea. A vague sense of dark energy is what they followed. They reached a clearing where the long tracks of farmland started their trip following the St. Lawrence River to the Atlantic Ocean.

They proceeded with stealth until they saw a blue dome off in the distance, no more than a hundred feet high, oscillating, and humming. The dome radiated tremendous energy.

"What do you think is going on here?" Shawn whispered.

"Brendel's tricks," Gwyn said.

"I can feel our recon party inside," Katherine whispered back. "I can feel Julien and Braden. We must hurry, they need our help!"

Shawn looked to the east and said, "Well, Victoria is on her way."

They proceeded on and worked their way close to the dome. This dome was different; it was much denser than any he had seen before. The hum of the energy penetrated his head, causing a disturbance in his mind. He had been a witch only a short time, but he could feel the tight supernatural spell surrounding this place.

"Let's move back away and think about this," he said. "The energy is too much here."

"It certainly is," Gwyn replied quickly.

They moved back, and Victoria came in for a not so graceful landing. Shawn knew Victoria would be upset and do anything to save her changeling. She was like Katherine when it came to their changelings.

"What has happened?" Victoria demanded.

They are inside the dome, as you can tell, and they are alive," Katherine sharply answered back. "I am as upset as you are—so let's try to stay calm!"

"The force field is different. There is a powerful spell attached to it," Gwyn informed Victoria. "I will use The Mother's Staff to see if I can penetrate it."

"Do it!" Victoria quickly commanded.

Gwyn stepped forward and lowered the staff unleashing a beam of white energy at the dome. The beam tore into the vault giving off a loud sizzling noise and a terrible stench. Shawn wrinkled his nose, raised Adeen, and prepared for the attack. The energy beam finally broke through the thick energy field of the dome, but as soon as Gwyn stopped, the hole filled back in. Looks of panic spread over Katherine and Victoria's faces.

"We need to stay calm! We will find a way! Can you still feel them," Shawn said as he turned to look at Victoria and Katherine?

Both shook their head, yes, then Katherine spoke, "Yes, I feel them, and they are alive, but they aren't moving."

Shawn pulled the communicator that Rachael had given him from his pocket. "Maybe human technology can open the dome. They've had a lot of practice at it so far. Within minutes Rachael's hologram face floated in front of him. He quickly explained the situation to her.

"I will contact Head Chair Fitzgerald," Rachael said. "I have been told that we have new technologies to penetrate the domes. Probably one of the reasons why they stopped using them."

"That will be appreciated. We are located south of the St. Lawrence River…"

"I know where you are," Rachael quickly replied. "You called me, and now I have your location. I know exactly where you are."

"We are going to need an answer soon."

"Understood!"

"I hope she understands," Victoria muttered.

"We will get them out," Katherine said, trying to be reassuring mostly for herself. "Let's follow the outside edge. Maybe we can find a weakness."

They followed the dome's edge and had gone some ways when a portal started to form. The entrance was small, and it quickly came together, then a figure stepped through, it was Samil. Gwyn lowered her staff, but the bald witch swirled her staff and formed a dark energy field around her.

"Easy filthy vampires! I am here to talk," Samil hissed.

Shawn whispered to Gwyn, "Wait, don't shoot."

Then he shouted to Samil, "What does the bald witch want today. Someday, I will take your bald head Samil. You know that!"

"I don't think so, Demon Slayer. Brendel protects me. Malin sends her regards. She waits for you in the underworld. She desires to see you again! To settle the score!"

Shawn drew Adeen and walked toward Samil. "Step away from the portal! Show some courage, you evil bitch."

Samil back closer to the portal and said, "Brendel sends the queens a message. He will release your vampires, but vampires are to abandon the humans and go to a designated area in South America. That will be the only place vampires can live. And there is one more condition. The queens and The Demon Slayer are to surrender to Brendel so they can pay for what they have done to Lucifer."

Shawn stood staring at Samil, not quite believing what he heard. *The arrogance of these creatures,* he thought. Then a roar through the night sky as four large aircraft sliced through the clouds above, rapidly descending, then arcing around the dome, traveling outward, turning, and coming back, human bombers making their run. The vampires heard eight loud swooshes, and eight high temp photon missiles flew hot, straight, and true to the blue dome. Samil quickly went back through the portal.

Shawn yelled excitedly, "We need to leave and quick!"

The vampires flew back as far as possible, then huddled, chanting and pulling the protective blanket of the Mother's energy around them. A thunderous sound traveled outward, and a dense swirling yellow fire and intense light engulfed the dome rose up and into the night, making the darkness as bright as a summer's day for miles. Then the light condensed in all directions, and the blue dome wavered and collapsed into itself. The fields and forest caught fire, sending bright yellow flames and thick smoke high into the air. The bombers moved off, and then another high pitch wine as human troop transports came into view. They circled the burning field, found a cool spot, and landed. Their ramps fell, and hundreds of human soldiers swarmed out and quickly moved toward the area where the dome once stood.

"Let's go," Victoria commanded as she drew a glowing Deceida. "They are lying in the middle. Are you with me vampires?"

"We are!" they all said as they took their slayers from their backs.

Victoria and Katherine immediately flew forward toward Julien and Braden with Shawn and Gwyn following behind. Also moving quickly across the field were a couple of thousand human special force troopers. The vampires moved to the area where Julien, Braden, and four other vampires were lying unconscious. The captives laid huddled and curled in on themselves, faces distorted with horror only they could see. Now with the destruction of the dome, the spell was lifting, and they were beginning to awaken. Another loud roar and a blue fire started to swirl, larger and larger into a circle until thousands of Kargarians swarmed from the opening firing their blasters. Streaks of blue light filled the night, and the vampires crouched in the tall grass to avoid the fire.

The human soldiers in numbers moved quickly across the field to put themselves between the Kargarians and vampires. An onslaught of human fire met the Kargarian fire as they took defensive positions to hold the assaulting Kargarian horde at bay. Blistering streaks of light seared the eyes all around, and humans and Kargarian soldiers fell to the ground. The boundary between the soldiers became a killing zone. The vampires quickly hid in the field grass, and Gwyn fired her staff at Kargarians, trying to make their way to the prisoners. Again, she fired, and the red soldiers thought better and turned back, continuing their attack on the humans. Shawn chanted a spell to help them wake up, and slowly the captives came too as the fight raged around them.

Two soldiers made their way to them and yelled over the loudness of the battle. "We can't hold them much longer. We are going to have to leave soon. Get your people out of here." And just as quickly, the soldiers turned and started to crawl back.

"Victoria yelled after them, "We are leaving too! Thank you for your help!"

Victoria and Katherine shook their changelings, slapping their faces and pulling them to their feet. Victoria turned to the other captive vampires and yelled, "Get out of here now!"

Gwyn chanted another spell and slammed the butt of the staff down. A shock wave of tremendous power traveled outward toward the swarming Kargarians killing them by the hundreds. The vampires using the shock wave for cover quickly lifted into the air to start their trip to Dalton and safety. Shawn could see the human soldiers making their escape, desperately trying to make it back to their transports. He had never seen such intense blaster fire.

Shawn turned to Gwyn and yelled, "Give the humans some help!"

Gwyn nodded and brought her staff to bear on the Kargarians and fired. The blast slowed the Kargarian advance enough to allow the humans to make it to the transports. The battle transports quickly lifted off only to have some struck by laser fire. The crafts would wobble and then fill with fire and smoke, falling back to the ground, exploding into a ball of fire. Still, with the help of The Mother's Staff, many of the human aircraft escaped.

Shawn knew Victoria would think different about humans, now. They had helped saved both queen's changelings. Saving Braden and Julien would undoubtedly buy the humans more time with vampires, and knowing Rachael, that was what she was hoping for. He felt Victoria's stare turned to look at her, and she nodded.

Chapter Fifteen

B rendel had just arrived on the American continent and stood south of the Chesapeake Bay on an abandoned military base. His plan to hold the queen's changeling hostage had failed. The humans had proven to be very effective with the physical sciences. Lucifer had finally given his permission to use the Tarragons in the fight, so he had brought their witches and wizards to this land. Soon they would start to bring the Tarragon Army through. Then he would commit his entire army against the humans. The domes were no longer effective in the attack, as the humans had learned how to penetrate them. He would assemble the Tarragon army along the East Coast and sweep across the heartland of the Americas. The Kargarians would attack from the south. Defeating the Army of The Americas would bring total collapse to the human resistance and deliver this world to Lucifer.

His father was unhappy that Shawn was still alive and at his pace in securing this world. Lucifer wanted The Demon Slayer soul, and Brendel was to send Samil to end the vampire's life. Samil had fallen out of favor with the devil, and this would be her award. Lucifer felt she had shrunk away from The Demon Slayer when the opportunity had present itself to kill the vampire. Witch's lives met little to Lucifer, and Malin certainly could testify to that. All life meant nothing to the dark angel only to use for his evil. The final battle would certainly go their way if Shawn was dead. Brendel needed Shawn killed. The Demon Slayer was a powerful creature, a foe he would prefer somebody else take care of so he wouldn't have to suffer the pain of killing him. He had agreed with his father and would send Samil and the Valaris wizards against the vampire.

★★★★★★

Shawn had gone back to Dalton and collected Rachael. She was glad to see him and relieved that they saved the queen's changelings. Queen Victoria and Katherine had graciously thanked Rachael and ask her to make sure she told her government the Herit Covenant was grateful. Now he and Rachael traveled north on a grand walkway known as the Northway. The ancient interstates used for wheeled vehicles provided a worn path for these ways. They were meticulously taken care of and offered wide smooth routes for hiking or recreational hover crafts. In this age, one of the human's favorite pastime was getting close to nature.

He wanted to travel by foot to see this land before Brendel's evil had a chance to change it, so he decided to take Rachael home this way. His maker long ago had instilled the need to slow his pace, to match his meandering lifespan, and travel the countryside by foot.

Victoria left for The Citadel to collect twenty thousand vampires and bring them to Dalton. Twenty Thousand vampires under Peter's command would protect The Citadel.

On this continent, Brendel was gathering a large army on the coast, out in the open, no longer confined to domes. Shawn knew the Americas would win Brendel this world. As he and Rachael traveled north, they saw hundreds upon hundreds of military vehicles hovering above the way following this route south to regroup and form an army to meet Brendel's hoards.

Shawn and Rachael traveled north and met many escaping humans on their way to the spaceport south of Montreal. They already had come under attack by Brendel's evil soldiers. These were mortals, refugees who had lost everything and wanted nothing but to escape the horror that had come to this world. Now they were leaving for what they thought would be the safety of space. Traveling with hover carts and what little possessions they had left.

They had come to a clearing and stopped for the night. Across the field, he saw the flickering fusion stoves of the many humans that had stopped for a rest. A smile spread over his face as the aroma of food traveled across the field to his sensitive nose. He never tired of smelling the many varieties of cooking food. He watched the symbols and maps appear around Rachael's head. These images would dance in front of her eyes, disappear, and new ones reappear. They came from nanochips placed in her head. Rachael was always in contact with her superiors through her chips.

"Giving your kind the latest on my travels," Shawn said with a wink.

"You know I am," Rachael replied with a smile. "And the number of humans traveling this trail. I'm afraid a lot of people are giving up on the fight."

"There is more arriving all the time," Shawn said.

"There is a lot of humans coming to this field."

Rachael then slid next to him and joked that she would warm him for a taste of his blood.

"Funny," he whispered. "Are you sure you aren't a vampire already?"

"Shawn allowed his sense to travel the human energies that surrounded this field, to travel across, and go amongst the mortals. To hear and feel the forces that they were so unaware of. They knew he was here, a vampire sharing the field with them. That was why they were on one side of the field, and he and Rachael were on the other. He also felt Rachael, and she raised her head from his chest and smiled. "I'm OK."

"You are stressed. Take a little of my blood. It will strengthen you for what is coming."

Shawn bit his wrist and offered his blood to her. Rachael took a mouthful, swallowed, and then took another. Shawn wiped the excess from her lips, lightly kissed them, and briefly saw her eyes the blue of the Herit Covenant but then fade away. Rachael's head went back, and she let out a soft moan, and then a smile spread over her face.

"I feel better. Your world calls to me now when I take your blood," Rachael whispered. "Sometimes, I am afraid of what is to happen!"

"Do not be afraid! A great life awaits you! If we survive!" Shawn laughed.

"You have seen the world change before! You have seen great calamity. What is it like to live through such great trials."

"Mostly, it brings hardship and uncertainty for the future. Humans will have to adapt. They did it once before, and they will have to do it again. Most important is to protect their technology. A day will come when humans will need it again."

Shawn returned his gaze across the field. It was a cloudy night and then a rumble of thunder and the beginnings of light rain.

Will they make it this time, he wondered? He stretched his memory and remembered The Great War and the dark age that came after, how the humans struggled to regain their science and life of comfortable living. Now they will lose it again. His thoughts sent a chill up his spine and blood tear to his eye.

The mortals kept coming in small groups of twos, threes, and fours, and again, he realized many humans were coming to the field.

"Rachael, don't you think there is a lot of people showing up?"

"Yes, there is. A little unusual, maybe. I don't think there is any danger. Keep an eye on them if you want." Rachael yawned.

Shawn saw Rachael was becoming sleepy. Not paying attention to him, so he held her, took a blanket from his sack, wrapped it around them, brushed the strands of wet hair from her face, brushed her lips with his to feel her warmth, and watched the mortals across the field. Humans preferred believing in their reality, and having no concept of other realities, the reason they were easy prey for the demons.

Shawn could smell the human's blood from here. The various scents, some blood sweeter than others, his life force, his nourishment, and the price humans must pay for Heaven's guardians. He sensed no evil among them, only fear of the unknown. The confusion of losing everything so quickly and the knowledge he was here.

Shawn's head nodded forward and then back up. Sleep was coming to him, too, and then he sensed the humans coming his way. Looking up, he saw the group of mortals walking hesitantly across the field.

He shook Rachael and blurted in her ear, "People are coming! Wake up, Rachael!"

"All right, give me a second," Rachael yawned.

"You are going to have to talk to them!" Shawn insisted. "See what they want!"

They both got to their feet and met the group. Shawn could see the apprehension on their faces. Rachael walked to them while he hung back. An explosion of various colored symbols formed around their heads as they made their greetings. Information on who they were and where they came from was quickly dispensed, and then they broke into the world language that humans spoke now. He sensed no malice from them, only fear. He looked at Adeen, and it lay quiet. The sword gave no sign, only cold steel now hiding its energy as Heaven did with mortals.

"You travel with a vampire?" one of the men said. "A little unusual, don't you think?"

"How did you know he is a vampire?" Rachael spoke sternly.

"Not hard to miss when you know about them. How they make you feel when they are near. And now looking at him, it is obvious. He is not trying to hide."

Four men and two women stood staring at him, waiting for his reply, not knowing what he would do. These people were not rich, only desperate. The fact that they would try and speak with him showed their anguish. They came from a city and had no transportation of their own. All their lives, they had only used city transportation. The mortals were heading north because they were human, part of this world, and were owed a seat on a spaceship to escape this nightmare. All they had to do was make the trip and survive.

"Greetings," he said in a robust, friendly way. He already saw into their minds and knew what they wanted. "What can I do for you?"

"You are traveling north. We were wondering if we could travel with you."

"Just you?" Shawn questioned.

"No, I mean all of us. All of us in this field. Are you a warrior guardian? I see your sword. There have been sightings north of the creatures attacking us."

"What have you heard, friend?" Rachael asked.

"Strange creatures are attacking north of here killing us. They don't want us to reach the spaceports. The military has helped, but they have to move south to fight this enemy. To buy us time."

"How many need protection?" Shawn asked.

"I don't know," the man said. "When we discovered who you were, we sent the message out, and as you can see, more are arriving all the time. We are desperate to leave this world. Our military can't protect us from these creatures."

"I will do what I can," Shawn assured. "But if humans don't stay and fight, you will lose this world."

"Fight what? Fight the devil! We have seen the power of these beings, and we want nothing to do with it. We heard if we leave this planet, the devil will leave us alone."

"Darkness will never leave mortals alone, and Lucifer is a master deceiver. But I will help you."

The humans started to go back across the field, but one woman turned and said, "Do you travel in the light? Or do you need the night."

"I also have the power of The Mother so that I can travel in the light. It will be safer for your kind."

The woman then asked, "Are you a strong vampire?"

"Strong enough," Shawn answered to the woman with fear etched across her face. He quickly sensed that she, too, was a mother and desperate to save her children.

Shawn and Rachael slept the rest of the night, and by morning more than a hundred people had arrived. He looked across the field and chuckled at the many-colored small rounded, camping domes spread out over the clearing. These were one-person domes protecting them from the elements. They gave a comfortable shelter, a soft surface to sleep on, and electronics woven through the fabric to keep a constant, comfortable temperature. When not in use, they would collapse to a small cube and easily fit into their travel gear. For the few that had domestic robots, he saw them standing next to the carts powered down with their heads bowed.

Shawn had woken to cloudy skies, a damp, chilly day, and a band of Saskatch shadowing them to the west, keeping their distance. He had spoken to Victoria about the Saskatch, and she said at this time, guardians shouldn't risk trusting them. Later if they were needed and survived this catastrophe, she would rethink the idea.

The humans and Rachael had their breakfast and soon were ready to begin the slow journey north. Rachael, for the first time-strapped her sidearm to her hip and gave him a deadly serious look. As the days and weeks passed, and the war went on, he could sense the escalation of dread and worry in her. She would secretly communicate with her council, and then the fear would show on her face. He knew what she told them about him, how the queen thought, and knew the humans believed they would not prevail against this evil foe, and they blamed the angels. Sadly, for him, he knew Rachael also didn't think they would win.

He would give her blood to bolster her confidence, but he had just given her some. *No matter,* he thought, *soon he would make her vampire.* When the humans weren't looking, he quickly bit his wrist, and Rachael took a few mouthfuls. Rachael wiped the drops from her lips, kissed him at the amazement of the few humans that had just turned their heads to notice. He heard her speak softly, "Funny, the one thing in my studies. I didn't find out about vampires is how they draw mortals into their world, how we end up wanting what scares us about you; what made us want to avoid your kind. Now all I want is you!"

"Someday, when all this is over, I'm sure Queen Victoria will let me change you."

A young teenage girl was glancing at him. He saw her curiosity, and he gave her a pleasant smile, and she shyly smiled back at him. The girl was maybe sixteen—that too, he could sense—and she always had a desire to meet a vampire. Long ago, he had learned that some humans marveled at vampire's age, but sometimes he too would marvel at how young humans could be. Sixteen years to him was a blink of an eye. To his surprise, she started to walk over to him. She was an attractive young human, brave, and he quickly smelled her sweet young blood. Shawn also sensed she was sad and easily heard the rapid beating of her young heart as she approached.

"What is it, girl? Why so sad?"

"I lost my parents to the strange red creatures," the girl replied and then started to sob. "They appeared out of nowhere and killed my family."

"Walk with me, girl. You have nothing to fear from me!" Shawn looked into her eyes and settled her heart and fear. Then he spoke softly, always keeping a friendly smile on his face. "What is your name?"

"Susy with a Y," the girl mumbled as her gaze traveled to his feet and backed up.

"Where are you from, Susy?"

"I am from Maryland City. There are so many red soldiers to the south of us. They keep coming from the blue fire. Not many of our soldiers around, though. They raided our city nightly, killing and plundering, and soon they will attack! Strange creatures come with them—tall and no faces –and they carry long sticks. They killed my parents! They don't take prisoners!"

"Where are you headed, young one?"

"I am traveling with my aunt and uncle and their family. We are headed to the spaceport and plan to travel to the belt. Take our chances there!"

"So, you are giving up on this world?"

"Yes! The only time we see our military is when it flies over our heads!"

"They have to get ready for the battle," Rachael spoke with a weary voice. "And we may need every able-bodied people in the end to save this world."

"And what are we fighting?" the girl quickly replied. "The leaders keep it secret from us. Where are these creatures coming from? And why so many?"

"They come from another dimension," Rachael told the girl in a low voice, looking around to make sure no one was near, making sure she showed no symbols. "They come from an evil place. Places the devil has ruled for thousands of years. You see, Susy, there are good forces and evil forces, just like the old religions said."

They all walked on in silence. Soon Susy said her goodbyes and rejoined her group. Shawn saw her speaking to the others and then the shaking of their heads. He sensed their fear, bewilderment, and anger at their government for not being able to protect them from this horror that was spreading over their world. And then a thought formed, and he asked Rachael, "Will your family stay and fight for this world?"

Immediately, he sensed Rachael's turmoil, the reason for her secret communications, and her betrayal. Tears came to her eyes, and she replied, "No, they won't, and I don't want them to. Your queen does not trust us, and most humans don't trust your kind. Civilians will leave this planet; it has already been decided."

Shawn mostly tried to stay out of Rachael's head as politeness, but now he sensed something. He entered her mind entirely and saw something had changed. The humans had learned what they were fighting. Quickly, he left to give her a chance to explain.

"What is it Rachael, explain yourself!"

He watched Rachael regain her composure from his assault on her mind.

"I was going to tell you, Shawn. I was waiting for the right time."

"As a mortal, you do not have to do as I say. But as my changeling, you will. I hope you understand that."

"My government found a way to send nanoprobes through the portals. They are programmed to do recon and then find a portal to return. We sent thousands, and a few came back."

"What did you find out?" Shawn asked as he felt amazement at how far human's technology had progressed. *Astonishing,* he thought.

"Their planet is huge, almost the size of Jupiter, but it is solid. Their sun is red, and it gives their world a dark tint. It is a spartan world ruled by a few central military elites that produce and control soldiers by the billions. They use the portal to come to our world and not just to ours, but to many worlds. According to you, other worlds are like this one. Controlled by the devil."

"You sent probes to another dimension, and some returned."

Rachael looked away then to her feet, where she usually looked when she was going to tell him something that would upset him, but he already knew what she was going to say. "Yes, we did. The combined governments of this world have decided we can't win this war. We will speed up the exodus to the belt. That is why you see so many people on the road."

"I am sorry to hear that. Humans must fight for this world, or the vampires won't. You know that Rachael and I have told your government the same. The devil will follow humans out into space. Rachael, Lucifer is deceiving you!"

"Space is much bigger, Shawn, than this world. Here, in this confined space, we can't last fighting numbers like that. You and your queen must know this." Rachael looked back up, her eyes filled with tears, and he saw her despair. "Now, I just want to go home to see my family!"

Shawn looked away, thinking he saw distortion in the air then looking back, he said. "We aren't far now. You should be home soon."

Rachael met his gaze. Tears came to her eyes again as she whispered, "Humans have recently rediscovered angels, and they treat us differently than your kind. They have hidden from us. That is why most of us don't have faith in them."

"Rachael, that is why the angels treat you the way they do. When humans believed in angels, you still didn't do as they asked. The Mother keeps this world for you, and humans almost destroyed it. The world is yours, not ours. You are the reason we are here! And humans need to defend it!"

"We do not have the numbers to defeat the evil your Mother has brought to us!"

Shawn stopped walking, took hold of Rachael by the shoulders, and looked her in the eyes. "I stay out of your head as much as possible. I give you that courtesy. Someday I will change you, and then you will know the angels." And then another thought came from Rachael, an uncontrolled, powerful, desperate feeling, an idea that stung him. "You are going to take your family to the spaceport!"

"I have to! I don't want them to die!"

"Do they want to leave their home?"

"Yes, under these conditions!"

"Humans won't fight. What will I tell the queen?" Shawn mumbled.

Shawn's attention was quickly taken over by a rise in dark energy. It grew to a tremendous level, and then a loud humming as a blue portal swirled and started to form. The humans stopped frozen in stride, petrified, afraid to move, looking at the developing entrance. The portal developed, and a platform hovering three feet above the ground came through.

Ten creatures stood solid and rode the platform, adorned with shiny silver armor and all kinds of weapons. These creatures were not the Kargarians but reptilian, looking with squat, powerful humanoid bodies. Their skin was dark green and had a leather texture. Their heads were not round like humans'. Still, they extended forward at the face with many small sharp teeth in their lipless mouths, remnants of their long-ago reptilian past. They were the Tarragons, from the lizard world, and they lowered their weapons firing laser blasts at the frozen and staring crowd of humans.

Shawn turned and yelled in a booming vampire voice, "Run!" The sound was the shock to their senses the humans needed. They woke from their trance and quickly scattered. The Tarragons again fired into the mortals, and many crumbled to the ground, still wearing their shocked looks. Burnt body parts and guts exploded outward from the blasts. Rachael drew her weapon and started to advance.

Shawn took hold of Rachael's arm and pulled her behind him. "Stay behind me!" he sternly commanded.

The power of The Mother grew in Shawn to join the might already give to him by Michael. He drew Adeen, then chanting a spell he formed and threw a fireball of white energy that tore into the carriage heaving it up and back, spilling the Tarragons to the ground. Rachael stepped out from behind him and fired her blaster, killing one as he lumbered to his feet.

"Careful!" Shawn again shouted.

"I am a soldier, and this is my job!" Rachael yelled as she again fired at the Tarragons. Rachael took off running, dove, rolled behind a tree for cover and continued to fire at the Tarragons. These were the times Shawn realized that Rachael was a well-trained human operative. Rachael had drawn the surviving Tarragons attention, Shawn raised Adeen, and charge the evil creatures. He quickly covered the distance to the remaining five surviving Tarragons, parrying their fire, and putting himself in their midst. He took the first creature's head, spun, and took another. A photon bullet from Rachael's gun downed the third. He charged the remaining two, plunged Adeen into one of the creatures, lifting him and throwing him to the ground. Dodging the other, he took his head as the beast fumbled at his weapon.

The Tarragons for all their ferociousness were slow-moving creatures and were slow in picking up on movements. Shawn approached the one living Tarragon, trying to crawl to where the portal had been. The creature turned and looked at him with his egg-shaped red eyes and gave a sideways blink of his eyelids. A strange clicking noise came from the lizard as he held his wounded gut with his reptilian hand, probably some way of cursing at him. Raising Adeen, Shawn brought the sword from Heaven down and took the creature's head.

Again, a hum that rose in pitch and soon a new portal started to form. Numerous blasts from Rachael's gun hit the entrance with no effect. The portal developed, and a hideous creature walked through protected by an energy field. Looking the same as the others but twice the size and adorn with elaborate gold armor, Shawn sensed a being of importance, a lizard commander from their dark world. His tongue flicked out like a snake, and he gave a look of loathing at Shawn with his red lizard eyes.

Another creature came through with a head like the soldiers, but this monster had four arms that held curved swords. The body continued with four short, squat legs like the body of a lizard and a tail that rose in the air and flung itself back and forth. The creature quickly approached Shawn swirling the sword and making metallic clanging as the metal blades struck each other.

Using the powers, the angels gave him Shawn changed to his vampire form, shapeshifting to twice his size. He crouched, raised Adeen, hissed at the creature, and charged. He met the lizard with full force, swinging Adeen with the speed of a vampire. The creature's four blades whirled and blurred in the air, then out and in, plunging at him. Shawn parried and blocked the creature's sword. Both stood locked in combat, looking for an opening.

Then with unbelievable speed, Shawn feign left, came back around, dropped, and took one of the creature's front legs. The Tarragon stumbled, Shawn rolled out and then came up with blinding speed and brought the slayer down with great force taking the monster's head. The body collapsed to the ground, and another creature, the same as the first, came through swinging his swords. The lizard commander stared at Shawn, flicked his long tongue at him, turned, clacked something to the elite warrior. They both turned and walked back through the collapsing portal, followed by two more blasts from Rachael's gun.

Rachael stood with her weapon drawn and kicked at the dead Tarragon lizard. "What the hell is this?"

"One of the lizard commander's elite guards, I believe!"

"Lizard commander?" Rachael gasped.

"That is what I got from their strange thoughts."

"So, another devil world is coming through these portals. How many hideous soldiers will come from them?"

"In the dark dimension, there are many worlds of Lucifer's. And the Tarragons are one of them."

Rachael's eyes glazed over as she looked away; she was receiving a message through her nanochip. "Asia and South America have fallen. And these creatures are now being seen south of here. It is only North America now, and we can't stop this!"

Shawn looked at the cloudy sky and the storm clouds to the west. The day was dark to match his mood. Only a continent now stood against Brendel and his army. For the first time, he felt the humans defeat. A cool rain started, and Shawn raised his face to allow the rainwater to wash over him to remove the blood and stench of these creatures. A quiet had settled in the forest, and only the sound of the falling rain came from the woods. A shocked scream broke the silence, and it was a woman standing over a body. The torn body was the girl he talked to earlier. A large hole seared through her, visceral spread out on The Grand Walkway, and her death face stared up as the rain washed the blood from her skin to join the large pool of red already spreading out from her body. He could feel Rachael's hard gaze, as blood tears came to his eyes. They, too, were quickly washed away by the rain.

Chapter Sixteen

S hawn and Rachael continued north. The humans stayed with them until they reached the spaceport. Fortunately, there were no more attacks from the Tarragons. They said their farewells and went onto Montreal. With Rachael's help, Shawn was able to secure a hotel room in the city. They made love again. Shawn wished he could turn her to show her vampire love, the intimacy of exchanging blood. Later that day, Rachael had left to go to her family in the city to prepare them for Shawn's visit.

He was tired, had slept the night, and now was taking a shower running the warm water over his tense body. Vampires enjoyed a hot bath; it gave them a pleasant sensation. This morning reality had come, he had not fed in a month, and now the need for blood was strong. Since meeting Rachael, he hadn't fed enough, and it was affecting his mood. He dressed in his fine new age clothes; after all, Bryces were very rich. Running a brush through his hair, he turned and looked into a mirror, something he seldom did unless he was checking his clothes. His face never changed, never aged, and any marks or bruises quickly healed, so there was no need to look. It was always the face of a twenty-five-year-old.

He was more than twelve hundred years old and could not remember what he looked like when he was a forty-year-old human. Vampires must become comfortable with the effects of time on their memories if they wanted to survive. He shrugged; these were thoughts for a time when he was drinking wine, not now when he was going to meet the family. Chuckling a nervous laugh, he went to the balcony, looked out at the sunny day with the white clouds leisurely floating by. He lifted off his feet, floated up, and out into the blue sky.

Most of his long life, he had flown at night, but now because of The Mother's power, he could survive in the day. His destination was a large nature preserve just south of Montreal. He flew at a sufficient height to look out over the countryside to see a landscape he rarely saw during the day. Landing in a small secluded wooded area, he walked out onto a walkway, which led to a sports complex where he was to meet Rachael and family. The day was beautiful, bright, sunny, and warm. He was sure the humans would think it pleasant.

There were plenty of people in the park, so he cloaked himself to hide what he was from them. They appeared stressed enough. Some gathered in groups and talked of the terrible calamity coming and debating whether they should stay or leave. He walked by them, smiled, and made them see what they wanted to see, a pleasant man taking a stroll. Then came the crack of a bat, and he knew he was getting close.

He hoped he didn't scare Rachael's family too much. He debated using his powers to ease their anxiety or to let them see him for what he was. He should let them, but he was uneasy and would continue to consider the idea. He walked on and came to the ball field, saw Rachael and her father, mother and sister with her new husband standing next to an aircar. Rachael waved to him, wearing a forced smile, and he immediately sensed that she was worried about what they would say to him.

He decided to meet with her family because of their history of past interaction with vampires. Now, he questioned the idea. Approaching the family, he smiled and decided maybe a little calming wouldn't hurt. Rachael made the greetings. In any other situation, her family would be gracious, pleasant, and friendly when greeting a stranger, but not today by the stern looks on their faces. They looked him up and down, but they were not afraid of him, which he thanked The Mother for.

"You are headed to the spaceport?" Shawn questioned while still projecting calm. He quickly got a tense stare from Rachael.

"Yes, the father said. "We have decided to accept our government's offer."

"I will ask the protection of The Mother for you," Shawn answered graciously.

"You will?" the fathers said snidely. "The angel that got us in this situation?"

"You are Rachael's family, and I will speak honestly with you. If it weren't for that angel, you would have been Lucifer's long ago. Most times, she is very successful in dealing with Satan's evil. And we better hope she is this time!"

Rachael's family was in turmoil; he saw the anguish on their faces and quickly sensed the despair that surrounded all of them. They were giving up their lives and homes, their way of life here on Earth, to escape a horror they knew little about. They had lost everything, and it terrified them. He also sensed that they wanted Rachael to come with them and had been pursuing this idea vigorously with her. He realized that some of their anger was because they thought he was responsible for them losing their daughter.

Rachael's father looked him up and down. Shawn saw his turmoil, and then he spoke, "My family knows vampires! We are not like other humans. I know you can let my daughter go. She should be with her family!"

"Mr. Bonnet, I do not control your daughter. It is your government that controls her. Everything she does is to save your world. Humans sent her to me. To spy, to learn about us. She decides on her path! And I do believe humans must fight for this world too!"

"Maybe, but we are not soldiers."

"Your daughter is."

"Please protect her," Mrs. Bonnet sobbed. "What she tells me of you, I believe you will. And I give you my permission to make her a vampire if it means saving her life."

Shawn looked at the family one by one as a blood tear came to his eye, and none diverted their eyes, and all had teared filled eyes. "I promise to do my best for her."

"Please take care of Rachael," the sister pleaded and then turned to Rachael. "We will see each other again. I know we will!"

"We will," Rachael sobbed.

Shawn watched the Bonnets say their goodbyes. Tears came all around and even to him. Humans, for all their technology and science, were sometimes so ignorant of the world around them. They always were so unsure of Heaven and the forces that moved their world, but Heaven was sure about them. The Bonnets left for the spaceport, and Shawn and Rachael stood holding each other, crying.

The next eve, Shawn, came to Montreal to hunt. No longer could he put it off, he told Rachael. It was a chilly, clear night, summer was ending, and most humans were inside. He leaned against a building watching the few humans and soldiers walk by. Mortals would pass him and pay him no notice, but a few would give him a second glance while a signal of recognition entered their minds.

Soon, the street became deserted. Shawn lifted slowly floating upwards, turning as he ascended, projecting his senses outward looking for the substance that would sustain him, and the reason for taking it. He was searching for that absolute darkness that lived in a few humans, a dark evil, and once he felt it, he knew they were the lowest of the human race.

Looking out, he saw the multitude of blinking colored lights and wondered how much longer they would sparkle. Montreal was a large city of this age, and many of the humans had left. The military was everywhere, patrolling on all towers and the streets. Soon Shawn sensed the evil, soldiers preying on the very people they were supposed to protect. Flying higher, he landed on the top of a high tower next to a broad transmission array. He crouched and searched the night for the locations of the soldiers. He sent his telepathic energies out looking for the evil mortals and the nectar that kept him alive that wicked blood Heaven allowed him to take.

There you are, he thought. *What is this!* To his astonishment, he sensed two Valaris wizards with the soldiers. Lifting into the night, he traveled toward them. Landing a block from where the treacherous soldiers were holding their meeting with the wizards, he chanted a mother's spell, cloaking himself and slowly drew closer. As he went, he quickly sensed the minds of the soldiers and saw their cold souls.

Shawn knew the soldiers were delivering humans to the Valaris Wizards to take back through a portal. Also, they were setting themselves up to help Brendel, to become his servant, to control the remaining humans left on this world once the battle had ended. There was one more entity, lurking in the darkness, hidden by powerful magic. The soldiers and the two Valaris Wizards went through a back door into a building holding a few mortals to start their betrayal. They had left only one soldier as a look-out. Shawn was hesitant because of the unknown entity, but he wanted to help the humans. He moved with blinding speed and was on the soldier snapping his neck before he could signal the evil inside. He quickly drained the soldier of his blood and wiped his mouth with the back of his hand.

Unfortunately, when the human's nanochip stop sending, the soldiers inside knew something had gone wrong. They piled through the door, their weapons drawn and stopped when they saw Shawn standing, changed to his vampire form with Adeen raised and glowing. The wizards came out, went to the front, and lowered their staffs, firing their dark energy at him. He swung Adeen like a bat, blocking the heat, sending some back to kill the soldiers, then flew straight up and came down in the center of the soldiers and wizards. Immediately, he took two soldiers' heads and watched the rest scatter and make their way out of the alley.

The wizards spread out, lowering their staffs as if they were protecting something. Then a new portal formed behind them, Samil and four powerful Valaris Wizards of Lucifer's stepped through. The wizards all were from his first order, all caring staff and small battle swords at their sides. The early two wizards step back through the disappearing portal. Now he could see what was hidden in the darkness. This was a trap.

"Samil," Shawn growled. "Coming here was a mistake!"

"Brendel has sent me to kill you, Demon Slayer, and I figured you would be looking for blood soon. Your life on this world is over!"

Samil lowered her staff, and the four powerful dark wizards moved towards him. Shawn swung Adeen side to side, and the sword from Heaven hummed as it sliced the air. The Mother's power formed in him, her energy surrounding him, and again he heard in his head, *why is Gwyn not here?*

Samil and the wizards spread themselves, trying to encircle him. He heard the sing-song language of the wizards, the sharp commands of Samil to the wizards, and pleas to make them understand the danger they all were in. Samil did not want to be here that was obvious to Shawn. Brendel had forced her hand. Lucifer was a cruel taskmaster that he knew. Samil and the wizards lowered their staff and fired at the same time. Again, he swung Adeen, blocking four of the plasma beams, but a fifth got through.

The Mothers energy built in him, surrounding him, but still, the energy penetrated and sliced his side. He fell to his knee, holding his wound but quickly sprung back up and with high speed charged forward, taking the wizards by surprise. He feinted to one side and then arced around to the back, taking one of the faceless heads. Leaping over them, he appeared in front and swung Adeen slicing one of the wizards up the stomach, into the chest, and through the wizard's heart. The stricken wizard fell dead, and the remaining two and Samil moved back.

Shawn had killed two in an instant with his vampire speed. The three remaining evil creatures were shaken. Samil chanted a dark spell, and their staffs glowed a deep blue becoming super-heated and now could slice through anything in this world. The mysterious creatures advanced swinging their staffs. Shawn swung Adeen, blocking the super-heated staffs. Samil worked her way to the side, tore her sword from its sheath, brought it around, and sliced him across the back. Shawn fell to the ground, rolled and got to his feet, and stood legs spread Adeen raised ready to strike. His eyes burned the blue of the Herit Covenant, his vampire face fierce, he cursed at Samil and the faceless wizards.

Again, with high speed, he charged forward parried the burning blue staffs, dodging and taking another wizard head as he blocked a thrust from Samil swords. The last blue staff swung at him, and he parried and feinted thrusting his blade through the wizard's throat then kicking him away. As he turned, Samil's blade penetrated his stomach and pierced him through. He fell back, stumbling, holding the wound, staggering, trying to regaining his footing. He stared at Samil, blood flowing down his arm from the wound on his back, blood coming from his mouth, and swallowing what he could. The Valerians had hurt him, and still, he had to take care of Samil.

He swayed and gurgled, "Come for me, Samil! Let's finish it between us!"

"Mighty Demon Slayer," Samil hissed sarcastically. "You don't look so tough now! I brought the best wizards the Valerians had, and you killed them. But vampire, you are spent, and now I will kill you!"

The Mother's power surge in Shawn and he advanced on Samil Adeen held ready to strike. Their blades rang out in the night as their metal struck. Back and forth, they drove each other as each looked for an opening.

He felt himself losing blood and becoming weaker, with sickening fatigue spreading over him. This is what Samil wanted. Exhaustion had taken him, and only for a second, he lowered his guard, and Samil struck, driving her blade into his chest, trying to pierce his heart. He fell back onto his knees as Samil brought her sword down to sever his head. What could have been the last seconds of his life, was stolen from the witch as The Mother's power surged in him. Instantly, he brought Adeen up, blocking her blade and then kicked her feet from under her.

Rolling with vampire speed, he appeared to form over Samil as she tried to get to her feet. He parried her thrust, kicked her back down, and drove his blade through her. The witch screamed and cursed, came up at him, slicing his side again and charged in madness and fear swing her sword. Shawn dodged the fiery witch, turned around, and took the bald witch's head. Samil body slumped to the pavement, her head making a thud as it hit the ground, the rolling leaving a trail of her putrid brown blood. Samil crackled and fizzled, and blue fire consumed the witch. Lucifer was quickly reclaiming the witch's body, not wanting anyone to see another humiliating defeat.

Shawn staggered and fell to his knees, head bowed, blood flowing from his nose and mouth. He looked around to see where he could bury himself, but there was only pavement, and now soldiers started to gather around him. He raised his head and sent his signal to those vampires that could hear him. *Help me. I am hurt!* And then he fell forward onto the hard pavement. He rolled to his back and stared at the faces of the gathering humans. He heard a soldier say, "Should we shoot him?"

And then another said, "No, he would only kill us; besides, I believe this one is on our side! We'll contact command!"

Consciousness was leaving him, as he desperately tried to remain awake. He heard the sounds around him, and then he heard a familiar voice.

Chapter Seventeen

R achael had risen early and sat on the balcony of her suite in Montreal. The sun was rising, spreading its warmth, showing the beauty of the early morning sky. A slight cool breeze blew against her face. How much longer, she wondered, would the world be this way? Shawn had not fed since Washington and had left early last night to seek out the evil blood he needed to stay alive. She wanted to go with him to watch the action, but as of now, he would not allow it. He still hid that part of his existence from her.

He would talk to her about the turmoil of young vampires when faced with the newness of taking blood. Shawn told her eventually for all vampires a time came when it was as natural as her eating her food. The thought broke her melancholy and made her chuckle. She would eat, and Shawn would sip his tea, watching her with his fake sad face, and tell her to enjoy her food for as long as she could. For him, he told her, the loss of it was the most significant sacrifice he made becoming a vampire.

She sipped at her hot, black coffee, a beverage that had always been her first choice of the day—picked at her porridge with a heavy heart. How would she live without her family? They had always been there for her even when she joined the intelligence division of her federation's army. When she was young, her father had talked of vampires, the reality of these creatures, how our uncle and family had known these creatures, and had been friends with them. She had followed her interest in vampires, joined The Vampire Corps, and it had led her here, in love with Shawn.

Off to the side just above her eyebrow, a small, red V formed disappearing and then reappearing. Her superiors were signaling that they were going to send her a secure message. Rachael's head went up as she heard the news. *A vampire was down in the city.* She immediately replied, *Keep back! Most likely other vampires will be coming and send transport for me!*

Rachael was taking the lift down to the bottom floor. She had changed into her uniform, so the first responders knew who she was. She moved at a good pace, out the front of the building, and into the waiting military transport. They dusted off, and immediately she started receiving information on the vampire. A portal had opened in the city, and creatures had come through and attacked the vampire. A battle had followed, and the vampire had killed the monsters, but they had severely hurt him, and he was down on Avon street. Intel then joined the conversation and told her they weren't typical red soldiers more like the ones that open the portals. What vampires call wizards.

The military vehicle was lit with a soft red glow, a low hum of the turbines, and the chatter over auditory communication was heard. Symbols and maps were forming everywhere in the air, a sign of a military at war. The transport hugged the buildings weaving and arcing, then quickly dropping to ground level, sending Rachael's morning's porridge up into her throat. The craft was landing, and she saw the body lying on the street and knew it was Shawn, knew it in her mind's eye, and amazingly felt it in her blood.

Rachael left the flyer and saw many military transports landing with hundreds of soldiers disembarking, forming a perimeter around the body. Shawn laid on a walkway close to an entrance to an alley. She went, sat next to him, gathering his head in her lap and saw the blood congealing in his wounds, his supernatural healing was progressing.

She then barked commands at the soldiers, "Form a perimeter around this block, let nobody through, bring in some heavy pulsars, and be prepared for more portals." She saw him open his eyes as she sent a message to command to send more soldiers.

A smile spread over his face, and he whispered, "I will be all right. Vampires are coming. Let the humans know."

She yelled to the commander, "Prepare yourselves for vampires." And then, with the help of Shawn's blood, she sensed powerful vampires coming. Around a tower, they came, descending rapidly, fifty warrior vampires, Queen Victoria, Katherine, and Gwyn landing on the street. Rachael still held Shawn and watched the queen walk toward her. She wore golden chest armor, shins and guards, a golden holly leaf crown on her head, and Deceida—one of the five original swords from Heaven—strapped to her back.

The soldiers parted as the queen came to her. Victoria reached down and lifted Shawn's limp body taking him away from her. She heard her whisper in his ear as she wiped the blood from his face and saw the love this queen had for Shawn. "You have won a great battle, my love. Samil is dead, and Lucifer curses your name again. I'm so afraid for you! Lucifer never forgets!"

Rachael listened to Victoria speak these words, and it turned her blood to ice.

The queen looked at her sorrowfully, then turned and yelled, "We are going to Washington to bury Shawn. Gwyn, bring Rachael with us." And then the ancient vampire shot straight into the air.

Gwyn quickly scooped her into her arms, and some soldiers mistook the action and moved toward them. Rachael immediately yelled to them, "Stand down!"

For the second time that morning, her stomach made a loop as Gwyn quickly lifted her into the air. They flew west, and she watched the scenery below rush by. The wind blew at her hair, and she felt the gentle brush of Gwyn's hand against her cheek and heard her whisper, "He will be okay." Rachael took notice that the vampires were flying in a "V" with Victoria at the point then Katherine and Gwyn and the rest of the vampires following. Victoria had passed Shawn's lifeless body off to Katherine. Shawn was her maker, and it was Katherine's responsibility to bring him home. Through the years, Rachael had learned about the vampire's rigid hierarchy and their rules of honor.

Gwyn had glimpsed her thoughts, a smile came to her, and she told Rachael, "Katherine will bury him and be the first to give him blood."

Sometimes, she would fly with Shawn, but still, she was not used to being suspended in the air without human technology surrounding her. Rachael rested her head against Gwyn's shoulder, willing herself to relax, knowing the trip to Washington would take a couple of hours. She felt the brush of Gwyn's lips across her cheek, and again she heard Gwyn whispered, "Try to rest; we have some ways to go."

Rachael woke to them circling the house in Washington, and the beautiful small lake with clear water reflecting its various shades of blue. They had split off from the warrior vampires, and her stomach floated as Gwyn slowed and descended on to the front yard, finally allowing her belly to come to a rest. The warrior vampires also landed, and all of them were older, more seasoned. They quickly surrounded and occupied the house.

Gwyn set her down and told her, "Follow me."

Rachael followed Gwyn, Victoria, and Katherine carrying Shawn through the front door into a large central room. Rachael immediately recognized the Crimmian servants scurrying to lend their masters a hand. The Crimmians had set up extra cots in the room to help the influx of their kind trying to find safety. Through the centuries, it was Crimmians that humans had used to learn about vampires. Once, she was involved in interrogating a Crimmian. It was her that had eventually stop the practice when she learned they were giving these people a death sentence. Vampires would kill any Crimmian that betrayed them, spoke of them to humans; it was vampire law.

She hurried across a large sitting room down a hallway and into a large room with paintings hung, on easels, or propped against the wall. She stopped and stared at a picture of Anne, Shawn's maker. She had always wondered what Anne looked like. How beautiful she was. Being here was like the holy grail for a human who studied vampires seeing an actual image of the vampire Anne. Shawn had told her stories about her, and the name Anne Bryce had come up many times in human research of vampires. She, too, was a Demon Slayer. Many considered Anne to be the greatest of the vampires. Across the room, they went through a sizeable old bronze door and down a stone, curved stairwell. She entered a large basement area, and immediately the strangeness of the place overwhelmed her. She had found the Bryce family's ancestral home, the center of the Herit Covenant and their burial chamber, and because of Anne the covenant that ruled vampires.

The basement of this house felt ancient. In the center, a large tile mosaic of a gold lion's head laid in the tile floor, and she knew this was the symbol of the Herit Covenant. Her mouth fell open when she saw rooms recessed into the walls filled with gold and jewels. She saw a gold pitcher sitting on a table prominently displayed in a corner with a large burgundy candle burning next to it. The pitcher resembled a drawing she once saw of the one that held Bricius's blood. She walked further into the basement and saw what looked like a swimming pool filled with dirt.

Gwyn made circles in the air with her staff chanting a spell that would keep the demons and evil witches at bay. Gwyn used her staff to draw a strange stick figure of a man in the dirt of the pool. Chanting a spell, she snapped her fingers, and the figure glowed a white light that lit the room and then faded. Gwyn told her it was the symbol of the defeated Esmanaa demons. It was a warning to any demon who came that this was a burial place of a Demon Slayer.

Katherine had taken Shawn to a marbled table and, with the help of Victoria, stripped his bloody clothes from him and washed his body with water. The head Crimmian, wearing a strange and ancient attire, brought the linen bandages to Victoria and then quickly left. Concentrating on her heart, trying to stop it from racing, Rachael realized she was witnessing a vampire burial. She saw Katherine bite her wrist with her vampire's teeth, cover the bandages with her blood, and fill Shawn's mouth with it. Chills went up her spine. Victoria laid the blood-soaked bandages on the wounds. She then tore her wrist and allowed her blood to pour into Shawn's mouth. Gwyn went to the dirt and held her staff, chanting a spell, the soil parted, and made a grave.

Even with her limited psychic ability, she could feel the tremendous power in the staff Gwyn held. It vibrated her very being. Gwyn went to the foot of the marble table, held the rod up, and again chanted a spell. The staff glowed, and a spirit of a fair lady came from the staff hovered over Shawn and then returned to the staff. Rachael's head spun, and she felt light-headed at what she was seeing.

Victoria lowered her head, and Rachael heard her whisper in Shawn's ear that they were there, would protect him, then she saw his eyes open and nod his head. Victoria and Katherine lifted Shawn and placed his naked body wrapped with the bandages into the grave. Immediately the earth filled in engulfing his body. Two lit burgundy candles held in large gold candleholders were set at the head of the grave. The final act was Gwyn drawing the symbols of Herit into the dirt of the grave. One by one, the vampires passed the grave, wishing Shawn well in his journey, and left the basement.

Chapter Eighteen

S hawn found himself drifting in the mist, and slowly the first plane of the spiritual world came into focus. He was sitting against the tree he came to when he had transcended from the physical to the spiritual. The tree that he had first found himself when he lost his mortality. All creatures of his world had this connection to Heaven, but in this age, few were aware of it. The green field that surrounded him stretched to the horizon, and there the intense white light glowed outward. That was where the city of light started. He had gone there before, but now he felt indifferent. He was tired of the fighting.

The beings that came from the portal where powerful wizards that distracted him, while Samil sword had come dangerously close to his heart. And now The Mother was upset with him. Eos wanted Gwyn to be with him, but he was a vampire, and his choir of angels was the Archangel Michaels.

He allowed the spiritual sleep to take over, and then he was floating in the light. Again, Heavens energies washed over and through him, renewing, and allowing him to accept the never-ending conflict of good and evil that would always be with him. Anne had sealed Shawn's fate the night she made him a vampire. Sometimes, he would think of taking Rachael and living away from all the conflict. He knew, though, that he could not ignore Heaven and certainly not the devil.

He floated in the light listening to the vampires that had come before him—Herit, Anne, and Marilyn—whispering to him to accept his destiny and fate. They would wait for him.

Eventually, the light dimmed, replaced by a white mist, and that to dissipate. He was awakening, perfectly healed, and could feel the fresh dirt all around him and the healing energies of The Mother penetrating every cell in his body. Blood lust rose in him, consumed him, a strong need that drove him to leave the grave and find nourishment no matter who.

A revival was the time Heaven's killers were the most dangerous to mortals, the reason Gwyn was with Rachael to keep her out of the way. He clawed at the dirt while his instincts told him to rise and find blood. He felt the powerful hands of Katherine and Victoria holding him back, reassuring him that they would give him blood, and there was no need to find a mortal. Warm water washed over him, rinsing the dirt from his face and skin, cleansing his perfectly healed body.

Shawn came from the ground three days ago and had slept most of the time since, but still, he felt weary. He sat next to the lake in a lounge chair looking out over the water, watching an osprey circling then diving into the water. The bird emerged, breaking the water and flying back into the sky, over the treetops taking its meal back to its nest. Gwyn had taken Rachael to Seattle during his awakening and had returned earlier that day. Last eve Katherine and Victoria had left to go back to Dalton.

He sat, hunched, staring into the forest, daydreaming of all the Bryces he had spent time with here. Still, he could remember the time of Anne, his maker, and Marilyn, how he loved them. After twelve centuries, he always could remember the first time he saw Anne, the touch of Marilyn's lips. He also remembered Anne's warning to him about becoming lost in time and how the burden of a long life could wear on a person if they weren't suited for it. Anne had told him she had gone through a melancholy when she was a thousand-years-old, the reason why she had taken Renee as a changeling. He remembered Renee and Caitlyn the Bryces that had lost their lives, saving his. Each of them, he had loved in his special way.

He replayed the fight with Samil and the wizards in his mind. They had almost ended his existence in this world. Lucifer had turned on Samil as he did with all his witches. Malin once told him Lucifer would turn on her someday, and he still remembered how Lucifer had abandon Malin, leaving her lying in an ugly death.

Shawn now sensed Rachael coming and turned to look over his shoulder at her. He smiled, and she returned the smile. Sitting on his lap, she gave him a hug and a kiss.

"You look much better than the last time I saw you. Actually, it is amazing how you look!" Rachael then unzipped his shirt, looked, and felt his chest. "Amazing!"

"Thanks, I think I look amazing too," Shawn laughed.

"I bet you do!" Rachael looked out over the lake, and a smile spread over her face. "Gwyn and Katherine told me of some of the lovemaking that has gone on around this lake."

"I am glad you are now getting along with Gwyn and Katherine. I'm surprised at how well."

"Me too!" Rachael laughed, then she looked into Shawn's eyes touched his cheek. "Make love to me! It's been a while."

Shawn rose from the chair, holding Rachael in his arms and flew across the lake to that special spot where he knew the grass and earth were soft. There he laid her on the ground and removed her clothes. He hurriedly took off his clothes and embraced her rolling in the grass. Shawn kissed her passionately, went between her legs until he heard her special moans, gently entered her, and felt her human warmth. He made love to her until they laid tired and satisfied.

They held each other in the grass, Shawn stroking her red hair, feeling her soft skin, making sure that her human body was warm enough.

"Oh, Head Chair Fitzgerald sends her wishes for a speedy recovery," Rachael whispered to him. "And there is something I need to discuss with you."

"And what is that?" Again, he felt that feeling of dread when he knew Rachael had not been truthful with him. That human condition of hers that came up from time to time.

"We haven't told vampires about a discovery we've made."

"Let me guess, and it is now something you need vampire help with!" Shawn knew humans were still learning how to deal with vampires, and strangely vampires were learning how to deal with humans. They didn't understand that vampires expected them to be truthful, not scheming for an advantage. Most vampires, he would remind Rachael, had forgotten about that part of everyday life for mortals.

"I have to do what my superiors tell me. I have to follow orders. I am in the military, Shawn."

"I understand, Rachael!" Shawn said, slightly exasperated. "Tell me what you want me to know."

"Since the portals started to open, humans have made some strides in understanding interdimensional travel."

"Really!" Again, mortals and their technology had surprised him.

"We built one prototype of a machine that can generate portals. Unfortunately, the lab was located on Hempstead Island and has since been taken over by Brendel's forces."

"Humans must have plans to build another."

"We do, but the machine has electromagnetic pads that are made of beridium. The only place to get beridium is a mine in Europe. And that place is also held by Brendel's forces."

"Well, that is bad luck! What would you like from me? I'm sure your government wants something."

"We want vampires to retrieve the machine, keep it, and protect it until we can take it off-world. And, one more thing, the machine is inside a silicon-based A.I. humanoid."

"You're kidding!"

"No, Shawn, I wouldn't kid about this!"

"And how do you think that is going to help humans? You cannot attack the Kargarian world. Humans cannot match their numbers, especially on their home world. And there are many more worlds in the dark realm."

Rachael's voice dropped low as if she was afraid somebody would hear her. "We would not send soldiers. We also have a bomb of unbelievable force. A bomb that never could be detonated on our world. It is a planet killer. A doomsday bomb!"

"Can the bomb be sent through the portals?"

"Yes, it can," Rachael whispered.

This had surprised him, but humans were always coming up with big bombs. The mortals had been working on a plan that could slow Brendel and his forces and with the vampires' help defeat Brendel, but humans were leaving this world. Then he realized that would not do; this world needed that machine and bomb. Vampires would secure the device, and then they would have to find and take the weapon along with a few scientists to work the bomb.

"Where do you keep the bomb?" Shawn asked while he cloaked his thoughts and probed Rachael's.

"I can't tell you that. You know I can't, Shawn."

Again, he read her thoughts, but she did not know where the bomb was and quickly saw a tense look spread over her face for him being in her head. *Of course*, he thought, *the humans wouldn't tell her where this bomb was*. Then he realized that Rachael knew he would try to steal the weapon.

"We will leave for Dalton with this news. I must tell the queen. Did you tell Gwyn?"

"No, I wouldn't do that! You are my contact. Could we take a flyer this time? Please!"

Shawn smiled at her and answered, "Sure, why not. I suppose it would be more comfortable."

"Yes, it would!"

Rachael banked the flyer around a sizeable forested hill, flew over a river, descended, and landed on the flats known as Dalton, now seat of power for the vampires of this world.

Flying was another skill that Rachael did well. The camp had changed since he was last there. Crimmians had built a large hall with the Queens Symbol prominently displayed on the oversized, wooden double doors. Also, the barracks were greatly expanded to house the increasing population of vampires.

Shawn, Gwyn, and Rachael disembarked the flyer, and Katherine greeted them. She immediately went to Shawn, embraced him, and kissed him. "How are you! You look much better. Do you have your energy back?"

"I'm fine, my love, good as new. I have to see the queen. I have some important new information for her."

Shawn watched Katherine go to Gwyn, embrace her, and give her a passionate kiss followed by an expression of mischief spreading over her face. Katherine turned her attention to Rachael. "How are you, dear Rachael?"

"Well, Queen Katherine."

Again, Katherine's mischievous smile. "You and Gwyn must come for a visit later. Shawn will be with Victoria. Follow me; the queen is in the hall."

They went through the large wooden double doors and into the hall. Victoria sat on the blue throne moved from The Citadel. To her left stood the remaining three heads of the covenants with various other vampires. He walked toward the throne, and Victoria raised her hand at the others to stop their chatter and commanded, "We will speak further of this tomorrow. You are dismissed."

Victoria stepped down from the throne and embraced him. "How are you, Shawn?"

He assured her he was fine, and then he told her of the news he received from Rachael.

Victoria's eyes turned a deep blue as she turned to Rachael and probed her mind. She abruptly stopped. "Are you sure of this, Rachael?"

"Yes, Queen Victoria!"

Silence fell over them, and he watched Victoria to see what she would do, and then she said, "I will have to think further of this. Shawn, come to my quarters later, I would like to discuss this with you." Victoria dismissed them and turned to leave, deep in thought, and then as an afterthought for the others added, "We will discuss this further."

Shawn had just left Victoria. They had made love and taken considerable time lying in each other's arms, discussing the latest turn of events. Victoria had seen the news his way and agreed they would take control of the machine and find the location of the bomb. This could be the development they had been waiting for. This machine could save the world. Victoria didn't trust mortals, especially now, when it looked like they were not going to stay and fight. And now they were starting to realize the humans only told them what they were doing when they had to. From his very beginning, Shawn had been a rider of vampire blood and had seen Victoria's beginnings. He understood where her mistrust for humans had come from. Her distrust came from an age when she was human.

He now stood on a large balcony that led to Katherine's bedroom. Stopping halfway across the balcony, he sensed Gwyn, and to his surprise Rachael. They were in Katherine's couch, making love to Rachael. Allowing his senses to travel past the fluttering windblown curtains into the dimly lit room, he felt Rachael's ecstasy and gave a slight chuckle. Rachael was getting the full vampire experience tonight. And then he felt his changelings in his mind calling to him, *come to bed,* but he declined. He felt a slight melancholy tonight and did not want to ruin their mood.

Shawn turned and lifted into a star-filled night, rising higher and higher into the darkness. Flying was still his favorite power, and he would sometimes travel as high as his vampire body would let him until he felt the pull on his strength and his life force. He was a vampire of the Archangel Michael's making and could never leave this world. Drifting in the high currents, where the air was thin, he allowed his mind to wander, while feeling only a whisper of a breeze on his face. Looking into the darkness of space, he thought what Victoria had commanded him to do. Again, he was sent to do the impossible, risk everything for the cause.

He had glimpsed Lucifer's world once, felt the deep darkness, and knew his evil would never end. Sometimes, since that time, he would feel the darkness creep over him like a heavy cloak and then leave. Now, he was to take Katherine and Gwyn, retrieve the machine, and bring it back to Dalton. Out of concern for Rachael's safety, Victoria had ordered him to leave her behind. He had spoken again with Victoria about Rachael's turning, but still, Victoria would not allow it. The time was not right, she would tell him, Rachael was more valuable as a mortal.

Chapter Nineteen

G wyn, Katherine, and Shawn had come to York to start their mission on Hempstead Island, where Rachael told him the machine was located. They had occupied a large suite with a balcony that gave them reasonable access to the sky for their comings and goings. Humans were abandoning the city in droves. The island was directly east of York and was the only part of Long Island the Atlantic had not claimed after the apocalypse. It was a small island and now held the closest forces of Brendel's to an American city. Before Brendel, Hempstead's one claim to fame was selling underwater tours of a now-submerged New York City.

Shawn took from his traveling bag a metallic disk the size of a quarter, gave it a soft squeeze with his fingers. Maps appeared in front of him, showing the town of Hempstead that the newly arriving Tarragons had made into a fortress. Audio came with the plans, and when touched, he heard an explanation of the layout of the town and the location of Tarragon forces. The tutorial drew particular attention to a flat, squat fortified building located on the eastern side of the town. The visual showed a heavily guarded building, and weaponry placed all around. The audio told them this was the probable location of the machine.

"It looks heavily guarded," Katherine pointed out.

Shawn ran his hand through his hair and said, "It certainly is!"

"Maybe we should have brought more vampires with us," Gwyn added.

"We can't," Shawn said. "The queen does not want to commit the vampire army fully. Not yet. She feels they are not ready."

"Why? Gwyn asked.

"It is the same problem," Katherine replied as she turned to Gwyn. "Not all warrior vampires of the earth are warriors. If you remember, it was the same problem I had trying to save Shawn."

Shawn pointed to an area on one of the floating maps, a spot next to the building. "There…that area looks to be a blind spot. We will land there, move to this door, overpower the guards, force our way in, and take control of the building."

"The place will be swarming in no time with Tarragons," Katherine reminded. "We won't have much time to find the machine."

"The building is not that big!" Shawn mumbled.

"Good thing we have The Mother's Staff," Katherine said as she strapped Alexa to her back.

"The Mother has put considerable power in this staff," Gwyn assured. "Unfortunately, she decides how much to release from it."

"We'll find out," Shawn added, as he strapped Adeen to his back. He went to the balcony. "It's time. We will fly at a speed that hopefully, the Tarragons cannot detect. But we will be there in minutes, so are we ready."

"Yes," they whispered.

They stood on the balcony, hoping that each would make it back. They were going to a place and an enemy they knew little about. The night was cold, with a stiff breeze blowing against their faces. They embraced and kissed each other, and then they disappeared, taking flight to the selected spot.

The guardians landed and crouched at the chosen area. The cold kept many of the Tarragons inside, and the few that were outside huddle around a waist-high glowing sphere of warmth.

Nobody was manning the weaponry around the building. These were the lizard creatures he saw on the trail to Montreal, and the way they moved around and stomped their feet showed they were from a much warmer climate. They were bigger and more durable than Kargarians. Still, their movement was clumsy on this world, and they were careless in guarding the building.

They all fell to the ground to hide. Shawn sent a thought to Katherine and Gwyn to levitate just above the ground. Using the tall grass for cover, they slithered to their goal, and to Shawn's surprise, the Tarragon's large red eyes stayed fixated on the glowing orb.

Shawn allowed his supernatural senses to travel toward the Tarragons. With great stealth, he entered one of the beast minds. It was a strange place for him. They did not think as he did. There was no love, no romance, only ritualistic procreation, and for these creatures only battle, how many kills they had accomplished in their lives. For them, a struggle was the only way to die; all others were a dishonor. Then he made another important discovery—they did not see by light rays but by heat rays, and that was why they had a hard time detecting vampires. The Tarragons might be better at fighting humans, but they were a poor selection to fight vampires. Vampires were cold; somebody hadn't down their homework.

Shawn put his hand on Adeen's hilt, drew it from its sheath, and nodded to the others to begin the attack. The vampires rose with breakneck speed. Quickly they were on the four Tarragons, and as they turned their gaze from the orb to them, Adeen and Alexa took their heads. Gwyn lowered her staff and blew the entrance door into the hallway.

They entered, and immediately Shawn and Katherine blocked searing laser fire from the Tarragons lumbering toward them. Gwyn chanted a spell, and a force field formed around them, blocking the deadly fire. They advanced down the hallway taking the heads of the Tarragons that blocked their way. A clacking and a strange screech came from the creatures as they fell to the floor, and their thin green blood flowed freely from their wounds.

A peculiar sounding alarm rang out, and the hallway filled with a red light, and then a door slid open, and a lizard guard came through, large with four arms, and four legs. The lizard had come from the room where the Tarragons were keeping the machine. The creature lumbered down the hall, swinging the four swords he held. Shawn met him with Adeen in combat. Their blades struck again and again, and the sound of metal rang out. The creature initially drove the vampires back down the hallway. Katherine joined the swordplay, and slowly they stop the lizard guards advance. Shawn parried then feign, and Katherine stepped from behind and drove Alexa through its lizard head. The lifeless Tarragon guard dropped with a thud to the floor, and the stench of the lizard's blood filled the hallway.

The vampires stepped over the creature, and cautiously approached the door the Tarragon came through. Shawn grasped the door and, with his strength, tore the door from its metal hinges and tossed it aside. The room was bare except for a shiny metallic table that was almost tilted vertical to the floor and strapped on the table, was an Artificial Intelligence being. The room still stunk from the Tarragon that had been guarding the robot. The vampires looked at each other, and Katherine whispered under her breath, "You never know what humans are going to do."

Shawn spoke first, "You may start yourself, robot."

A hum rose followed by a twirling sound and then all subsided to where no human could hear the sounds of the A.I.'s existence.

"Can you hear me, robot?" Shawn shouted.

"I can hear you, guardian—no need to yell. Your term *robot* is incorrect. I was hoping humans would rescue me."

The robot was now looking directly at Shawn. The A.I. appeared human dressed in human clothing, slightly unkempt, probably due to its captivity with the Tarragons. The A.I. eyes were the only part that did not look human. The pupils were unusually large, and their irises opened and closed in a circular, mechanical way.

Shawn stood and stared at the creature and then shook off his surprise and answered, "The humans are a little busy right now, fleeing and all, so they sent us. They told us the machine was inside a robot, and you are the robot."

"I am the so-called robot you are looking for. And the machine is in me."

Katherine then warned the others. "There are a lot of Tarragons coming; we need to leave. Can you stand, robot?"

"I am fully functional, and you can call me Max. I am Max28SD. Special design, I might add."

Shawn broke Max's restraints. "If you don't want to be taken apart piece by piece, follow me, Max!"

The group went back down the hallway. Shawn peered through the door opening, and a large amount of laser fire from the Tarragons greeted him. Dust and pieces of the building flew inward, covering the vampires and Max. Smoke and the smell of ozone filled the air.

Shawn yelled back to Gwyn, "Use the Mother's Staff to clear some of the Tarragons away and cover for our escape!"

Gwyn went to the door and sprayed out a plasma beamed that disintegrated any Tarragons that it touched.

"Katherine, take Max!" Shawn yelled. We will go out the door then straight up."

They went through the door dodging laser fire, then with blinding speed flew straight up out of harm's way. Within minutes, they had arrived back at the hotel with their strange prize.

The next day, Rachael flew Shawn to New Chicago, and he now sat with her in the council room of the relocated world government. Victoria wanted a meeting with the human government, and they had agreed. He stared across the table at the empty chairs of the remaining Head Chairs of the world government and the nervous smiles of the human assistants mulling about. The heads of what was left of this government were discussing the latest turn of events from the vampires.

The queen wanted the humans to give the doomsday bomb to her. He had negotiated the queen's terms all day with the humans. The queen did not trust them, he explained, therefore vampires would keep the machine and robot.

"Queen Victoria knows you plan on leaving the planet, another fact you humans have not shared with us," Shawn said.

He told them that vampires planned on staying and defeating Brendel. The reason the queen wanted the doomsday bomb with people to operate the device. Shawn had caught the humans by surprise with these demands.

Shawn told the heads the queen knew the federation was buying time to get their remaining population off the planet. They would only commit their armies for this task, and they desperately needed the vampires' assistance. Another fact that mortals had not shared with vampires. For Victoria, the humans were using vampires, and now she considered them a long shot to win. Mortals believed space was their salvation.

The heads of the federations entered, with dire expressions, took their seats, and motioned for all to find their places.

Madame Chair Brune, head of the European federation, look directly at Shawn. "Brendel's forces have overrun South America and are now entering the District of Mexico. The Kargarians have destroyed the Southern Federation Army, and the Army of the Americas are moving south to engage the Kargarians. Also, it looks like Brendel will soon start his attack from the east. The European and Russian federation armies will take a position to counter this attack. As you can see, Shawn, the final fight for this world survival has begun. The humans expect your queen to commit fully to the battle now!"

Shawn stood, and his eyes turned and glowed blue. "We will commit our forces, but what you want is cover to leave this world! You do not plan to defeat Brendel's forces! You plan to leave! Vampires can't leave this world; we have no choice. We have to stay and fight! What have you decided about the bomb?"

Head Chairwoman Fitzgerald of the American Federation stood suddenly with contempt on her face looking at the other chairs. "It wasn't humans that brought this on the world! It was your kind that brought their wrath! Evil was perfectly satisfied with the few souls harvested from this world. Your angel Eos has cost us everything we hold dear. Maybe you don't know this, Shawn, but we have some pretty powerful machines that can calculate almost anything and give us an answer. Not once have these machines told us we could prevail against this enemy and their numbers. Do want to know why we can't win! It was the easiest calculation of all!

"Enlighten me, please!"

The councilwoman again looked around the room this time she kept her voice low and measured. "Because your mother kept our population low. We do not have the numbers now!"

An uncomfortable silence came over the room. The humans looked at each other, afraid of what he would do. Shawn could sense their extreme tension. *They still did not understand vampires.*

Shawn looked down at the tabletop, ran his hand through his hair, and mumbled, "She is your mother too."

"We have decided on the bomb. There are two built. We will give vampires one, and we will dismantle the second and take it off-world. You will not need extra humans—the A.I. Max is capable of operating the equipment. I hope that pleases your queen. We are certainly aware you would just take it anyways!"

They continued the rest of the afternoon to work out details on the transfer of the bomb. Shawn again was told that humans desperately needed vampires to go south and commit to the battle. He told them he would do everything he could to convince the queen to fight for them. The heads gave Rachael a choice to join her family or continue with him and her mission. Rachael chose to go with Shawn. The following evening, Shawn and Racheal made the return trip to Dalton.

Chapter Twenty

S hawn had spent days at Dalton trying to convince Victoria that now was the time to commit the vampires to the fight. Lastly, he reasoned with the queen that humans felt Eos and vampires were responsible for bringing Lucifer's wrath to this planet. This had softened Victoria's take on the humans. Deep down, Shawn knew that Victoria felt the same way. Finally, Victoria had given her consent and sent ten thousand vampires under Katherine's command to support the Army of the Americas in the southwest. She had given him a warning that her patients were ending with the humans.

The day before, Shawn had come to the desert by flier with Rachael and Gwyn. The human army had made camp in the El Paso Territories part of the District of Mexico. The camp stretched for miles, and the vampire army had arrived two days earlier, led by Katherine, and was located in the center of the encampment. During the day, vampires would rely on human protection. Vampires stayed in tents with little else but their bedrolls and armor and slayer. They did not need air conditioning, just a place to get out of the harsh sunlight, unlike humans that had many more needs with their shelters.

The vampire location had taken a half-day to negotiate with the humans. The mortals were nervous having that many vampires in their midst.

Shawn sat outside Katherine's command tent, having his morning tea after sleeping through the night. He didn't have a shelter; besides, Katherine had been queen once, and she commanded this army, so her tent had plenty of room with amenities. Earlier, Rachael and Shawn had to say their goodbyes. She had received orders through her nanochip to travel five hundred miles to the rear to the mortal's central army command in Denver City.

Duty had called, and soon Shawn and Gwyn flew to a forward human observation post. On arriving, they met with a young human captain named Mike. He was scruffy-looking, sporting a week-old growth of whiskers, and much sweat covered his now dark, weathered skin. He was sure the humans strongly felt the heat here. Captain Mike brought them to the observation bunker, which was little more than a hole dug in the sand with sandbags for the walls and a synthetic plastic type of material used for the roof. The content absorbed the heat on the outside surface and produced coolness on the inside. That made the temperature slightly bearable for the mortals.

The humans in the bunker quickly moved aside as he came near. Shawn peered through the opening at the Kargarian army that fanned out for a hundred miles. He saw the heat waves come off the desert's baked sands, the bleak hazy horizon, and the cobalt blue sky overhead with a massive burning sun. Humans had buried Photon cannons and rail guns in the desert, only their muzzles showing. He looked farther off pass the first defenses of the Kargarians. Then to his dismay, he saw the enemy's witches and wizard gathering to counter the vampires. Because he was annoyed with this discovery, he brushed off the captain's attempt to hand him binoculars. Then he heard Gwyn say to the captain politely, "It's okay; he doesn't need them."

The Army of the Americas, with their superior weapons, had halted the Kargarian advance. Still, it was only a matter of time before the enemy army, and its overwhelming numbers would start their progress north again. They had already made their slight turn to the east, and it was apparent New Chicago was their goal.

Shawn sent his psychic energies across the sands and probed the strange alien minds of these creatures. The heat also bothered them, and he found many of the Kargarian with the same thoughts. How could so many have the same thought? He pondered the idea while gathering sand in his hand, watching it sift through his fingers back to where it came from. Then it hit him; they were a collective with a central mind authority. Briefly, he remembered the Kargarian gigantic world swarming with their numbers, a world overflowing with red soldiers. And then the signal that made him wince, Shawn faced the captain and told him to sound the alarm that the Kargarians would attack before the morning was out.

He peered out over the desert, looking at the hordes in front of him and then he realized, Captain Mike probably would not live through the day. These humans were brave. They faced death, though unlike vampires, many were not sure what that fate would bring. He had faced danger for over a millennium, but he always knew what would happen to him if he loss, unlike these humans that didn't know. *Who was braver,* he wondered.

Shawn and Gwyn went back to the camp and met with the commander of the army and told him to prepare for an attack. Then Shawn went to Katherine and found her sitting in her large royal blue tent with her captains gathered around discussing tactics. Shawn had often wondered where Katherine got her military mind. When human, she had always been a person in charge.

"What did you see?" Katherine asked as she stood and moved through her captains to greet him.

"The same, more Kargarians than you can imagine. They are going to attack soon. They want the sunlight."

"Then they certainly know we're here," Gwyn added.

Shawn leaned toward Katherine, a dire look on his face. "They have brought witches and wizards this time. We must be careful."

"That is certainly a complication," Katherine said.

"We will go to the portals and attack there that is our best chance," Kathcrinc said. "We all know we are here to support the humans not to win this war. If I take to many casualties, the army will leave. You know that, Shawn!"

"I am aware. I know what Queen Victoria has ordered." Shawn met Katherine's gaze and said, "Rachael told me what the human strategy will be from now on. They will kill as many Kargarians as possible until they are overwhelmed and then pull back, dig in, and repeat the process. Buying time is what the humans want so they can get as many of their kind off this world and into space."

"Then Victoria is right," Katherine said.

"Yes, she is, but I might have discovered something about the Kargarians. I have been probing their alien minds."

"How could you look into these creature's minds?" Katherine asked as she screwed her face up in discuss.

"It's not easy. This morning when I was at the observation bunker, I could see thousands of their minds. They all had the same thought! Also, in my early contacts with them, I noticed many of them moved in unison."

When Shawn finished talking, the sirens blared, and then the thunderous noise from the thousands of Kargarian particle cannons firing all at once. Plasma bombs after plasma bombs came from the guns, and the sound was overwhelming.

"We will talk more of this later," he heard Katherine yell, and then he heard her call to arms and saw the vampires scrambling for their armor, blasters, and slayers. The Kargarian's red balls of plasma streaked through the sky, landing all around them, their explosions shaking the ground along with his bones. The chaos of battle and the horrific noise overpowered the senses. The land became quickly soaked in death for hundreds of miles. Then came the whine of human rail guns and the multitudes of high energy photons streaking through the sky toward the Kargarians. Humans had been killing the Kargarians by the millions, yet still, they came, and the slaughter went on.

The vampires put on their armor, and by the hundreds, they lifted into the sky. Vampires used their abilities of physic projection to send the battle plan throughout their ranks. Ten thousand vampires formed a large arrowhead with Kathcrinc in the lead. They filled the sky and, in unison, turned and headed toward the portals in a desperate attempt to slow the numbers coming through.

Flying over the desert, Shawn saw the hundreds of thousand Kargarians storming across the desert toward the human's defensive positions. The sky filled with streaks of lasers and photons and their thunderous noise. The blistering fire from the human weapons would wipe out the first ranks, but the Kargarians kept coming. Thousands upon thousands of red soldiers would bash themselves against the human defenses, dying by the tens of thousands, again and again, until the Kargarians finally overwhelmed the humans.

He saw the obliterated outpost where he had met the captain. With his vampire's eyes, he located the partially exposed dead face of the man protruding from the debris. Onward he flew behind Katherine, and he felt Adeen's metal vibrating on his back in anticipation of the battle. Katherine turned, and the formation followed, then she descended, and they streaked over the desert until the five portals came into view. The Kargarians were bringing through supplies and their battle platforms.

The vampires flew toward the portals, and Shawn sent a telepathic message to the vampires, *harden yourselves, use your blasters, use your strength and speed and destroy as many as possible. Try to drive the burning wreckage back through the portals.* They banked again, and ten thousand guided missiles broke formation and flew straight for the Kargarians portals. In mass, the vampires attacked the war machines coming from the portals, driving them back or into the ground. The stronger would just penetrate the war machines with hardened bodies, tearing them apart, sending them to the ground in balls of fire.

Kargarian battle tanks floated from the portals bristling with plasma cannons and lasers and a never-ending stream of troop transports carrying red soldiers. The vampires would land amongst the Kargarians quickly, taking their heads and then driving the transport platforms into the ground. The battle went on, and Shawn heard the constant explosions, and everywhere hot plasma bombs and high energy photons streaked back and forth between the two armies. Death filled the sky. Vampires fired their high-velocity pulsar basters at the Kargarian war machines, tearing them apart, sending their burning wreckage whirling off in flames.

The Kargarians had located a staging area for their equipment a half-mile from the portals, and the vampires turned their wrath on the multitudes of battle tanks and troop transports. The vampires destroyed row upon row of the equipment. Still, the Kargarians poured from the portals. The vampires had to abandon the storage area and returned to the portals. The Kargarians were staging their final massive, all-out assault on this world. Shawn flew at the machines firing his blaster, dodging their fire, penetrating their war machine's armor, and destroying as many as he could.

The front of the portals became filled with laser fire. Many vampires were struck bursting into flames, their fiery bodies streaking to the desert and their spirits toward Heaven. The vampires began to push the war machines back into the portals, causing massive explosions. Finally, the portals wavered, plumes of blue fire shout outward, and then they collapsed in on themselves. The Valaris Wizards would need time to reopen them, but still, too many of the machines had come through.

The battle went on for hours, back and forth the plasma and photon bombs flew, the concussion of the explosions shook the ground the soldiers stood on. Eventually, the sun became too much for the vampires, and Katherine ordered a thousand to fly north to the Santa Fe territory and build a secret camp to protect them from the sunlight. The rest continued the attack, but finally, with little choice, Katherine ordered the vampires to the camp. Still, there were hundreds of thousands of the Kargarian battle tanks and troop transports moving north.

The vampires flew north over the desert, and Shawn positioned himself in the rear, looking for stragglers. The sun had drained much of the younger vampire's strength, and they were weak from the exposure. Shawn flew alongside, encouraging them. Large fireballs of plasma would shoot into the air as the Kargarian continued to fire on them. He saw millions of Kargarian soldiers swarming across the desert and over the human camp. All along their line, the mortals fired their lasers and photon cannons, giving cover for the retreating human army. Again, there were just too many of the swarming Kargarians, and again they move in precise unison.

Then without warning and no thought for the vampires, the humans detonated their atomics they had buried in the middle of the desert. The blast sent a large fiery mushroom cloud shooting up and out into the sky, killing a million Kargarians. Shawn accelerated away from the blast, but many of the young vampire stragglers where consumed by fire. He could feel the strong cry and despair of The Mother. Her plan had brought destruction to her world. The human army was going north, to ready their defenses again, and prepare for the next attack of the Kargarian army.

Shawn made it to the day camp that the vampires had prepared, and Katherine immediately came to him.

"How many stragglers made it back with you?"

"What you see here."

Katherine hung her head and shook it. "Mother, look at what is happening to your world."

"How many vampires do you think we lost?" Shawn asked.

"Five hundred," Katherine whispered. "The wizards killed many of them." Then her blue vampire eyes met his eyes, and he was surprised. He expected to see fear, but he saw her anger and resolve. She had been the first queen and had lost many vampires under her command. She had won a great battle at the

Gates of Hell, and that did not come cheap. She was a genuine military tactician, and now he knew she would not waver.

"We destroyed a lot of their war machines," Gwyn added.

"Nowhere near enough!" Shawn said.

Off to the east, Shawn saw two vampires flying toward them. They landed, their armor burnt and dented, their faces drawn and tired. Victoria had sent them, and immediately they informed Katherine and Shawn that the Tarragons had started their attack in the east. Unfortunately, the Russian and European Armies were in retreat. The Europeans were exhausted from the war they had borne the brunt of.

The scout told them the Tarragon's numbers weren't as many as the Kargarians, but they had more war machines. The vampire also informed Katherine that they were burning every city and town they came to on their way to New Chicago.

Brendel was going to treat the Americas differently and show this world how cruel he could be. The demon would send an evil message to the humans left on this world, submit to him or die a terrible death, and then they would deal with his father, Lucifer. Brendel would show this world his cruelty, his power.

Katherine nodded at the vampires. "Go rest…you have done well."

The messengers then told Katherine the queen was upset with the human's use of atomics, and she expected to know how many vampires the humans killed by the blast. Queen Victoria also commands you to stay for one more attack and then bring the vampires back to New Chicago.

Katherine then looked back at Shawn, gave him a weak smile, and told him, "We will talk more later after you have rested."

Shawn was tired and went to Katherine's tent to sleep and was now resting comfortably as he always did with Katherine and Gwyn next to him.

"Brendel has an unlimited number of soldiers and war machines," Shawn reminded. "Humans cannot win by themselves. Brendel has to be killed!"

"The Mother looks to you, Shawn, and my staff to kill Brendel," Gwyn whispered. "The Mother knows that is the only way, and I don't think Queen Victoria will have any more faith in the humans after what they did today."

"I know," Shawn said.

"We will attack the portals one more time," Katherine added. "Then, we will return to New Chicago and join the queen. I know Victoria wants to abandon Dalton and is sending ten thousand warrior vampires back to The Citadel. The war has quieted down there. The queen feels now the Citadel will be more defensible."

"I am not surprised. It is time to prepare for the future," Shawn added.

He laid thinking, trying to come up with something that would slow the Kargarians. This world needed a break. When the next attack started, he would try to find a central authority for the Kargarians. Unfortunately, today the humans had not helped their cause with the queen.

Chapter Twenty-One

T wo day had passed since Shawn came to the vampire camp. He had spent his time resting and thinking about his plan to find the central intelligence of the attacking Kargarian Army. Killing this mind would be different than killing their generals. When he destroyed the central brain, the whole Kargarian Army should come to a halt. He hoped. The central authority must communicate telepathically with all the others. That should make it easy for him to find the source.

Shawn sat outside Katherine's tent and sipped at his tea. Looking out, he saw the glow of the multitude of heaters boiling water for the vampires' awakening tea. The Kargarians finally broke off their attack, and now the humans had made camp a hundred miles to the south. Katherine ordered all vampires to stay out of the sunlight to save what ability they had to withstand the light. Some of their causalities had come from the bright desert sun. The sunshine was not unexpected but was becoming a problem for the vampires and their ability to help humans. Brendel understood vampires quite well.

Katherine and Gwyn sat next to him, and he told them of his plan to destroy the central brain. He saw the worried look on Katherine's face. A second messenger sent by Victoria had finished briefing Katherine. Julien, along with Braden, was with Victoria and the vampire army to the northeast. The messenger told her they beg the queen to let them into the fight, but he didn't think they saw action. Victoria was on the move headed to New Chicago with her army. Once Katherine joined the queen with her army, there would be thirty thousand vampires, half their army, to defend this continent.

"Julien will be all right," Shawn said. "He is with Braden and Victoria. She will certainly watch over them. They no longer are changelings. I know it is hard!"

"I'm sure you're right. We will stay for one more attack and then go to New Chicago. I hope your plan works, Shawn."

Shawn had turned in a little after midnight and now was awakening to a call to arms. The Kargarians had not waited long and were attacking again. It was early morning, and the sun was low in the sky, which was a break for the vampires.

They again took to the air, heading toward the forming portals. The reek of death and a haze of smoke covered the desert sand. Katherine had sent vampires to the west to set fires to the scrub pine forest. Now he saw fire and smoke billowing into the air giving cover for the vampires. This time they received much more fire from the Kargarians moving over the desert. Katherine sent a telepathic message for the vampires to fly higher and spread out. Shawn and Gwyn separated from the main body of the vampires and flew down low, avoiding the fire from the Kargarians. He used his vampire senses and probed for that commanding thought, and as he expected, it was easy to pick up. He looked to Gwyn for her confirmation and saw the nod of her head. They gained altitude and followed the mental signal south past the opening portals.

They had flown considerable distance from the battle when they came upon a small red dome placed on the hard-packed sands. They landed, and Shawn could feel the mind inside the dome. How many of these minds controlled the Kargarians, he couldn't guess, but in this world, it was this mind. Inside the vault was where he felt Lucifer's darkest of evil. Lucifer only had to conquer the central authority of the Kargarians to give him their world. The devil would find it much more difficult in this world. Humans are very independent, with many more minds and much to conquer. Small portals quickly opened, and elite Kargarian soldiers and many Valaris Wizards came through. Shawn and Gwyn had stepped into a hornet's nest.

Gwyn lowered her staff pulsed white energy at the Kargarian soldiers burning many were they stood. Shawn sensed the dome that was sending Brendel's commands to the red soldiers. The one command the brain was repeating, *Attack, move forward, kill the humans.*

The wizards fired their staffs, and Gwyn formed an energy shield with her staff and stepped in front of Shawn, absorbing the dark energy. The creatures continued their attack, but slowly through constant assault, the vampires advanced. Shawn gathered The Mother's power, stepped out in an attempt to clear a path, and threw the energy, killing two of the wizards.

The faceless wizards formed portals, step through, and disappear. Then the portals would develop in a different location, and they would step back through and continue their attack. Eventually, Shawn and Gwyn fought their way and put themselves between the hut and the wizards. Gathering Heaven's energy, Shawn pushed his hands toward the shelter. The energy with a loud thump hit the dome cracking it open, throwing some of the strange material up and away, leaving a large ugly looking creature behind.

The beast was shaped like a massive undulating transparent crimson blob, large at what looked to be the head, and then it tapered down at the other end. Four small appendages stuck out from its quivering pink body, probably what used to be legs. At the big end were little beady red eyes and a small slit that had been its mouth. Black streaks would form at points near the head and shoot through the body and disappear. The creature was mostly brain, surrounded by quivering fat, and it was the sole sender of the mental energy.

Gwyn continued to use her shield, and again Shawn drew on The Mother's power and pushed his hands outward toward the mind. Before the heat hit, the strange creature opened the small slit, and a loud piercing shriek came from the beast. The sound was painful to a vampire's brain, and it briefly stunned them both. The energy hit and blew the creature apart. Shawn and Gwyn fell to their knees, and Gwyn brought the staff around, spraying out white energy destroying the frozen Kargarian soldiers. The wizards missed their opportunity and did not charge but went back through the portals to Shawn's surprise. To check on his actions, Shawn allowed his senses to travel outward. In his mind's eye, he saw the attacking soldiers come to a halt, and some aimlessly wandering around, trying to regain the signal that gave them direction and purpose.

At first look, Shawn though his plan was going to work, but then a large portal opened, and thousands of Kargarian soldiers came through with their war machines. A second portal opened, and the wizards came back through surrounding another red dome with ragged beams of blue energy shooting up from their staffs. The energy formed a blue plasma field of protection around the dome. Shawn immediately sensed the tremendous energy coming from this Kargarian brain, as it reactivated the soldiers, which quickly resumed their advance. Shawn and Gwyn huddled behind the energy shield as the Kargarian soldiers and wizards returned their blistering plasma fire at them.

Then the Valaris wizards and the red dome floated into the sky, moved west, and disappeared. They used The Mother's protection to shield them from the fire. Shawn threw white energy at the soldiers, killing many, but as they did with the humans, they used their numbers, and slowly advanced on the vampires. Then a battle tank pulsed a plasma ball at them, blowing them back out onto the sands. The force had stunned them both and burned their clothes. They got to their feet, faces, and arms scorched by the blast.

A fit of terrible anger shot through him. "How dare you do this!" he screamed with Adeen raised in one hand and the other a Kargarian blaster plucked from the burnt earth. He fired and fired until the blaster glowed red from the heat, threw it to the side, and again screamed his rage at the Kargarians. "How dare you do this to my world!"

Gwyn again had formed a shield with her staff as the Kargarians responded with intense fire of their own. She yelled over the noise, "We have to leave, Shawn, there is no way we can stay here!"

"We have to kill these bastards!"

"We can't! They will destroy us, and where will that leave humans?"

Shawn looked through the shield with his vampire's eyes. He saw the multitude of Kargarians and their war machines preparing for an all-out assault on their position. He shook his head in anguish and realized Gwyn was right. They had failed to stop the Kargarians. They destroyed the first brain, but like everything else, the Kargarians had replaced it with another, and now they had to leave.

Fear for his world filled Shawn, as he and Gwyn lifted into the air and made their way back to the main portals, to Katherine, and the attacking vampires. Smoke rolled upwards into the air from the battle. Horrific explosions and then the concussion of the blasts hit them, pushing them back as they flew closer. Up and down, the forces of the explosions buffeted them as they made their way back to the primary battle.

Finally, they made it to the portals. The vampires swarmed the area, driving the war machines into the ground or back through the entrances. Some of the portals would waver then collapse, but this time new portals would open, as more and more of the Kargarians and their war equipment came through. He met Katherine on the ground and saw the hopelessness in her face as she looked over the battlefield.

"We failed!" Shawn shouted over the sounds of the explosions. "We destroyed one but a portal formed, and they brought another through with thousands of red soldiers. There were too many, and we had to leave."

"We are going to leave too! Katherine shouted back. "I have lost too many vampires on these portals. There are too many, and this is not the way vampires should be fighting them."

Suddenly, Gwyn's head went back, her eyelids fluttered, and she stared blankly off at the horizon. The Mother was sending her a message. Then she came back and warned, "The Mothers says leave here as quick as we can! We must hurry and gather the vampires!"

They took to the air and sent their telepathic messages screaming to all the vampires' senses. *Leave as quickly as you can! Fly north, hurry!*

The vampires broke off their attack almost in unison then flew up and north to safety with Katherine in the lead. Shawn and Gwyn flew over the battlefield and saw the devastation. Thousands of plasma bombs streaked over the desert toward the humans. In return, thousands of photon bombs came back toward the Kargarians. This carnage would not let up. He had never seen this much death in one place, not even through the Apocalypse.

The humans had lost half their army in these two battles, and they had killed millions of red soldiers. The Kargarian bodies littered the desert for hundreds of miles. The humans desperately kept up their fire, as their soldiers almost in a panic started retreating north toward the mountains. And then Shawn saw the hundreds of missiles coming from the north. They carried the explosive R486. The humans had discovered the material centuries ago, and it still was the most powerful conventional explosive ever devised. The substance was dangerous to make and was in limited supply. The humans were desperate, and most likely, this was all they had. Shawn and Gwyn accelerated upwards until they came to the edge of space and then turned north. Still, they could see the massive explosions from the battlefield; again, the humans were desperately trying to cover their retreat with no thought for the vampires.

Katherine had gone on with the vampire army to meet Queen Victoria and her army south of New Chicago. Shawn and Gwyn, with a thousand vampires, were following and giving cover for the retreating Army of the Americas. What was left of the army had split in two and moved north through two mountain passes, the McKenna Pass and the Lone Mesa Pass. Hovering troop transports and battle tanks stretched for miles in these two passes. Shawn and Gwyn traveled alongside a medical unit traveling slightly behind the main body of the retreating army.

There was a constant hum overhead of human fighter aircraft traveling south to engage the Kargarian bombers before they could reach the retreating army. Still, some bombers got through, and the horror of this day continued. Shawn heard the cracks and booms of the particle weapons, their beams searing through the atmosphere overhead carrying deadly plasma bombs toward their targets sending the humans into a panic. Fighter aircraft battled overhead; some would start their death spiral, sending particles of brilliant colored fire outward like fireworks at a summer fair. The medical transports would constantly pull over and unload the dead soldiers. The sides of this mountain pass were lined with the dead. Shawn would lead vampires into the sky to attack the fliers, but again they just became too many. Vampires did everything they could to protect the humans, and the mortals could see their extreme efforts.

The Army of the Americas was headed to Cape Girardeau Spaceport on the Girardeau plateau south of Denver City to protect the launchers while the humans made their departure. The spaceport was the largest in the world and one of the few still in operation. The mortals were committed to a constant cycle of transports lifting off with their human cargo. Once in earth orbit, they would load onto larger transports. When the transports were full, the humans connected them one after another until they made a train that stretched for miles. Last connected was a massive ion engine that pushed the train to the belt. The transports would return and repeat the cycle.

Shawn and Gwyn continued to follow the army north through the passes and watched as the humans took terrible losses in their retreat. He had sent word to Victoria that he needed more vampires to help protect the spaceport. Eventually, the human army made it to the Giradeau Plateau and set up defenses on the high ground, looking down at the valleys below. The next day, Shawn and company met a thousand more vampires sent by Victoria and made camp to the west of Denver City. Vampires did not want to stay with the humans, it was too dangerous, and Brendel's forces bomb the humans constantly. The newly arriving vampires informed Shawn that the Tarragons had defeated the eastern army, and it would only be a matter of days before they reached New Chicago.

Shawn stood at a bluff, looking down at millions of advancing Kargarians. Plasma bombs sailed over his head on their way to the spaceport. Photon bombs passed them as they traveled down into the valley to try and slow the advancing Kargarians. Behind him were plumes of smoke and fire as the spaceships kept up their frantic pace delivering their human cargo to the orbiting transports. Shawn decided he would use his forces to raid the Kargarians camps at night and try to do as much damage as possible to the enemy and their war equipment.

Humans now realized that the Kargarians would soon overrun the spaceport, and there would be no transports for them. Large groups of mortals were preparing to go into hiding, to disappear into the forests and mountains. This would be the second time in Shawn's long life he would watch humans learn a different way to live to survive in a new world. This civilization was in its death throes; soon, Brendel would defeat the humans, and that would leave only vampires. Certainly, The Archangel would then command The Queen to protect the few humans left. *Would Victoria except this? Again, humans hadn't warned vampires about the coming danger.*

Two eves had passed, and Shawn stood on a bluff overlooking a Kargarian camp. The vampires were preparing for another attack. The humans had finally stopped the advancing Kargarians. They held the cliff and had made the Kargarians pay for keeping the low ground. At his back, two thousand warrior vampires now stood ready, waiting for the order to attack. The portals had closed two days ago and had not reopened. This was a significant development, and Shawn wondered had the Kargarians finally spent themselves.

He looked and nodded at Gwyn. "Are you ready?

"I am love!"

Shawn raised his hand, motioned forward, and again the vampires lifted into the night sky formed, banked right and then down into the Kargarian camp. They would enter the camps at vampire speed, dodging fire and killing any Kargarian in their path. Another target was destroying their war machines before returning to the sky and back to the bluff. They had spent the last two nights attacking the Kargarians in this way. The camp was big, and it was hard for the red soldiers to know where the vampires would begin their attack. The vampires would repeat these attacks throughout the night, terrorizing the Kargarians, and then eventually fly north to their camp to avoid the daylight. This was a tactic that Shawn had learned long ago when he defeated John Brown's army at the end of the last Apocalypse.

Shawn was awakened midday by a vampire and a human military officer standing by his side. The human had a message to deliver. The Kargarians were leaving, moving northeast, and Denver City was in their path. The humans believed the red soldiers were taking too many losses here and were bypassing the spaceport, running north to Denver City, and on to join with the Tarragons.

Shawn looked at the nervous human. "Have the Kargarian portals reopened?"

"No, they have not," the human answered plainly.

Shawn went to the bluff and watched the massive Kargarian Army breaking camp their attack fliers lifting off and traveling north. The enemy was moving north, and Shawn still could sense Rachael in Denver City. He hoped she was making arraignments to leave the city and go north. With the looming destruction of the humans, Shawn decided it was too dangerous for her to be away from him. He would send a message to the queen and tell her because of the deteriorating position of the mortals; he would have to take possession of Rachael.

Chapter Twenty-Two

B rendel now traveled with the Tarragon Army. They were in full pursuit of the human army that had escaped across the sea. This time the Europeans were too weak and did not put up much of a fight. They would not escape him, and soon their end would come. The humans were defeated; it was only a matter of time. The Kargarians had petition Lucifer and complained about the losses they had suffered subjugating this world. They had asked for more compensation for their losses, and his father was not happy about this. He needed more Kargarians to drive a wedge between the two armies, to cut off the American military from the European Army. That would give him New Chicago and this world, but those filthy Kargarians had closed their portals, and by the time the negotiations were through, it would be too late.

Anger still seethed in him because of the loss of Samil. He had grown up with her, grown used to having her near. Now his rage was at his father as much as it was with Shawn. Samil magic had kept him looking like a young human, but now she was gone, and his black oil of darkness was coming to the surface for all to see. He must be careful, and he must defeat the vampires of this world, and that meant he must kill Shawn and the whore queens. Lucifer expected this of him and would not tolerate anything less of him, or he would end up like Samil. Shawn was the most powerful of vampires, and he must kill him first. Eos and the Archangel had given him high power, and even he must be careful with Shawn, or all could be lost.

The Demon Slayer was always in his way, and now, he knew why his father hated Shawn.

The key to Shawn was his new human lover. Brendel gave out a deep evil laugh. *How this vampire enjoyed love. How he loved these mortals. This time, it will be his undoing.* The human woman was in Denver City, and Shawn was not with her. He sat, pondered. *Was it time for him to make his move on the bastard who killed Samil?* He would direct the Kargarians to move their army to Denver City, to create a diversion and allow nothing to move north and wait for his arrival. He could only imagine what it would be like to tear Shawn's heart from his body or maybe watch his head fall to the ground.

☆☆☆☆

Shawn had woken early from his day sleep at their camp next to the White River a hundred fifty miles west of Denver City. Brushing a lock of hair from a sleeping Gwyn's face, his protector sent by Heaven, he kissed her lips lightly and went outside. He looked out at the sea of tents the vampires used for protection from the sunlight. The sky was hazy with smoke from the fires of the battles and the ones set by the advancing Kargarians. A dark, foreboding ring had formed around the sun from the smoke.

Earlier, one of his scouts told him the Kargarian Army was moving north through the Gunnison Pass and would certainly occupy Denver City. And for some reason, a large force of Tarragons was moving from the north toward Denver City. Rachael would have to make her escape and soon. The scout also told him the Army of the Americas had broken camp. The army had taken another pass, bypassing Denver City, so they would not be cut off from New Chicago and what was left of the European Army. It was apparent to Shawn; they were certainly not going to Denver City. In a few hours, he would wake his vampires, go to Denver City, and rescue Rachael.

Shawn now stood with Gwyn and his marauding vampires. They had drunk their tea, donned their armor, blasters, and stood at the ready. But the vampire's mood was sour. The humans had given up and now were fleeing this world. They were preparing to move their government to the belt. Humans were continually transmitting warnings into space not to approach the planet; evil and death await anyone who comes here. The human race was isolating their homeworld.

Stepping out, Shawn shouted to his vampires, "We go tonight to rescue a mortal. She is our link to the humans, however long that might be. Vampires will have to carry on the fight, and we will need her." He could see the vampires did not quite believe what he was saying, but they would follow The Demon Slayer, a Herit, and the maker of one of their queens.

The vampires lifted into the air, formed, and turned west toward Denver City. They followed the Arapaho Pass, hugging close to the mountains for cover. Smoke still drifted in the night sky that helped hide them from their enemies. Shawn led them forward, always with his senses at their highest. These were dangerous times. Soon Denver City came into view. He looked down and saw a small, quaint city with no towers. The inhabitants felt the mile-high city was high enough. All that was left was the inner part of the old city, and the outer areas humans had leveled centuries ago and now were pine forests or parks.

The Kargarians streamed into the city in large numbers, but still, a part of their army was also by-passing Denver city. Shawn could see heavy fighting around the government buildings located in the center of the city. Unfortunately, that was where he sensed Rachael. He felt the shock waves from the blasts as the two sides pounded each other. It was clear the humans would not last long in their defense of the city. Shawn used his vampire eyes and senses to look past the city and felt something was not right; something was hiding in the darkness like Samil did that night. He probed more into the ether for the subtle signal, but he couldn't see it.

He felt Gwyn's hand on his shoulder turned to see the worry on her face. "I don't know about this. Something is not right. Can you feel it?"

"I feel something, but it's elusive. Maybe it is signals from the north. Maybe the Tarragon Army. I can't leave Rachael!"

"I know! But The Mother does not want you to stay here long. That I know!"

Shawn turned and told the vampires. "A quick strike—if we can't reach her, we will leave. Are you with me!"

The vampires shouted their bravado, and then they took to the air, flew straight and true toward the government buildings. Plasma bombs came quickly and in large numbers at the vampire formation. The ground fire became intense, loud shrieks and intense light as the bombs went by. The buffeting caused the vampires to close ranks, but Shawn signal for them to spread out to better dodge the fire. Shawn looked down on the streets and saw the humans and Kargarians fighting, thousands of the enemy but only a few hundred humans. He saw photon bullets streaking through the streets and large hunks of the buildings torn from their smooth pristine walls, thrown out onto the ways, and now like the other cities, fire and smoke billowed into the sky.

Shawn and the vampire formation darted around a high-rise, preparing to dive toward the government building. Still, the vampires hit a large amount of pulsating energy, and then a blue dome formed around the government building. The vampires banked to the side and up to avoid the barrier. Then came the overwhelming sense of Tarragon as their battle fliers flew in and fired at the vampire formation. Shawn signaled the vampires to break off and headed west to their camp.

Shawn and Gwyn took cover on a terrace across the walkway from the blue dome. They crouched hiding on the terrace peering over the railing and then the sickening feeling of a demon. Shawn had felt this before but never this strong. He still could remember over a millennium ago with Victoria the sickness he felt, the overwhelming despair when he first came upon a demon. Grabbing Gwyn's arm, he said to her, "Focus, Gwyn do not let him into your mind."

Then came the hard-gritting sound of a million insects and maggots covered every surface their eyes could see. Brendel was near and showing his power.

"Focus," he repeated as he slowly willed the evil signs away. "Are you all right, Gwyn!"

"I'm all right! The demon is in the government building!"

"Damn it! Rachael is in there!"

"Now we know why the Kargarians stopped to attack Denver City," Gwyn whispered.

★★★★

Rachael had turned in early it was Ten, and she had just turned off the news of the evading Kargarians. The reports were always the same Kargarians were coming, and they couldn't stop them. This government complex had a day, maybe, before it was overrun. She would escape the city in the morning. She had occupied her thoughts by packing what few belonging she had left. The war had cost her everything her family, her belongings, her job, and now her planet.

Orders had come for the final departure, and she was to proceed with the other government officials to the spaceport at

St. Louis to be transported to the belt. That was not her plans, though; she would go north to the vampires and Shawn. His blood was in her, and she could feel the pull on her to his world. And it was this blood that allowed her to know he was near. She had showered because who knew where the next bath would come and had gotten into bed with her reader. She did not sleep well; a fear was always with her these days.

Rachael still remembered the first time she saw Shawn. How handsome he was, and he radiated warmth, a friendliness that was different from what she saw or felt from other vampires. From her studies, she knew all vampires were Heaven killers, and even with Shawn, that danger was felt. Sometimes she was suspicious of how quickly she fell in love with him, but Katherine told her she had felt the same way. Gwyn had told her he would not trick her because he knows it would be only a matter of time before you would know.

One, two, three loud booms, she heard, and the building shook and swayed. Rachael's world lost texture, it blurred, her head spun, a dark mist spilled into the room, flowed and hugged the floor, and it came with a sickening thick stench. A grinding noise like crickets sounded in her head, and the bedding crawled with maggots. Gasping, she brought her hands to her gagging mouth to hold back her supper.

Her door glowed a bright blue, and she could feel the slap of intense heat to her face as the door melted away. A medium-built man walked through, and nausea and fear followed him. When he entered, cold filled the room that made her lips quiver and teeth chatter and freezing her face with a look of horror. She gulped the cold air hoping it would help her with the intense fear she felt toward this man.

With great effort, Rachael's military training came to her as she rolled herself off the bed to stand but fell backward against the wall and slid to the floor, staring up at this man. Flashes of demonic visions went through her mind. Her walls became transparent, flowing with dark currents, and through them, she saw only darkness and a castle on a rocky hill. Massive black iron gates cracked open, and evil specters took flight, coming toward her and this world.

The man was not big but had used his magic to create a handsome face and body that would be pleasing to her eye. Still, his evil had grown to such a state it filled him, and he had so much darkness it erupted in small black pustules on his skin. The wounds would break open, and the demon would dab at them with a filth handkerchief. His eyes and hair were as black as night, and he wore a constant smirk on his purple lips. She knew this man was the destroyer of her world; this man was Brendel.

The demon walked over to her, looked down, and a smile spread over his face. He spoke with a pleasing voice, an alluring voice. "Rachael, I presume." He reached his hand down, took hold of her hair, and yanked her up. His face was so close it terrified her, his breath smelled of rotted vinegar, felt like ice, and it tore at her skin. She wretched and tried to turn her head, but Brendel held it firm and her head filled with darkness, enclosing her, wrapping itself around her, almost suffocating her. His voice resonated in her head, filling her with terror. "Can you feel him, Rachael? Feel the Demon Slayer. He is close! Isn't it exciting! He wants you! And for me to kill such goodness! I know you can feel him with his vampire blood in you."

The demon jerked her head and turned it to see a dark, sinister figure of a human rise from the corner floor. It stared at her with burning red eyes and flicking its long thick red tongue at her. The figure had darkness so deep no light could escape. Darker than the darkest of nights. She felt an unbelievable pleasure between her thighs, a sexual warmth, and then a hiss of a voice in her head. *I will see you soon.*

"Don't you want to go with my father?" Another deep laugh and the evil figure melted back into the floor and disappeared.

She tried to regain her senses and tried to regain her defiance. She forced herself to speak, only to hear a weak and terrified voice. "Shawn will kill you!" She tried to tear her arm away, but his grip was unbreakable.

"You humans are already defeated, and your vampire will do something stupid in trying to save you. He will be the one to die because of his pathetic need for love!"

"He is not going to save me. He is going to save humanity."

"We will see. You must know The Vampire Queen doesn't like humans." Brendel laughed and then got close and whispered, "I have a secret to tell you. Going to the belt will not save humanity." Again, his laughter filled her head. A sneer came to his lips, and he hissed, "It is time for us to go. Shawn is already getting ready to do something reckless, and it is not quite yet time. I want him to suffer a little more, become more desperate while I take care of you humans."

Brendel clapped his hand, her body lost all weight, and she rose from the floor into his arms. Her skin crawled, and again she wretched. He carried her out into the hall were a Tarragon stood, and by his size, this one was a lizard commander. The armor covered creature clack something to Brendel.

"Get your soldiers to the roof, we are leaving," Brendel commanded.

Rachael lost consciousness; the fear was just too much. She woke on the roof with two of the horrible creatures carrying her and dumping her into a flier. The inside of the flier wreaked with a terrible smell, and a thin layer of green grease covered the metal. She slipped and crawled to the back and sat holding her knees, shivering while the filthy creatures stared and clacked away at her.

★★★★

Shawn could feel the demon Brendel was after Rachael. The dome was small but thick and only covered the building Rachael was in.

"Fire your staff at the dome!" Shawn yelled in a panic.

Gwyn chanted a spell while lowering her staff and shot the energy of The Mother at the dome. The dome wavered but held firm. This brought Tarragon fliers firing at their position on the terrace. Shawn and Gwyn broke through the glass behind them, diving and rolling across the floor as the photons blasted through the walls covering them with debris. More fliers than came and joined the others firing at the building. The walls and floor shook from the blasts.

Shawn yelled at Gwyn, "This building is going to come apart! We can't stay here!"

Gwyn again chanted a spell that created a force field around them as they broke through the door and went into the hallway. Photons fired from the fliers punched through the walls of the hallway. Debris flew everywhere, creating dense clouds of dust and ash. Shawn and Gwyn made their way down the hall to a personnel lift. Shawn forced the door open and tore the lift from its shaft as the building continued to shake from the blasts. The vampires quickly climbed the elevator shaft to the top floor, broke through the ceiling, and crawled out onto the roof. Tarragon attack fliers filled the sky, and Kargarian troops were quickly surrounding the two government buildings.

Gwyn fired her staff, bringing a few fliers down, and they both flung the energies of Heaven down on the soldiers. But more and more of the Kargarians streamed into the area joined by even more Tarragon fliers. Plasma bombs landed all around Shawn and Gwyn, as they dodged their way to the edge of the roof.

The dome suddenly disappeared, and Tarragon transports filled the roof of the building. They were warming their engines, preparing to take off. Easily Shawn could sense the flier Rachael was in.

"Can you sense the flier she's in, Gwyn?" Shawn shouted as despair quickly overcame him.

"I can!"

"Shoot at the others and leave that one alone!"

Gwyn fired her staff, hitting one and sending it skidding off the roof and cascading down the outside wall to the ground in a ball of fire. Suddenly, the area darkened, as if a large dark cloud moved in front of the sun, and the stench of death filled the air. Brendel appeared, walked to the parapet of the roof, stopped, and looked across at them. He could feel Brendel's darkness probing, trying to penetrate his mind, but he threw the evil off and turned to Gwyn and shouted, "Shoot the bastard!" Gwyn sent an intense white plasma beam at Brendel, but the demon shot straight up, and the energy sizzled by him.

Brendel came back to the roof and then brought his arms up, gathering the dark energy and pushing it at them. Gwyn raised her staff just in time, blocking the evil power, but still, the force threw them from the building across the way and into another building. They fell to the ground, and Kargarian soldiers quickly surrounded them. Shawn raised Adeen, and the slayer hummed and glowed as he pressed the attack.

"Come on, you filthy bastards!" Shawn screamed as he watched the flier that held Rachael leave the building, turn, and head east. Tarragon attack craft quickly surrounded the flier.

Shawn swung his slayer with abandon cutting the Kargarians down in waves. Still, they came. Tarragon attack fliers flew in, circled, and dove at them firing their weapons.

"We have to go after Rachael," Shawn yelled in desperation.

"It is too dangerous; we could destroy the flier and kill her."

"We have to try!"

Then Shawn felt Gwyn's hand on his shoulder, jerking him around, and he saw anger in her eyes. She screamed at him,

"She is already dead! We have to leave this place before they kill us! The Mother will not allow me to let you go! The Mother cares for this world, not a single mortal like Rachael!"

Then Gwyn grabbed his arm, pulled him across the street away from the Tarragons and Kargarians, and pushed him into an alley. He forced himself from Gwyn's grip and yelled, "You are my changeling; how dare you do this to me!"

"You left me no choice. You are my maker, but I answer to a higher authority. I told you when we first met that I would not be a typical changeling. First, I am a mother's witch and then a vampire. And you need to learn to accept The Mother's power; you must also show allegiance to her not always to Michael."

Shawn looked east and whispered a promise, "I will find you, my love!"

Shawn still could see Gwyn's anger, and now she stood squire in front of him, holding her ground. A changeling defying him was knew for him.

"What did you expect?" Gwyn said, as the anger left her face and replaced by a look of concern, a look of deep love. "A Demon Slayer that Lucifer himself swore to destroy with a mere mortal woman—how long did you think she would live?"

"I was supposed to protect her. She was my responsibility."

"And now she is with Brendel and probably dead."

"She is not dead!"

Shawn brushed pass Gwyn and walked out onto the street, looked to the sky, and only saw Tarragon attack fliers. He turned to Gwyn and nodded. They lifted into the air and traveled back to their camp in silence.

Chapter Twenty-Three

S hawn's mind raced as he flew back to camp. The fresh air blew against his face, giving him no relief from his fear. Every so often, he would scream out in anger. Gwyn flying to his side would look at him as if he was a madman. He would find Rachael, her blood was in him, and Brendel couldn't hide her forever. The demon had taken Rachael for a reason, probable to draw him in. Who knew a demon's motive; usually, it was pure evil. Whatever the reason it didn't matter, he must go after Rachael, and the beast knew it. Then a more intense fear burned its way through his body. *What if the demon killed her, to spite him!*

Shawn was responsible for two thousand vampires. He would take them back to New Chicago, then find Rachael and finally kill Brendel. The afternoon was late when they arrived at camp. A smokie haze still filled the skies from the fires. His marauders had taken refuge in their tents, waiting out the sun. A tired Shawn and Gwyn went to their tent, and inside found Julien with armor and slayer at his side.

Shawn looked at Gwyn with complete surprise and moaned, "Does Katherine know you are here? This is not a good time. This is a dangerous place right now."

"I know it is, Shawn. And I left without telling her! I told my maker the world is burning, and no vampire is safe anymore! Every vampire must fight! It has been over a hundred years since Braden and I were turned. Our makers still try to control us. I will fight alongside vampires. I chose you. I hope you don't mind!"

Shawn stared at Julien, probably with his mouth open and then spoke. "Well, I hope she is okay with it. She will have to be for now!"

Shawn saw the apprehension in Julien's face. He was a young vampire, and he might not live to be an old one. Coming here took courage. Katherine probably wasn't able to talk him out of this. Surprisingly, Braden wasn't with him, but Victoria wasn't easily tricked or pushed around. He knew how Katherine was and knew the fear she was feeling for Julien.

"I need to honor my family," Julien said, "to show the Bryces that came before me that I can be a great warrior. That I am worthy of their name!"

"We will be fighting creatures that are more powerful than you," Shawn said. "And I know you are not used to that, but you are Katherine's changeling and a Bryce. I will do my best with you." Shawn finished speaking, and then he felt the dark energy of the portals cutting their way through the boundaries of space into his reality. He yelled to Gwyn, "Portals are opening!" They quickly ran outside amongst the tents yelling, "To arms! To arms, portals are opening!"

The vampires poured out of the tents pulling on their armor, slayers, and blasters. Then the rising hum of the dark energy, the swirling blue fire, and two portals formed. A lizard commander strutted from each opening, and then a loud shrill came from both as they brought their blasters down and pointed them at the vampires. When the lizard commanders went silent, to Shawn's horror hundreds of Tarragon Wizards, adept in black magic, flew from the portals directly at the vampires.

Shawn shapeshifted and grew himself into his most fierce vampire form. He raised a glowing Adeen and shouted, "To battle! Follow me!"

The vampires flew up and toward the Tarragon Wizards, clashing in mid-air. The meeting of their energies created a boom that echoes down the valley. Shawn parried the intense fire and, with blinding speed, took two wizards' heads. Turning, he eyed the two lizard commanders standing near the portals. He flew at them using Adeen to block the fire coming at him. Still stinging from the loss of Rachael, in his vengeance, he brought his fist around, smashing it into one of the lizard's face, caving his head in. The beast fell to his knees and then crumpled over dead. He swung around, driving his slayer into the neck of the other, lifting him from the ground, screaming his hate at the lizard commander. He flung him aside and watched the creature stagger toward the portal. Again, Shawn was on him driving his slayer into the monsters back and to the ground.

He stood above the lizard commander and shouted, "Is that all the fight in you? Vampires will kill all of you!" Shawn brought Adeen down and took the lizard's head.

He turned back and flew into the battle, striking down wizard after wizard. He would block their dark energy, dodge, fly up, loop, and in an instant, came back around behind them and took their heads. Wizard, after wizard, tasted his blade and fell from the sky. Many of the vampires, especially the younger ones, were also lost due to the dark energy of the wizards. The vampires continued to press the attack, swarming the Valaris Wizard with their vampire speed, swift use of their slayer, and an assist from their blasters from time to time. The marauders slowly took the upper hand. Now was the time to show the wizards who was the better.

Shawn looked across the battle and saw Julien fighting alongside Gwyn. He was a young vampire, and Shawn could see he was tiring, yet Gwyn protected him and kept the wizards from him. They pushed the Valaris Wizards back, and when defeat was near for the wizards, they broke their ranks and flew back toward the portals. The wizards went through the portals, and all went quiet.

When evening came, Shawn, Gwyn, and marauders flew northeast toward St. Louis through the thick smoke billowing into the air from a burning Denver City. This was the second time in his life he had seen the mountain city destroyed. On this continent, the demon armies were burning everything that was of value. Shawn flew over the countryside and saw what was left of humanity, making their way north.

The vampires turned north and soon came to a large, flat, wooded area. Ten Tarragon attack fliers were circling shooting into the trees at targets on the ground. Quickly, Shawn realized there was at least a division of America's Army in the woods firing back at the fliers. Shawn led the vampires in a circle around the wooded area and then signaled for the vampires to attack the fliers.

When the Tarragons saw the vampires coming, they broke off their attack and tried to head east, but the vampires quickly overtook the fighters. The fliers banked and looped, trying to avoid the rapid pulsing photon bullets of the vampire's blasters but to no avail. After the last Tarragon flier took its plunge to the ground Shawn, and the vampires circled, landed in the trees where the humans had taken refuge. This division of the American army was now ragtag much of their fighting equipment destroyed. To Shawn's surprise, they were protecting what remained of the human government and by the looks of it were heading west, not toward St. Louis and the spaceport.

Madame Chair Brune and Head Chair Fitzgerald greeted Shawn. They and a hundred government officials were all that was left of the human government in this world. Shawn offered a weak smile, but their dirty faces returned none. Now their once fine clothes were soiled and tattered, and only anguish came from them.

"What has happened? Shawn asked quickly.

Tears came to Madame Chair's eyes. "The European Army has been destroyed. There is no army left to stop the devil's armies from taking New Chicago."

"Where are you going to go?" Shawn asked as he felt his spirit sinking. This was the end of the world.

Head Chair Fitzgerald answered, "The Army of the Americas is now heading west. They will set up a line of defense along the Cheyenne River. That will allow this government to make it to the Seattle Spaceport. It is the only spaceport left."

"What about the rest of the people?" Shawn demanded.

"The spaceport will stay open longer to allow for stragglers. There are not many people left. They have left for the belt, or the demon's forces have killed them. We must ask you and the vampires to look after the few that are left behind."

"We will do our best," Shawn said. "Your action in the last two battles didn't do much to win the queen's trust."

Madame Chair Brune then said, "We had to leave the bombs behind. Unfortunately, they are in St. Louis, and the Kargarians now occupy the city.

"Why would you do that?" Shawn demanded his anger now starting to show. "Those bombs were going to save this world."

"There was no time. It happened so quickly," Head Chair Fitzgerald mumbled. "Our intelligence did tell us that the Kargarian army is half the size it was, and for some reason, their reinforcements have stopped."

"Where are they located in St. Louis?" Shawn asked.

An image of a map appeared in front of them, and Madame Fitzgerald pointed to an area. "The bombs are deep under this armory. The Kargarians have occupied the building, but according to our sensors, we believe they are not aware of the bombs below."

Then an architectural drawing appeared in front of him. Head Chair Fitzgerald points to a spot in the cellar of the building. "Behind this protective wall is a secret, secured door that leads to stairs. The vault is a hundred feet down. You must use the combination I am going to give you. If you try to force the vault door, they will fuse shut, and the bombs will be destroyed."

Head Chair Fitzgerald then handed Shawn a small silver disk. "All the information you need is in here. Your queen has

Max, and the A.I. knows how to do the calculations and assemble the bombs. Listen to me carefully. You cannot use the bombs in this world. The bombs will start a nuclear chain reaction in the planet's core. Any planet you detonate them on will be destroyed. The A.I. will not detonate the bombs on this planet. Do you understand!

"I understand," Shawn answered.

"I hope you do!" Madame Chair Brune replied.

"We haven't heard from Rachael," Head Chair Fitzgerald said. "Do you have any information about her?"

"I do," Shawn said, trying to hold back his anger. "You left her exposed, and now the Demon Brendel has her!"

"Pity, we could have used her."

Shawn watched the Madame's faces, but there was no change. Their faces already wore the mask of shock from the destruction of their world. A low hum could be heard over the trees as transport fliers landed amongst the trees. Overhead fighter aircraft circled to give cover.

"It is time for us to leave," Madame Chair Brune said. "Thank you for what you have done for us."

A hologram appeared, and an exited pilot told the humans to hurry, enemy fighters where on the way.

"Go!" Shawn said. "We will cover your escape. I hope someday you can come back to your world."

"Do you think Rachael is dead?" Head Chair Fitzgerald asked.

"She could be, but I will try to find her. Go, there isn't much time!"

The humans quickly went and boarded the transports, lifted into the air, and accelerated west at high speed. Minutes later, Shawn heard the whine of the Tarragon fliers as they approached. Shawn and the marauding vampires met the aircraft, and for over an hour, the sky battle rage. The vampires and attack fliers swarmed the sky overhead with sharp turns and loops. Burning Tarragon fliers spiraled to the ground, followed by long tails of smoke. Eventually, the losses became too high for the Tarragons. The will to stay and fight left them and they broke, making their escape. Tarragons did not accept the kind of losses the Kargarians would.

A few hours later, a tired Shawn and marauders landed at Victoria's camp, their faces dirty, and their armor dented and burnt by battle. The vampires broke rank, scattered, and went to their tents exhausted. An approaching Victoria and Katherine, followed by Braden, greeted Shawn, Gwyn, and Julien.

"How many did you lose?" a solemn Victoria asked.

"I am sorry, my queen. I lost a hundred and fifty-eight vampires."

Victoria just nodded and mumbled, "Well, we will probably lose more. We must prepare ourselves."

Katherine embrace Julien and Shawn saw the fear on her face as she spoke, "It looks like you had a time. Was it what you thought it would be?"

"No, it wasn't. There is nothing grand about war."

Braden stood with his shiny untouched armor and asked. "You have seen battle, brother?"

"I have," Julien answered wearily.

"He has seen battle," Gwyn shouted for all to hear. "And he fought well! He is a Bryce!"

"Maybe the queen will now," Braden mumbled as he looked at Victoria, "allow me to bring honor to the Kenmare name."

"Not here. We will speak more of this in private, Braden." Victoria said sternly then turned to Shawn. "There has been a development with humans. I need to meet with you, Shawn."

Victoria turned and started toward her tent. "Braden, I want to talk. Follow me!"

"You and Gwyn can stay in my tent," Katherine said. "I am so sorry about Rachael."

"I have not given up on Rachael!" Shawn said plainly. "I will find her, and Brendel will pay for what he has done!"

Hurriedly, Shawn, Katherine, and Gwyn made their way through a multitude of tents on their way to Victoria's. Gwyn and Shawn had cleaned the grime of battle from their bodies and rested. Shawn had continuously thought of Rachael, how to save her, and where Brendel might take her. Probably the demon took her to the center of the Tarragon Army for protection.

As they walked, Katherine spoke in a shaky voice. "Rachael is probably dead."

"She is not dead, or I would know. I have taken her blood, and she has tasted mine. Rachael is alive!"

"Brendel loves to torment," Gwyn reminded. "Remember, he is the devil's spawn!"

"Let's see what the queen wants. I'm sure she knows about the bombs."

They approached the large, blue dome tent of the queen. The five covenants banners were waving in the breeze. They went in and saw Victoria, Wodan, Gormal, and Amrit, the remaining leaders of the covenants. The covenant leaders greeted Shawn and Gwyn, and coolly greeted Katherine, still a little bad blood from his saving.

"Have a seat," Victoria commanded, as she waved to some chairs.

"I would like to inform all what I know at this time. The European and Russian Federation armies have been destroyed, and survivors have blended into the countryside. What's left of the human government has fled New Chicago and are heading west to the Seattle spaceport. The humans did not deliver the doomsday bombs to us and, as usual, did not live up to their agreement. We do have Max, which we found out is perfectly capable of handling the bombs and opening the necessary portals."

"The humans have given up!" Wodan spat with disgust on his face.

"They have!" Shawn said. "They are leaving for space and left us to defend this world. The Army of the Americas is retreating west toward Seattle to protect the only spaceport left in this world."

"The humans have lost this world!" Gormal declared.

"We have one positive outcome," Victoria answered. "The Kargarians have suffered great losses in their battles with the humans, and their reinforcements have stopped. No portals have opened for them. And stranger still, they have camped at St. Louis."

"I believe I have the answer to that," Shawn quickly added. He took out his little silver disk and asked to see the drawings. The drawing of the city appeared and then the drawings of the building where the bombs are kept. "This is the building the bombs are in. Here in the basement is the door to the lift. The bombs are a hundred feet down."

"How did you come by this information?" Victoria asked.

"We ran into Madam Chair Brune and Head Chair Fitzgerald. We fought off the Tarragons for them. Shawn then looked at the rest in the tent, the commanders, and the covenant leaders. "The Queen is right! Soon we will be the only ones left to defend this world. And we need those bombs."

"Then we will have to get them," Victoria declared.

"The Kargarians are vulnerable," Shawn said. "There are a half-million of them at the most, and their equipment is damaged. We should attack them full force. I mean, you should attack full force. I am going after Rachael."

Shawn could feel Victoria's eyes burning into the side of his face, and then he heard her angry voice. "There have been only a few times in our long existence together that I have wanted to throttle you, and this is one of them." Then to Shawn's surprise, emotion took over Victoria, and she slammed her hand on the table. "I command you! You will stay with me! And you will help me retrieve the bombs!" Then Victoria softened, and her love for him showed for all to see. "You just can't help yourself. You have to try to save everybody."

Shawn had known Victoria for more than a millennium, and he could see the stress in her eyes. When the humans left, she would be Michael's only legitimate ruler of this world, and it would fall to her to save it. She was desperate to retrieve the bombs. Braden's revolt on her authority was not helping matters, and he also sensed worry for Peter in Amsterdam.

The meeting went on for a considerable time while they worked out the battle plan against the Kargarians and St. Louis. The vampire army would waste no time and attack the next eve. They would enter the city at three locations. Victoria decided Wodan, Amrit, and Gormal each would lead a third of the vampires in the assault on the town. With Katherine as the overall commander of the attack. Thirty thousand warrior vampires would attack the Kargarians and unleash their supernatural powers on them. This would distract the Kargarians, and then Shawn, Victoria, and Gwyn would enter the armory and retrieve the bombs.

Chapter Twenty-Four

I t was late afternoon the next day. The setting sun painted the horizon with reds, pinks, and purples. The smoke from the battles had settled for now. Shawn stood with Victoria, Katherine, and Gwyn, watching thirty thousand vampires taking flight in groups of hundreds. The three covenant leaders also were standing with them, ancient and powerful vampires, and the young ones Julien and Braden. There had been considerable tension with them, but they had won out and now would join the battle. Katherine had assigned Kalila Sadik, a vampire she had met centuries ago in Istanbul when she hunted one of Drakes killers, to be with them. Kalila had become a powerful vampire and schooled in the art of handling a slayer. She was known to be smart, cunning, and skilled in the art of killing Lucifer's witches.

The vampires would circle until all had taken flight, and their leaders had joined them. Then, they would fly directly to St. Louis, and it would only take minutes for them to arrive. Surprise was the name of the game this evening. There had been great animosity between Katherine and Amrit during the time of his rescue. Shawn still could feel the tension between them, especially when she gave him an order. He saw how they looked at each other. The ancients were never fond of Katherine being queen. They thought she was too young, and they were far more important. Still, Michael was upset with the covenant leaders, wanted to put them in their place, and young Katherine, a descendent of Anne, became the first queen.

Shawn was hopeful about tonight. Something had gone wrong with the Kargarian portals, and the vampires were well-rested. They would give the Kargarians all they could handle and hopefully more. They wore their armor and slayers, and human weapons, pulsars on their backs or blasters at their sides. If all went well, he would leave the vampires and search for Rachael. Victoria did not want him to be close to the humans, though. She always had a fear of him being with humans, a fear that had come from Heaven through Drake, but he would not abandon Rachael and leave her to a horrible fate with Brendel.

All the vampires had taken off and now circled above, blocking out the stars. Victoria took Deceida, held it high, commanded Katherine and the ancients, "Go and lead my vampires in battle! Lead them well!" She turned to Braden, and Julian gave them a weak smile, trying to hide her fear for them. "You two stay with Kalila! If you must go bring honor to the Herit covenant, and if you perish—I will see you in Heaven!" She then turned to Kalila and whispered, "Watch over them!"

The vampires split their ranks into threes and then streaked to their targets. Shawn, Gwyn, and Victoria lifted into the air to follow. They had considered bringing Max with them but decided it was too risky, so they instead would bring the bombs to the A.I. Soon the towers of St. Louis came into view, and then the Kargarian outer defenses began their assault on them. Plasma beams streaked past them, silhouetting the towers against the early evening sky. As planned, a section of the vampires veered and attacked the plasma cannons.

Katherine's company followed Wodan's division and came directly into the city from the east. Thousands of vampires landed in the streets at ground level and with blinding speed set upon the Kargarian soldiers killing them by the tens of thousands. They pushed the evil army back down the streets, scattering their ranks throughout the streets of the city. The vampires moved so fast the enemy couldn't target them. Photons from the vampire's blasters seemed to appear out of nowhere and tore the red soldiers apart.

The Kargarians set up plasma pulsars on the towers and fired hot balls of energy down on the vampires. The extreme temperature of the gas killed many. Swarms of vampires came streaking down from the sky, attacking the Kargarians on the towers to quiet their intense barrage of bombs. A massive explosion shook the city, a high tower leaned and then collapsed upon itself, sending fire, smoke, and debris billowing into the sky.

Shawn, Gwyn, and Victoria landed in the center square, ten blocks from the armory, and quickly took cover in a narrow alley between a small building. The plasma cannons had made it too dangerous to fly directly to the armory. A detail they had not planned on. Destruction was everywhere, and fire, chunks of buildings, and steel from the towers rained down all around them.

Shawn, with Adeen in one hand and a blaster in the other, shouted, "Follow me!"

He flew across the square, followed by Victoria and Gwyn, with plasma bombs landing all around them. Into another alley, they darted, and Shawn scanned the area, and then hugging the buildings they worked their way down a street that led to the armory. Bombs from nearby towers landed around them. Shawn would roll out his hand, sending the energy of The Mother streaking to the target, blasting the red soldiers out into the air, and an extended tumble to the ground.

Victoria pointed to a rooftop. "Let's fly to that roof. We can see better."

On arriving, they took cover and soon saw two hovering pulsar tanks coming down the street.

"I don't think they saw us," Gwyn whispered.

Shawn looked over the parapet. "When they are underneath us, we attack." Gwyn and Victoria nodded, and within seconds they all jumped over the wall and landed on the tanks. Shawn drove his slayer down through the metal, burning its way into the tank's power supply. The hatch slid open, and laser fire shot out. Shawn stuck his blaster down into the tank, firing multiple shots until the sides blew out. Gwyn and Victoria did the same with the other tank. They jumped from the burning wreckage, and moved down the street, building to building, sometimes flying to a roof to survey the area. They returned to the streets and continue to work their way to the armory. Finally, they arrived at the fortress buildings were the bombs were kept.

Shawn pointed. "That is the building we want. Cloak your thoughts. No one can know our purpose here."

Kargarian soldiers and two pulsar tanks guarded the steel entrance door. Using his supernatural senses, he forced himself to see into their minds, found their controlling mind, and sensed wizards escaping west with the brain. Shawn ducked back around the corner, shook his head to get the sensation out.

Victoria commanded, "Gwyn, use your staff to take out the tanks. Shawn, as soon as Gwyn destroys the tanks, we attack the soldiers."

Shawn nodded, and they all stepped out into the open. Gwyn lowered her staff and fired a white plasma beam of energy striking the tanks and laying them open, spraying metal and fire out over the street. Shawn and Victoria raced across the square their slayers from Heaven swinging. They plunged into the Kargarian ranks, stabbing, slicing, and taking their heads. Within minutes, they killed a hundred Kargarian guards.

"Step aside," Gwyn yelled from behind. Then a beam of white energy hit the door, melting it to the ground. They entered slowly and quickly felt multiple massive explosions shake the building. They steady themselves, went down a hallway, and came to a large command room with its equipment and electronics destroyed. Suddenly, more explosions and the building shook violently. Victoria grabbed Shawn's arm and, with a tense voice, asked. "Do you think this building is going to stay together?"

"Hope so!" Shawn replied. "It is an armory!"

"That's reassuring!" Gwyn answered.

They continued and came to another metal door. Shawn took the small disk from his pocket, asked where the changing room was, and a map of the building appeared in front of him. He studied it briefly and then waved it away and nodded toward the door in front of them. "This is the changing room. Gwyn, we have to go through this door. If you will do the honors."

They step back and again, Gwyn made short work of the metal door. Row after row of blasters held in their carriages filled the large room, and many cases of small metal cylinders that held the firepower for the weapons.

Shawn pointed across the room. "Through that doorway is the lift that leads to the basement."

They reached the lift, and Shawn forced the sliding door open, looked down the shaft allowing his powerful senses to scan for any sign of life below.

Shawn turned and said, "There is nothing alive down there."

They stepped, floated to the basement and entered what looked to be an underground firing range.

"The stairs are back in the far corner behind that shield wall," Shawn pointed and said.

Gwyn disintegrated the security door, and down the stairs, they went. They traversed a long flight, hit a landing, and continued down another long flight until they came to a metal vault embedded in a concrete floor. There were no signs, markings, or any warnings of what was in the vault.

Shawn asked the silver disc for the combination, and it appeared in front of him. He keyed in the code and opened the vault door. Inside were four metal briefcases, and each case held a silver cylinder, half of a bomb. Suddenly, all kinds of warnings appeared, floating in the air, telling of the horrors for any who dared tamper with the cylinders.

"Damn," he whispered. "Who would build such a thing?"

"Humans," Victoria sighed. "But this might save us."

They closed the cases, went back up the stairs, and made their way out into the square. It was empty, and ash floated down like a winter's snow, covering everything in sight. Shawn listened and heard the fighting now on the western outskirts of the city. In the sky, swarms of vampires circled, preparing to attack their next target. Now only a few plasma beams were seen lighting the sky, as vampires had destroyed most plasma cannons.

Victoria wiped the soot from her face and told Gwyn, "Take the bombs back to our camp. Shawn, you and I will join Katherine."

"Please, my queen," Gwyn said, "The Mother wants me to stay with Shawn!"

"He answers to Michael! Like all guardians! Do as I say!"

Gwyn looked at him, and he shrugged what could he do. Gwyn tried to hand the Mother's Staff to him, but he told her to keep it. He had Adeen. Gwyn again looked at Victoria with a questioning look, but no words were returned. Shawn watched her hesitantly take the cases and leave for the camp. Shawn knew Victoria wanted to go where Braden was, or she would have taken the bombs.

"Your witch likes to question me!"

"She is a witch and then a vampire, and unlike you, she has to answer to The Mother. And I would not be here if it wasn't for her and The Mother."

Victoria nodded her acceptance and sighed. "We all fight for the same idea. Let's go!"

They left the building their slayers drawn and holding a blaster. The explosions had subsided, and Kargarian blood covered the streets. Ash continued to sprinkle down, fire and smoke billowed into the air, and more towers had taken their fiery trip to the ground. The destruction of St. Louis was almost complete. They came upon a patrol of vampires covered in Kargarian blood. Surprise to see Victoria, they bowed, and one told her, "We have defeated the Kargarians, My Queen. What is left of them have left the city and are retreating west. They are probably trying to join the Tarragons."

"Have you seen any portals opening?" Victoria asked.

"None, my queen."

"Have you heard from Katherine?"

"Katherine has selected a rallying point, and as soon as our patrol is over, we are going there. My queen, we have made a discovery. We think it might be of importance. If you would follow us?"

Shawn and Victory followed the patrol to a destroyed police precinct building. They went in, and the vampires showed them a room with bodies lying on the floor covered with a sheet.

"We thought this would be important!"

Shawn knew immediately who these people were, and Victoria did too. Shawn walked over to a body, pulled the sheet back, and reached to the next and did the same. They were Madam Chair Brune and Head Chair Fitzgerald, and the rest of the bodies were government officials and aides to the head chairs. The last of the human government had not made it to the spaceport.

Victoria turned to the patrol. "Return to your duties." She then said to Shawn, "This is how it ends for the mortals."

Shawn stood, staring at the bodies. "Mortals aren't finished. They will be back, remember that, Victoria. And guardians must avenge them."

"Why?" Victoria questioned.

They are the face of humanity! The leaders of humanity and I will avenge them! I will kill Brendel for what he has done!

"Again, I tell you, you can't save everybody!"

Chapter Twenty-Five

B rendel slammed his hand on his table. He was having his evening meal when a Tarragon had informed him of the vampire's victory. He had selected the Kargarians for their numbers, but they were weak. He also was told the queen, The Demon Slayer, and his whore witch had forced their way into the armory. He had asked what they were after, but these filthy lizards did not know. All the Tarragons knew was battle, no finesse came with them.

Brendel screamed at the Tarragon commander, "Find out why or I will have your head!"

Eating was one of his favorite past times in this world. The servants always made a production when he ate. His table was full of earthly delicacies. After all, gluttony was one of his father's favorite sins. The Kargarians were finished, he had led them to the slaughter and had watched the humans kill them by the millions. Killing seemed to be a skill the humans were good at. There would be no more Kargarians, but there were the Tarragons, and they were better soldiers.

There were few humans in this world now, and soon he would begin the hunt for the ones left. First, he must subdue the vampires, but it would not be an easy task. He needed more Valaris Wizards. Lucifer was using his unique type of persuasion with the Valaris Wizards. Still, it would cost the devil more power than he cared to spend. He looked down the table at the human woman picking at her food. Humans, how he hated them for their weakness, so easily killed. There was no fun in killing one human, but he did want to snap this one's neck. Not now, though; that would come when he was finished with her.

"No appetite tonight, my dear Rachael?" Brendel sneered.

A low weak voice came back. "It's the company."

Brendel gave a deep laugh; how quickly a look of disgust had replaced this human's look of fear. What bravado she tempted to show, but he knew she was afraid; her fear radiated from her, and he could see her thoughts of suicide. She would do anything to escape him, but that thought quickly changed when he informed her what killing herself would bring. He certainly would make sure she died but not yet. Her price for falling in love with The Demon Slayer would be her soul.

"Your vampires have been victorious," Brendel hissed back. "The Kargarians are defeated in this world."

"You will not conquer the vampires. They will kill all of the Tarragons as well."

"We will see my dear Rachael." Then another evil laugh. "That will lead to your death and my father having your soul."

The commander returned, and Brendel could see his fear. Rarely did the Tarragons show fear, but with him, they had learned. The Tarragon whispered in his ear, and Brendel's fist hit the table, as he screamed at the lizard, "How did you not know this? Those stupid Kargarians! We must retrieve those bombs! Send the Valaris Wizards."

Unlike the Kargarians, the Tarragons had wizards of their own. He saw the smirk on the human's face and sent her a vision of his father's realm, what her future would be, watched her crawl to the corner and cower in fear. "Have your fun now, Lucifer awaits you, my dear Rachael."

✯✯✯✯

Shawn and Victoria traveled to the rallying point just west of St. Louis flying over large amounts of destruction. The city streets were littered with destroyed Kargarian war machines. Their bodies covered—and in some areas—layered the streets. Victory immediately went to Braden, standing with Katherine and Julien, kissed him, and wipe the brown streak of blood from his forehead. His armor was now scarred and stained from the battle.

"Now, you know," Victoria said tenderly.

"It was horrible!" Braden replied as he hung his head. "So much death."

Shawn saw the sad looks on Julien's and Braden's faces. They had seen death and destruction on a grand scale, unlike anything this world had seen. And the young Herits would undoubtedly see much more. Shawn embraced Katherine, brushed the hair from her face.

"Are you all right?" he whispered to her.

"I'm fine," Katherine sighed, then turned to Victoria. "The Kargarians are destroyed, and still no Kargarian portals. What's left of them are making their way west to the Tarragons. Tarragon portals are slow in opening and sending reinforcements. They paid a heavy price defeating the Europeans, and you would think they would be sending more supplies through."

"Do you know where they are located?" Victoria asked.

"The Tarragons have occupied The Territory of Washington and have surrounded The Army of the Americas and Seattle. The human armies are finished. But there are reports that small portals have opened west of New Chicago, and My Queen, Brendel, now occupies my family's home."

"How do you know this?" Victoria question.

"Our Crimmian servants."

"Appoint a reliable commander and send a thousand vampires to the human armories. Tell the commander to bring the blasters north to Queen Silva and the Saskatch. Tell him to inform the queen that the battle to save our world is near, and I will give her what she wants." Victoria activated a map and pointed to a northern section of the Washington Territory. "Have the Saskatch take up positions here."

"Have you heard anything about Rachael?" Shawn asked Katherine.

"She is with Brendel and is alive."

"We will not follow the Kargarians," Victoria said. "We will go back to the camp to retrieve the bombs and Max. It is time we send a gift to the Kargarians and Tarragons. A gift from the vampires!"

"Are you sure, my queen?" Katherine said. "We might not get another chance at the Kargarians."

"I have sent word to Peter to bring the army from Amsterdam, follow the night east, and come to Washington. We will destroy the Tarragons there, and what is left of the Kargarians won't matter."

Something came to Victoria, Shawn could tell, she had focused her attention on a vision. "Something is not right," she said. "Small portals shouldn't be opening where they are. Our camp is exposed, and few vampires are there with Gwyn and the bombs. Gather the vampires, Katherine! We are leaving!"

The vampires again took flight heading north to their camp. Shawn and Victoria flew ahead, and fifteen minutes later came to within sight of fire and smoke rising into the night sky. Many Valaris Wizards were moving through the camp, finding a lone vampire, surrounding, and killing him. Gwyn and the vampires had fortified their positions with boulders and large stones taken from the piles left at the sides of the farming fields.

Shawn and Victoria flew along the river's edge its dark waters lit by the setting moon. The morning light was getting ready to show itself. Shawn and Victoria were the first to arrive. He drew Adeen, lifted over the treetops swooped down into the camp with high speed, followed by Victoria. He landed turned and charged two wizards coming around a tent and took them by surprise. They tried to raise their staffs, but he was on them, thrusting his slayer through one, pivoting, and slicing the faceless head from the other. Shawn quickly realized many wizards were moving through the camp. Much more than he would have expected.

Victoria yelled, "We have to get to Gwyn and the bombs! Follow me!"

The vampire camp was more than a mile long, filled with blue, green, purple, and red tents. The colors that represented the covenants. Most of the tents were now on fire with licks of yellow flame shooting into the air. Gwyn and the bombs were at the eastern section of the camp, next to the farm field. Gwyn and about a hundred vampires had quickly made a rock fortress and now were defending it at a terrible cost to the vampires.

Shawn followed Victoria's lead as they moved through the burning tents. She was an old and powerful vampire, given great power by her maker Erdin Kenmare, and she had drunk the blood of Bricius. The Archangel Michael had also given her tremendous strength. Wielding Deceida, one of five original covenants swords given by Michael, she was Heaven's death, moving amongst the tents striking down any Valaris Wizards that approached. A wizard stepped out from a shelter and threw dark energy at them. Victoria using Deceida, block the dark energy and then was quickly on him, taking his head, swinging the slayer around, taking another hiding wizards head.

Since the time of Malin, Shawn always could feel The Mother's energy inside of him, and now he felt it build. He turned and threw her energy at the wizards charging toward him, bright white plasma washed over them, burning them, and their lifeless bodies fell to the ground. Valerians would come from nowhere, stepping through portals throwing energy, and then step back through. Shawn and Victoria used their vampire speed to make themselves disappear and reappear, coming from behind, taking the wizards' heads, and slowly making their way to Gwyn.

The sun rose, and it was early morning when the sky darkened by the vast swarm of vampires arriving for the attack. The vampires dove into the wizards, and the tide of battle turned against the Valerians. The wizards' dark magic was strong, but the power of Heaven was stronger.

During the fighting, Shawn had sensed that Gwyn was hurt. He glanced at Victoria and knew she felt it too. They fought desperately to reach her.

"We must hurry!" Victoria shouted.

Shawn nodded his head as he drove his slayer into another wizard. Fighting with abandon, he killed any Valaris Wizard that stood in his way. Finally, they made their way to the fortification and Gwyn. Shawn flew over the rocks and found Gwyn hurt, propped against a stone, her chest bloodied with a weak smile on her face, her staff still at the ready. The tip of a wizard's staff had pierced her chest with dark energy. The tip had barely missed her heart but had seriously hurt her.

Max stood motionless next to her with his head slightly bowed. The A. I. had powered himself off. The evil that came through the portals even repulsed silicon-based life forms. Victoria joined a group of vampires that had surrounded the bombs, and they would strike down any Valarian that came over the wall. Shawn sat next to Gwyn, bit his wrist, and poured his blood down her throat.

"Drink my love. Take as much as you need."

"No, Shawn!" Gwyn said as she pushed his hand away. "You will need your strength."

The vampire army swarmed the camp and escape portals for the wizards started to open. The Valaris Wizards began their retreat from the battle. A break for the vampires, the sun was becoming a problem for the younger vampires. Shawn heard Victoria's telepathic warning and instructions to all vampires.

Quickly, vampires, fly to New Chicago and take shelter in the tower buildings!

Victoria turned to the vampires protecting the bombs and commanded, "Take the bombs and follow us!" And then she shouted, "Shawn take Gwyn, and I will take Max!"

The vampire camp was in flames; fire, hot embers, and smoke flowed into the air, and so the army headed north toward New Chicago. Shawn and company flew ahead of them. He knew Tarragons had occupied the city, but he hoped not in large numbers. Following Victoria, they entered the city, veered slightly east, and took refuge in a high tower next to the great sea. The water was at their backs, and that was what the vampires wanted. The remainder of the army arrived, swarmed around the tower, and slowly took cover in the buildings. Shawn and Victoria went to a hotel midway up the tower and forced their way into a stylish lobby.

"Lay the bombs on that table and stand guard at the door," Victoria commanded the vampires.

Shawn laid Gwyn on a large sofa. "How are you doing?

"I am okay. A little weak."

"Maybe you should go to the ground?"

"No! I can't be buried now, and you know that! I know what you are going to do!"

"Let me give you some blood." Shawn bit his wrist and extended it to her. He watched her hesitantly take his blood, and then her expression changed to horror, and she pushed his wrist away. He saw the fear in her face. She also was a vampire, and through his blood, she knew exactly what he was planning.

Gwyn shouted at him with fear and anger in her voice. "No, Shawn, you can't do that! The Mother forbids it! Rachael is lost, and you must accept that!"

"I don't accept it, and you can tell that to Eos!"

Then the distinct whine of turbines sounded as waves of Tarragon flyers flew in for the attack.

"You stay here," Shawn ordered as he grabbed The Mother's Staff and headed outside. A clear mid-morning day greeted him, and the sun was bright in the sky, not favorable conditions for vampires. The Tarragon flyers flew in and fired at the steel girders of the tower, melting them, and the tower began to shake violently. Swarms of vampires would fly out and attack the flyers, destroying some, and then they would return to their buildings, and another swarm would come out. Shawn lowered the Mother's Staff and fired the white-hot plasma beam of the staff, destroying any flier it touched. The air battle went on for over an hour. Eventually, the losses became too much for the Tarragon flyers, and they withdrew.

Shawn looked out over the city with his vampire's eyes. He saw the Tarragon soldiers finally mobilizing and heading toward their tower. Quickly, he moved back into the lobby. Max had activated himself and now stood over a table that held the bomb halves. He had diagrams and schematics floating in midair, as he did his calculations. Then he reached down and put the halves together and made two bombs.

"We should try to hurry, Max!" Shawn warned. "There isn't much time!"

"I am aware of that, guardian," Max responded, as he punched in the correct formulas into the bombs. "Destroying worlds takes time, and we wouldn't want to make a mistake with doomsday bombs."

Again, the schematics changed, and his figuring started over. The robot waved some drawings away and brought up long, complex formulas waved them away and brought more. Eventually, the A.I. froze with a loud hum coming from his circuits. Max reached out one hand and ten feet to the side, a portal opened. He reached out with the other, and again a portal opened. Turning, Max said, "At your command, Queen Victoria."

Victoria looked at him then at Gwyn lying on the sofa and back to him. Shawn nodded, yes.

"Do it, robot!" Victoria commanded.

Max picked the bomb up to his left and threw it through the left portal, and then he threw the second bomb through the right portal. Just when the anxiety of failure built to a crescendo, the portals wavered, sputtered, and bright orange flames shot from them. Screams and wails accompanied the fire.

Shawn yelled, "Shut them down!"

Max immediately closed the portals, and all was quiet. The fighting had stopped outside, the Tarragons had come to a complete stop, and confusion went through their ranks. Out on the prairie, what was left of the Kargarian Army stopped and fell to the ground. A strange type of hibernation came over them. Kargarian war machines gave out large grinding whines, veered, pitched down, and plunged to the ground destroying themselves.

"It worked," Victoria whispered. "Thank the Heavens!"

Shawn walked outside to the railing of the platform and looked out over the city. His flesh went cold, and frost started to form on the railing. A stench that would make any creature gag, and then the maggots. Shawn knew a demon was near.

A small portal opened, and Brendel stepped through. "You think you are so clever!" he screamed. "You know better, Shawn. You have seen my father's realm! I still have my power, the Tarragon Army, and the Valaris Wizards! That will be enough to defeat the vampires of this world."

"This time, you will not win!" Shawn yelled. "The Tarragons do not have the Kargarian numbers, and they are no match for vampires!" Then Shawn felt Brendel's dark evil. The evil made him shudder.

"I have your mortal woman, and at sundown, I will kill her and send her soul to my father. Lucifer will have no mercy with her, and there will be no way for your angels to save her."

"She is nothing to you. Just another human. What joy is it for you to kill her?" Shawn pleaded with his hands out.

"That is true, and she is nothing. Only a human. Killing a thousand would be a start to make me happy." A crooked smile appeared on his grotesque demon face. "But she means something to you. That is where my joy will come from, and I will kill her at your family's home."

"I will not let you!" Shawn screamed in desperation.

"I know…I am counting on it. Welcome to Queen Victoria, you will be next. I will see you soon, Demon Slayer!" Brendel spat out with cutting sarcasm, then he turned and stepped back through the portal.

"You are not going, Shawn," Victoria said. "I am your Queen, and I forbid it."

Shawn embraced Victoria then smiled mischievously, the same way he had many times over the centuries. He gazed into her eyes, the very same eyes he had fallen in love with so long ago. He kissed her softly. "I have to. I can't leave Rachael to that demon. I promised her that I would protect her. I promised her family. You know how I am with promises."

"She is a human, Shawn! You can't save her! Tonight, Peter is bringing the army, and he will attack from the west, the Saskatch will attack from the north, and we will attack from the east. We will finish the Tarragons, and then we will use the staff to kill Brendel!"

"And Rachael will be dead and her soul sent to Lucifer by then," Shawn said sadly. "Long ago, Anne made me a vampire and gave me the blood of the angels. The blood made me powerful, but it also gave me an unquenchable thirst for love. More than most vampires, I think. I have spent my existence looking for this love. And there have been times I found it. I found you, Katherine and Gwyn. Now I have found Rachael."

Shawn saw the blood tears come to Victoria's eyes, he could feel her desperation, and then she spoke. "Katherine is coming, can you feel it? Wait for her!"

"No, I can't wait for her! She would try to make me stay!"

Shawn reached back and felt his sword from Heaven to reassure himself. He debated whether to take The Mother's Staff, but he didn't want to leave Gwyn undefended. Then he felt Victoria's powerful arms wrap around him. "Please,

Shawn! I have lived for so long in this world. I am tired! I don't want to go on without you!"

"I feel the same." He kissed Victoria and told her how much he loved her. Told her after twelve centuries, he still looked forward to her visits and being with her. He broke Victoria's hold, wiped the blood tears from her cheeks, kissed her, and took flight heading west to his home in Washington.

Victoria fell to her knees and cried out. "Don't go! Don't leave me!"

Chapter Twenty-Six

F or twelve centuries, Shawn had loved Victoria. He, too, could not imagine living without her or knowing she was not alive in this world. Even now, he could remember that strange night at the vampire party when he saw her for the first time. He remembers how beautiful she was, how she carried herself as if she had always been nobility. The surprise he felt when she returned his interest. He remembered Anne and Marilyn, how he loved them. They were the vampires that had found him. In a time when he was young and before he had learned the angels' real purpose for him.

He flew over the high peaks and landed on a mountain ridge that overlooked the valley below. He used his vampire vision to see the Tarragons quickly setting up their defenses, getting their war machines ready. Their numbers were low now, maybe a half million. They had delayed reinforcing themselves after the battles, and Shawn knew there would be no more reinforcements. It was too late for them. The Tarragons had placed their defenses in a long arc around Seattle, touching the sea at each end, and a small force of Tarragons circled the Bryce family home.

The Tarragons had spread themselves out, a mistake for them. He could sense their confusion. They had lost contact with their world, and only now were realizing their world had been destroyed. Now they were at the mercy of Brendel's cruelty and soon the attacking vampires. There would be no mercy shown for the Tarragons. *If only humans could have lasted a little longer.*

Shawn veered north and followed a sharp valley between two mountain peaks. He came to a pine forest and skimmed the treetops cloaking his thoughts, trying to hide from Brendel. Another small mountain came into view. He flew up, hugging the trees, and landed at the crest. He could see his family home by the small lake, a place that had given him so much happiness, but now Brendel had drenched it in his evil. How pleased Brendel must be that he had taken his home and made it his own.

There was considerable damage done to the property by the encamped Tarragons. Only Brendel's frigid coldness came from his home carried by the strong northern wind, traveling through the valley to lap at his face. Shawn could not sense the demon, but he knew Brendel was there. He could feel the chill against his body, the evil, and that meant Brendel knew he was near.

The sun hugged the horizon and soon would go down. Now, it was time for him to make his move. He looked to the mountains, how majestic they were; he had always loved the beauty of this world. He heard the voices of Anne, a sound he barely remembered after all these years and The Mother in his mind telling him not to go. *I have to,* he thought. *I promised her, and I have drunk her blood. I cannot leave her to Lucifer, what would that say about my life. My soul! And what about her soul?*

Shawn licked his lips, felt the fear travel through him. Looking at the ground, he saw the maggots all around his feet.

"Yes," he whispered, Brendel knew where he was. The white light of specters formed and flew around him, trying to drive him back. He reached back and drew Adeen, held it high; its metal rang, and it cast off a bright light. He felt the power of the Archangel travel through it and into him. He shaped shifted into his most furious vampire form, and another bright light formed, but this was much brighter. The light was Eos, and he heard her silver voice in his mind. *"Don't go, Shawn. All the vampires of this world are coming. Wait for them. Wait for Gwyn and the staff. I have played my old trick. I hid Jessamine's power in the staff, and that will kill the demon."*

"I can't! There is no more time!" he yelled to the light. "I must go! I have seen Lucifer's world. I could not bear it if Rachael went there."

Shawn felt The Mother's disappointment, the guilt that her grand plan had turned out this way. Eos, with all the time in the universe, had run out of time for her grand scheme. She hadn't seen the hold the human women would have on him, and his deep love for humanity. Still, she gave her power to him; all she could give him in this world. Then he took flight and headed home. He felt the demon gathering his strength, preparing for him. Shawn landed in the side yard by the lake. Reality was different here. He had punched through a barrier into the dark realm, and it felt the same when he saw Lucifer's world. What he felt was a dismal reality, nausea that squeezed at his stomach, the constant hum of flies, an evil that brought a melancholy to one's soul. Here he heard the sing-song of evil calling him to join them. His heart broke for Rachael that she had to experience this.

Blue specters came and flew at him, veering off at the last moment. He whispered a spell from The Mother to ward off these entities. Small points of bright light formed around him and then condensed into two warrior angels, Anne and Marilyn, they flew at the specters driving them back. Again, in his mind, he heard Anne, *"Leave this place; we will try to save the human's soul."*

"I cannot leave!"

Brendel came out the side door down the stone stairs and out onto the lawn dragging Rachael by her hair with one hand and holding a dark metal sword in the other. He threw Rachael to the side, leaving her sprawling on the grass, she raised her head, and Shawn saw a look of horror on her face. Brendel raised his hands, spoke an evil spell, and an energy dome formed around her. Brendel then spoked to Rachael, "Darling, look who's here. And I bet he's here to rescue you."

Shawn saw that Brendel had shapeshifted into his demon form. He had jet black hair, slicked back and tight, grey, oily skin with elfin ears, teeth that came to a point, so much evil it boiled to the surface of his being, and a stench that would turn any stomach or blood sac. A look that certainly was very stressful for Rachael.

Brendel raised his hand, asking his father to give him the power to show his might. He lifted his leg brought it down, and with a single stomp on the ground, a circular shock wave of dark energy traveled outward. The trees bent back sharply and then sprang forward, their pine needles blown from the branches. With no mercy from the demon, the evil energy disintegrated the Tarragon guards where they stood. A bright shield of light formed around Shawn, as he fell to his knees and brought Adeen in front of him. The dark energy blew around and washed over him, warded off by powers of Heaven. Still, it lifted him up and out over the lake, leaving him floating in midair. He quickly flew back and landed on the lawn, not wanting to show any weakness to the demon.

Brendel screamed his bravado, "You come to challenge me. You will need more power than your angels are willing to give you!"

Shawn chanted a spell, felt The Mother's energy travel down his arms, and at its peak, he pushed out his hand and threw white energy at the demon. Instantly, dark energy surrounded Brendel, and the two energies collided, sending out a loud boom that echoed through the valley.

They began to circle each other, each preparing for the attack. Again, blue specters formed flew at Shawn, and like before. The white lights became Anne and Marilyn to ward off the evil ghosts. A smile came to Brendel's face, and then he said mockingly, "Your dead family, how nice. They will not save you. Their spirits have no power over the physical."

"I won't need them to save me. It is time for you to pay for what you have done to this world."

"I do not think so, Demon Slayer. The odds are not with you this time. And now you have made a mistake. A blunder I knew you would make."

"And what's that?"

A deep laugh came from Brendel. "You came alone."

Shawn cloaked his mind so Brendel wouldn't know a massive vampire attack is coming.

"What are you trying to hide from me, Demon Slayer? I know your vampires are preparing to attack. I will kill you, and the Tarragons will defeat your vampires."

Shawn lowered Adeen, chanted another spell, and a white searing plasma beam shot out from the blade toward the demon. Brendel did the same, and a blue plasma beam collided with Shawn's, the beams suspended in mid-air, sizzling, filling the air with a strong smell of ozone. Like Gwyn had shown him, he would whip his beam, bringing it over the demon catching him and knocking him back. They circled each other fencing with the energy beams. The dark energy would come near, and white light would form around him, ready to absorb some of the energy. He would gather the Mother's power in his hand, throw it at the demon, and quickly blue energy would form around the beast absorbing Heaven's power.

The fight went on, back and forth with their energy beams, bringing cracks and booms echoing over the lake. Again, the blue specters flew at him, trying to distract him, and in their dark light, he could see distorted faces of the evil dead. He was tiring and expending too much energy at this. The situation had become apparent; he was not going to outlast Brendel. The smell of his burnt flesh pierced Shawn's nose. He had to decide, charge him with Adeen, or withdrawal. He could not leave, so he withdrew his plasma beam, raised Adeen, shouted to the Archangel and The Mother to be with him, then he ran at the demon. The demon readied his sword, and the two met with a crack of metal that sounded deep into the forest. The momentum of the collision threw Shawn sliding across the dew-covered lawn.

He sprang to his feet, but Brendel was on him, driving his blade into Shawn's back. Shawn flew out, gasping, and came back at the demon. Brendel formed his energy, catching him, again throwing him back onto the lawn. Shawn raised himself back up and heard a grave evil penetrating laugh and realized it did not come from Brendel. He saw a dark figure of a man standing near Rachael and realized it was Lucifer. The devil was smiling and nodding. He heard both Anne's and Marilyn's voices in his head, pleading with him to leave this place.

Raising Adeen, he again charged Brendel, and their blades rang out as they parried with their swords. Shawn saw an opening, pivoted, and sliced the demon across the stomach. Brendel bellowed and fell back, cursing at Shawn. The beast charged in rage and brought his sword down on Adeen, again and again, and Shawn used all his strength to ward off the blows. Then in an arc, Brendel brought his blade around, slicing a deep wound across his chest. In shock, Shawn fell back, and the demon drove his sword once again into Shawn. He could feel his hold on this world slipping, and he came back at Brendel landing on him, pushing his slayer down through his back, but the demon threw him off again.

Brendel's eyes burned red, and he snarled, "You do not have the strength to defeat me. Now I know that!"

Shawn got back to his feet and knew the demon was becoming cocky; sometimes, he had used their arrogance against them, but this time he saw no weakness in his defenses. Shawn circled Brendel but was losing blood. He willed his powers to heal him, to stop the flow of blood, but it would take time and energy, and that was something he didn't have. Brendel charged him, and Shawn threw off The Mother's power, stopping the demon, holding him where he stood, trying to gather his energy. Brendel quickly recovered, broke free, and was again on Shawn, their blades striking and ringing as they fought back and forth, each looking for an advantage. Brendel again was on him, bringing his sword repeatedly down on his. Brendel pivoted, and Shawn felt his blade cut slightly across his throat. Shawn fell to his knees exhausted, rolled away, and then got back to his feet, ready to fight on.

His situation had become desperate; Shawn knew he must wait for an opening and move in on Brendel, tackle him maybe, and remove his head. Shawn also knew his attack must happen soon. Brendel moved around him and then charged in swinging his sword back and forth, and again their metals clashed until Shawn parried and sliced the demon across his arm. Brendel cursed, lunged at him, slicing deep into Shawn's chest. Shawn dropped to his knees, severely wounded, exhausted. Still, finally, the fight was affecting Brendel; his putrid brown blood was staining his clothes.

The demon stood in front of him, planting his feet, swaying back, holding his sword. Shawn's vision was blurring, blood spilled from his mouth, down his chin and throat to stain his shirt. Blood trickled from his nose and ears, and his consciousness came and went. Shawn felt his strength spilling to the ground. He looked out over the lawn to his home, remembered the first time he saw this strange reality, walked it with Marilyn, and watched Anne come over the treetops landing in front of him. He had only been a vampire for a couple of days. *So long ago*, he thought.

He found himself falling forward. "Herit!" he screamed. "Where are you? Don't let them have my soul!"

Brendel raised his head and shouted, "Father, I give you The Demon Slayer!"

Suddenly a bright white light rose and spread over the area, giving clarity to the evil.

Chapter Twenty-Seven

Victoria sprung to her feet, gathered herself, wiped the blood tears from her eyes, and quickly walked back toward the building. Katherine arrived and came up behind her as she entered the building into the lobby.

"Where is Shawn?" Katherine demanded.

"He has gone to your home in Washington!"

"Why didn't you stop him?" Katherine shouted, almost in a panic.

"I couldn't stop him! You know that! I tried, but he wouldn't listen. He couldn't bear leaving Rachael to that monster."

"Brendel will kill him!" Katherine shouted with fear spreading over her face.

"I know," Victoria whispered, as blood tears came again to her eyes.

Victoria wiped her eyes with the back of her hand and turned to Max. "Show the location of the Tarragon Army." A map appeared in front of them, and Max pointed to their spread-out position in The Washington Territory.

Victoria turned to Gwyn, who had gotten to her feet and was now leaning on her staff. "Can you fly, Gwyn?"

"I can my queen, and I will fly to Washington," Gwyn assured. "He shouldn't have gone without the staff."

"Both of you listen to me!" Victoria commanded. "The sun is going down, and we will attack the Tarragon forces. Peter will come from the west and Saskatch from the north. Katherine, you will lead our forces and will attack from the east. When we arrive, you will take command of the forces. Gwyn and I will go on to Shawn. Can you make it, Gwyn?

"I will, Victoria! I will make it!"

Victoria turned to the robot. "Max, you are on your own. I suggest you find somewhere to hide for a while."

Victoria took Deceida from its sheath held it high. "Hear me, Michael, send my command to all vampires and the Saskatch. It is time to attack Washington. The final battle has begun."

Victoria followed Katherine out onto the plaza with Gwyn at her side. Katherine was the first queen the hundred-year queen and was known to vampires as the warrior queen because of her battles at the Gates of Hell. Katherine had relinquished her crown to her because she had become tired of leading. Now she would lead this army. Victoria knew Katherine had learned long ago the angels would not allow Herits to live a quiet existence. The vampires gathered in the sky, circling and forming for the attack, their numbers were many. The same amount would come across the Pacific and attack the Tarragons from behind.

Through the twilight, Victoria and the vampires flew. The night was starting to show itself. It would not take long for them to reach the Tarragon fortifications. Victoria knew Gwyn was severely hurt, but she would make it to Shawn. Victoria also knew Shawn was still alive. They had drunk each other's blood for over a millennium. They knew each other thoughts, where they were if they were hurt or not, and Shawn was still alive, in a desperate state, but still alive. There was no other way they must attack the Tarragons first. They had to destroy these lizards, and Shawn knew this before he left.

Victoria sent Gwyn a telepathic message, *He is alive, but we attack the Tarragons first and then fly to the Bryce's home.* Victoria could feel Gwyn's resistance to this and saw her glance of defiance. Gwyn would not stay long with the attacking vampires.

Over the mountains and then down into Seattle, Victoria flew with the vampirc army dodging the intense fire from the ground. The Tarragon plasma cannons lit the night sky. Peter had arrived first and was already attacking. As expected, Gwyn turned north to go to Shawn's aid. Sixty thousand vampires were now attacking the Tarragons, all along their arcing line of fortifications, bringing death to the Tarragon Army. Massive explosions echoed from the city, and towers tilted, and then the deafening sounds of tearing metal and explosions as the towers collapsed.

Circling the burning town, Victoria saw the Tarragons destroying and setting the city on fire for no reason other than revenge and chaos. They were on the verge of a great defeat, and they knew the guardians of this world had destroyed theirs. The twisted mind of a Tarragon was to take as many as possible with them. Victoria drew Deceida and flew at a Tarragon attack flier, firing into a tower trying to destroy its support columns. Victoria hardened herself and hit the flyer driving Deceida into its turbines and then pushing it into a metal girder. The war machine split and tumbled down the tower to the ground in fiery flames of fire.

She flew up and out of the city following the Tarragon fortifications north. Plasma canons from the Tarragons and fires turned the night into day. The Tarragons had spread out their defenses, and the fire from the lizards was too spread out. Flying vampires easily dodged the burning plasma. All along the line, Victoria saw swarms of vampires attacking the Tarragons with such speed they had no chance of seeing them in time. The Tarragons were slow-moving creatures, and the vampires killed them by the thousands, and still, there was no Brendel or Valaris Wizards to help them.

Satisfied with how the battle was going, Victoria veered slightly east and came upon the Saskatch, now attacking the northern part of the Tarragon defenses. The Saskatch were fearless creatures. She turned and flew down to the command part of their line. At first, the Saskatch were suspicious of her approach, and some blaster fire came her way. Still, she dodged photon bullets, landed, and immediately approached a surprise, Queen Silva.

"Greetings, Queen Victoria, this is a surprise," Queen Silva confessed. "I would have thought we would see The Demon Slayer.

He is trapped to the west at his family home," a desperate Victoria said. "He fights Brendel."

"I see…that is not good! Surprisingly I liked him! For a vampire!"

You must move your forces to Gunner's Pass," Victoria commanded. "I know you don't like to take orders from vampires, but I need this. I need your help, and I won't forget it. You must keep Tarragon forces away from Shawn. Do not allow them to reinforce Brendel. Do you understand?"

"I will follow your orders, for now, Queen Victoria. No Tarragons will reach Shawn."

"Have you seen the Valaris Wizards?" Victoria asked.

"They know the war is lost and they have left the fight. Soon a great victory will be yours, Queen Victoria. And the Saskatch expects you to keep your word!"

"Vampires will keep their word."

Victoria took to the air traveling east and soon came upon the Bryces home. An intensely bright light met her eyes. The entire Bryce property turned to daylight. Gwyn had unleashed the power of the staff on the demon.

✮✮✮✮

Shawn watched Brendel raise his sword for the final blow, then saw a flash and heard Gwyn's voice and to his surprise Jessamine's. "We are here, my love!"

An explosion of intense light that even surprised his vampire's eyes. A ball of white energy struck Brendel, lifting him, and throwing him through the wall of the house, and into the parlor. The house heaved with a loud groan, tilted and settled down slanted to one side. Shawn called on Michael and The Mother to once more give him the energy to continue the fight. He rose to his feet and flew crashing through the house wall. Shawn saw Brendel slowly rising, dazed, and putrid blood pouring from every opening in his body. He flew into the demon, driving him back out the front of the house on to the lawn.

Shawn wrestled with the beast, both slipping on the wet grass. With all that was left in him, Shawn beat the demon down. Brendel was stunned, like a boxer trying to stay on his feet for a few more seconds. A burnt, acidic stench came from the monster and tore at Shawn's senses. Shawn used all his remaining strength and held Brendel to the ground. He reached for Adeen in the grass next to him; his hands bloodied, making the hilt slippery and hard to grasp. His vision blurred and then came back to see the pummeled and bloody face of Brendel and his exposed neck. Bringing the blade to Brendel's neck, he cursed, "To hell with you, demon! Lucifer will not have this world!"

Adeen brightly burned as he pulled the blade across the demon's neck and then heard Brendel's last words as his head fell away from his body. "You, Demon Slayer, will not live in this world either."

Shawn felt pressure to his chest, felt Brendel's last movement in this world, his hand piercing his body, and wrapping around his heart. He felt the veins being torn from his visceral one by one, the suction as it left his chest. He looked down and saw Brendel's hand fall to the ground holding his heart, and still, he felt the heat from the demon's burning body.

The world and the home that had given him so much joy faded for him. Falling from the demon's burning body, he rolled away, stared up at the night sky, and then he felt himself coming apart, heard a roar in his ears, and knew his time in this world had come to an end.

He loss all weight and felt himself forming as a spirit, his energy coming together, rising toward a large bright light in the sky. Many dark specters formed and came at him, dragging him away from the light toward Lucifer's dark world. A harsh trumpet sounded, and the devil came through the darkness to claim him. Then a blast from another horn and the warrior angels of Heaven came from the light led by Herit, Anne, and Marilyn. A blast of another trumpet, and Eos and the Archangel came forward. They drove Lucifer and his dark angels back to his evil realm.

Herit took hold of him, led him to Heaven, and his long-awaited rest. He floated in the light and heard Anne and Marilyn's voices. *Rest, for now, we are together again. The devil has suffered a great loss, he has squandered much of his power, and mortals will not hear from him for many years. Heaven still rules the earth.*

✯✯✯✯

Victoria flew through the intense light, shielding her eyes with her forearm. Briefly, she sensed joy over the news that the vampires had vanquished the Tarragons and had won a great victory. Then she felt Gwyn's agony and the knowledge, the overwhelming thought that Shawn was dead. She landed next to Gwyn standing, her staff propping her up, and the witch was screaming like a madwoman, "I have failed you mother! I have failed Shawn!"

Victoria froze as horror spread through her being, watching her love of more than twelve centuries fall apart in front of her. The unthinkable had happened Shawn was leaving her. She cursed at the angels. They had made it impossible for him to live in this world. Lucifer would never allow it. She looked to the sky and saw five bright lights ascending surrounded by many white specters of angels. Herit's long-ago promise that Lucifer would never have his soul was fulfilled.

Katherine, with Julian and Braden, came next. Tarragon blood covered them. Victoria watched Katherine rush to the pile of dirt that once was Shawn. The wails that came from her she thought would drive her mad.

"How could this have happened," Katherine screamed! "What about that dam staff, Gwyn!"

Gwyn, propped up by The Mother's Staff, stood and stared.

Victoria knew that Katherine at first would try to find something to blame, but it would pass it had before. Julien went to her side to try and console her, but she brushed him off. Both Julien and Braden stood in shock. Victoria watched Katherine take a sack from her cloak, wipe her bloody hands on the grass until they were clean, and then she scooped Shawn' fine grey dirt into the bag and put it back in her cloak. She reached for a now cold Adeen lying in the grass, still soaked with the demon's blood, took it, and handed it to Julien and sobbed to him, "I hope and pray someday you will be worthy of this slayer. Honor it always."

Peter landed next, and Victoria heard his cries of anguish. She stood with blood tears streaming down her face, and then she heard the cries of agony coming from the mortal woman. Victoria walked to her and looked down on her, trying to raise her chest from the ground. All over Rachael's body were bruises and cuts, her legs were broken, and she had a terrible wound to her head. Brendel, in his perverse way, had repeatedly assaulted her, and her survival was doubtful.

She certainly was not happy with this human and felt in a way that Rachael shared some blame in Shawn's death. But Shawn had loved her given her his blood and made her a promise, a promise she would keep.

Victoria turned to the others, wiped the blood tears from her eyes, and shouted, "Who here will turn this mortal! Who will make her their changeling? Teach her what has been loss for her and her kind!"

"I will!" Katherine sobbed as she walked toward Rachael. "And hopefully one day she will be worthy of what has been sacrificed for her. I will make her a Bryce and a Herit!"

Victoria watched Katherine come and scoop a moaning Rachael into her arms. Then an overwhelming smell of Jasmine filled the air. Katherine's blood teeth went to the mortal's neck, and slowly Rachael went quiet as Katherine took her blood. Then Katherine laid Rachael on the ground, tore her wrist, and poured her blood into her mouth. Katherine put her head in her lap, took her hand, stayed with her, and waited. Two hours went by, and Rachael opened her eyes. They were vampire eyes and the blue of the Herit covenant.

Chapter Twenty-Eight

T wenty-five years had passed since Shawn's death, and Victoria still held sadness in her heart, a melancholy that was always there for him. All of the Herit Covenant did, and only now was Katherine becoming bearable to be with. Fortunately for Rachael. Never again would she see Shawn's physical form in this world. The loneliness of her existence without Shawn still hung over her and never went away.

There has been no sign of Lucifer, his demons, or witches in this world, but still, there was evil. The reason why vampires went to the human tribes to collect the few condemned mortals and their evil blood. Human blood in this world was now a delicacy.

Drake had come to her, told her, Shawn was in Stasis and would be for a hundred years. He had lived a hard life. Drake told her the heads of the seven choirs of angels held counsel on Eos and her handling of this world. The council had decreed that Eos would share watching over this world with Shawn when he awakened. Drake told Victoria it was a good thing because Shawn would be the only angel she would accept as a fledgling; after all, Eos was a Lesser God.

Victoria had stayed in the Americas and now lived at Dalton. Her old home on this continent was destroyed long ago. The army had mostly disbanded over time, and vampires had gone back to their homes. Peter had taken a small army back to The Citadel, and Victoria kept a small army in Dalton. Julien and Braden had gone off together to search out the surviving

Tarragons, to be emissaries for the Queen of the Vampires, and make peace with the stranded creatures that came through the portals. They were twins, and when she found them as mortals, they had been on their own since childhood and always were together. As vampires, Julien and Braden were fiercely loyal to their family and covenant but still wanted to be on their own. Shawn was like that; she remembered when he left Anne all those years ago.

Victoria felt the loneliness, and she pushed the bad thoughts from her mind; this eve, she did not want to feel sad. Now vampires wore their slayers and were expected to be warriors, no more carefree life living on evil blood. Victoria commanded that all vampires must be ready to defend this world.

Ten thousand vampires had perished in the fighting to save this world, and again the Bryce family had paid a horrible price, the loss of Shawn. The Archangel had sent word through Drake that Lucifer's power would be weakened for a thousand years. And he would certainly think twice before attacking this world on such a grand scale again. She knew that Brendel had underestimated the killing power of the humans, something she had always known about the mortals. A point that Drake had also strongly agreed with. Michael also warned that Lucifer would undoubtedly keep up his deception to keep evil alive in this world, and vampires must be on guard.

Victoria was with Katherine, Gwyn, and Rachael on an overgrown paved way that traveled west. They were not far from home and had decided to take this eve to hunt for deer blood. The humans of this world now lived as nomads, as tribes of a few thousand banded together. Humans would make their villages of tents and lodges heated by the old technology left behind. They had kept some of the human-technology but most was lost and they showed little interest in finding it. If the science didn't benefit them, the humans had no interest, but they were very well armed. This world had an abundance of weapons left behind by the armies that had fought so savagely here.

Victoria raised her head and looked down the road. Mortals were coming, still some ways off, but they were coming, then a screeching deer came from the trees and down the road it went. Suddenly, a flash of movement, Rachael sprung from the trees and quickly overtook the bellowing creature and drove it to the ground, sinking her blood teeth into its neck. A rare smile came to Victoria's face as she shook her head. Katherine was following closely behind yelling instruction to her.

Rachael was becoming used to being a vampire. Still, she was growing into its challenges and strangeness, a task that was made more difficult because of the loss of Shawn. Katherine was still somewhat closed off from Shawn's death, but she loved Rachael and treated her the same as she had with Drake and Julien.

Life was different now for her, and she would protect Rachael with her life, she was part of her covenant, a Bryce, and a Herit. Rachael loved Katherine. She saw Shawn in her, was extremely loyal to her, and shared her bed. Braden would come and share Rachael's bed when Katherine would allow it. Rachael, with her smile, a smile Shawn had loved, was always asking her about Braden. Gwyn came from the woods, wiping deer blood from her chin. She still carried the Mother's Staff, but it no longer had the power it once had. Jessamine had returned to The Mother. Unfortunately, Gwyn still held guilt for Shawn's death; hopefully, someday it would leave her.

Gwyn nodded down the road, and Victoria saw the humans coming around the bend. Six of them—four males and two females. They wore their blasters slung over their backs, and all sorts of weapons hung around their hips. Humans knew better than to hold a gun in front of a vampire. Now humans were grateful to have vampires around and understood the laws of the species they shared the world with. Victoria watched the humans. They were still hesitant when approaching vampires. They made their clothes of dark dungaree cloth, drab browns, and dark greens, black high-top leather boots. Colors that

272

reflected the mortals' mood in a world that was still in shock from the great calamity that Brendel had brought.

The humans stopped a reasonable distance back, a custom they had developed toward vampires.

"What is it you want?" Victoria shouted down the way as if she didn't know. She always gave the humans the courtesy of not letting them know she was in their heads, an honor she gave to Shawn's memory.

A slight bow and the leader spoke, "Greeting to the vampires. Please excuse our interruption of your hunt. Our leaders would like to speak with Queen Victoria."

They were not far from home, but still, humans always seemed to know where she was. *Someday she would have to get to the bottom of this*, she thought.

Victoria knew the meeting was about spacers. She told them, "Tell your leaders you found her, and we will be along shortly. They will have to wait a while before they go to bed."

They stopped at a brook cascading down a forested hill, the roar echoing through the trees. They washed the blood from their faces, straightened their clothes, and continued onto the village.

Upon coming to the village, they passed a shrine to Shawn; most communities had one. Surrounding the small crude wood or stone sculpture were small silver discs. When activated showed him standing with his smile and then a human speaking of thanks, great respect, and love for this guardian. Shawn had become this world's savior, an unintended result of The Mother's schemes. These perfect likenesses of Shawn always brought tears to her eyes.

Campfires glowed in the night, children, and crying babies were heard amongst the huts and tents. Since the war, humans no longer had difficulty bearing their children, and nowadays, when vampires entered a village, the children always outnumbered the adults. Fearful looks still came from the elders, not so much for what they were, but for the memory's vampires stirred in some of them.

Food was cooking, and Victoria smelled the exotic aromas of the meals drifting through the air. She remembered how Shawn loved the smell of food. She shook her head as if it could drive these thoughts from her, always memories of Shawn, and then she saw Katherine staring at her, knowing what she was thinking. Katherine still wore the look of sadness not erased by the passing of time, but at least she no longer looked for someone or something to blame for Shawn's death. *Maybe someday we will be whole again,* Victoria thought.

The leaders of the village greeted them and told they had come across spacers. The spacers said that they were part of a scouting team of the United Federation of Humans and had representatives in Denver City. They were using the Girardeau spaceport and wanted to meet with vampire leaders. Victoria listened to the humans; for her, most humans had abandoned the planet and bore some responsibility for Shawn's death. She knew the humans would return when vampires had defeated Brendel, to reclaim the earth, the jewel of the solar system. It was the human's way, but this time they would find a different world, a world that held other creatures, not just them. The Saskatch to the north and bands of Tarragons still roamed this part of the world. These few survivors of the war were trapped forever on this planet. Victoria decided to deal with the spacers, to see what the humans wanted, and told all they would be heading south.

That morning, they took shelter for the day. Rachael still was a young vampire and not able to handle that much sun. The next eve, they entered Denver city. The city lay in ruins like most cities in this world. Everywhere they saw destroyed and partially collapsed buildings, few buildings were left intact. Debris covered the streets, and vegetation was slowly reclaiming the city. The vampires had immediately sensed the humans and realized there were more than a few. They took positions on a roof of a building that fire had gutted, and all that was left was burnt steel girders and a partial roof that made a good vantage point to scout the city. Blaster fire hit the side of the roof, throwing debris into Victoria's face.

"Humans," she muttered as she focused her harsh glare on them. "Looks like we found them."

Then a strange dialect came from a man and then a familiar dialect from a soldier running down the street, waving his hands. The man was screaming like a madman telling them not to fire; they were vampires.

Victoria watched Rachael look over the parapet at the soldiers with Katherine telling her to be careful.

"The ones firing are Martians or Spacers, and the soldier running is an Earther," Rachael informed them.

"How do you know this?" Victoria asked.

The patches on their sleeves. The red patches are spacers, and the blue are Earthers. It seems they have worked out their differences."

"United Federation of Humans," Gwyn pondered aloud.

The sound of a human voice yelling. "We have representatives here to talk to guardians. Would you consider this?"

Victoria yelled down to the human, "I am Queen Victoria, and I will speak with your representatives. Tell the spacers not to fire their weapons at us again."

Then a laughed from Gwyn as she yelled down, "Take care, spacers! We are curious to find out what Martian blood tastes like."

Victoria watched the spacers lower their weapons, as the Earthers explained what Gwyn had said. They turned their frightened faces on each other, and she heard their exited gibberish dialect.

Katherine turned to Rachael and winked. "Do you think it tastes like Earther blood?"

"I don't know! Probably it tastes a little different." Rachael chuckled.

"Tell your representatives we will meet with them. Where can we find them?"

"They are in the government complex at the center of the city." Then the human's voice became nervous. "You can follow us if you like."

No!" Victoria shouted. "Move on; we will find them!"

They left the roof, floated to the ground, and continued their trip to meet with the humans. They came upon soldiers questioning refugees that had stayed behind. Later they forced their way through large gates and made their way onto a large central plaza of the government complex.

The spacers had already cleaned the destruction from the square. A group of humans quickly came out to meet them, accompanied by many well-armed soldiers. More soldiers came into the plaza, and they too were armed. The spacers were cautious; they did not know what they would find on Earth or who would be their enemy here.

A soldier stepped forward. "Welcome to Queen Victoria. I am Commander Collin. A pleasure to finally meet guardians. I have heard so much about you." The commander had a very flattering way. Pictures of Katherine and Gwyn formed in front of him and then disappeared. Then the man said, "And to you, Queen Katherine and Gwyn, a mother's witch." The man forced a smile and said, "I believe that is correct."

Victoria motioned Rachael to come and stand by her. She then asked Rachael, "What do make of this?"

"They are all military, and that man is of very high rank. Most likely here scouting the conditions on this world. And they aren't very trusting, as you can see by their numbers."

"Your weapons will do you no good here," Victoria informed.

"That is what I have been told, but I have to follow protocol," Commander Collins said. A picture of Rachael, dressed in a military uniform, appeared in front of the commander. "You are Colonel Rachael Bonnet. Many a tale has been told about you over the years." Excited conversation went through the group, and then the commander asked. "How do you find this world, Colonel?"

Katherine stepped forward and informed the commander. "She is no longer a colonel or human!" She is my changeling, a guardian, and her name is Rachael Bryce. And she will need my permission to speak to you!"

"My apologies," the commander said.

Katherine turned to Rachael and nodded her acceptance. Rachael's eyes turned the blue of the Herit Covenant, and she showed her vampire look to the humans. She walked to them and stopped in front of them to give them a formal military report. "The invaders are defeated, and their worlds destroyed by your doomsday bombs. Evil was swept from this world by guardians using your technology." Rachael stood in front of the soldiers, looking them up and down a blood tear came to her eye. "The guardian Shawn killed the demon Brendel, and Brendel killed him. Lucifer is gone for now, but there is still evil in humans that we know." She stared at them, her blue vampire eyes blazing. "Guardians lost a great deal keeping this world in the light. And they and human's loss Shawn Bryce. Humans fled this world, and you will never know what guardians sacrificed for you." Rachael abruptly turned her back on them, walk away from the human race, went back, and stood with the vampires.

"All humans have heard of Shawn Bryce. Our government sends its sincere condolences. His letters to humans are displayed in our government center in the belt."

Victoria declared, "Do what you want with this world. It is yours. The angels declared this long ago, but there will be no war! Or you will hear from The Mother! You will live next to other creatures in this world, and some will surprise you! You will honor the pact we made with the Saskatch. They also helped save you."

The vampires left the city and began their trip home. Victoria veered off from the others, told them to go back to Dalton; she wanted to be alone. Then she lifted into the sky and headed west.

Victoria landed on a bluff that overlooked Denver City. Looking out, she saw the lights shining once again in the city. To the south, she saw the bright lights penetrating the dark sky, and the roar of spaceships descending to the spaceport. An armada of transports waiting for the signal from the commander. The humans were returning to claim their world. They would find a different world, a world with supernatural creatures, but this was their world. The angels had made this world for man.

Victoria slowly floated off the bluff into the night. She felt the breeze against her face and saw the stars blanketing the clear night sky. Stretching out, she pointed her hand west and then accelerated toward Washington. Later that night, she landed on the front lawn of the Bryce family home. A stiff breeze rippled the lake waters, washing the pine needles onto the shore, and bending the tall grass of the now unkempt lawn.

The house in Washington laid destroyed only monuments placed by vampires to honor Anne, Marilyn, and Shawn. Around the memorial were many small stones laid by humans, some with chiseled words thanking The Guardian. The house had collapsed in on itself after Shawn's and Brendel's fight. Human gypsies that traveled through the mountains looted the treasure stored in the basement. Someday she was sure Katherine would have the home rebuilt and send vampires to find her family's riches.

Victoria walked to the large stone next to the lake. Shawn's had finally joined Anne and Marilyn's, and his dirt was with theirs buried underneath the unmarked stone. She still could picture the first time she saw Anne and her changelings so long ago.

Blood tears came from her eyes as she turned her thoughts to Shawn and whispered, "I told you not to leave me."

Gwyn had stayed buried close to a year after the battle to heal her wounds and mind. Soon after rising from the ground, Gwyn came and told her of a vision The Mother gave her in Heaven. She sent her to the Hall of Souls to find Shawn's newly added listing. There Gwyn found Shawn' true destiny, to sacrifice himself for this world and to kill the demon, Brendel. Victoria and the Bryces always thought Anne made Shawn to kill the Esmanaa demons and bring the first queen into their vampire world. She had lived many centuries thinking Shawn's purpose was fulfilled, and someday they could live together in peace. The Mother and Michael always knew differently and always knew Shawn's real purpose. Shawn had told her once even the angels sometimes didn't tell the whole truth.

How she had loved him, and now she missed him more than anyone could know. She missed his touch, his laugh, the feel of his lips on hers, and his mischievous smile. She had always known that it would be humans that would cause his death. She almost could see him now standing by the water's edge, reaching out she touched the stone and looked at the fading dawn stars, the stars she had looked on for over two thousand years. How tired she felt since Shawn's death, but she knew Michael was not finished with her. Michael would not let her relinquish the throne as he had with Katherine. The Archangel had told her she was still needed to lead the vampires, to lead his Heavens killers here on earth. Through Drake, Michael told her she must stay and look for another champion that only she would recognize.

A crack of a far-off branch breaking brought her out of her thoughts. She saw the band of humans following the shoreline around the lake. They carried their provisions, and some had old blasters on their backs, still unaware their world was going to change once again. She thought about all the tales she had heard over the millennia about vampires, bloodsuckers, and the undead. Now mortals would know them for what they were, Guardians here to protect them from the dark angels. Someday mortals would hear from Shawn. Not the way they could imagine, but they would hear from him. The humans stopped and stared, they knew what she was, and then some grinned and waved. Victoria smiled and waved back like Shawn would have done.

Richard R Hall

THE END